STAY

JENNIFER SUCEVIC

Stay

Copyright© 2015 by Jennifer Sucevic

Cover Design by Mary Ruth Baloy at MR Creations

Editing by Andie Edwards of Beyond the Proof

Home | Jennifer Sucevic or www.jennifersucevic.com

1

CASSIDY

With a shake of my head, I watch as my roommate, Brooklyn, busts out all her best moves on the makeshift dance floor. She's the tall blonde dancing with her hands twisting in the air, almost as if she's doing a very sad Stevie Nicks impersonation.

I almost wince.

Yeah…it's that bad.

If I had to guess, I'd say that she isn't feeling the slightest bit of pain. I'm sure the liquid refreshment currently on tap is to be thanked for that. I'm hoping tomorrow will be a completely different story. She deserves the hangover-to-end-all-hangovers for dragging me to this god-awful excuse to drink beer, get rowdy, and troll for a hookup or two.

My plan for the remainder of this evening consists of staying inconspicuously tucked away in the back corner and sipping my tepid diet soda, because being a girl and walking around a drunken fraternity party is apparently an unofficial invitation to have your ass groped by a random dude. Or should I say random *dudes,* because this has now happened twice. And a third time will likely push me over the edge of my douchebag tolerance limit for the evening.

The objective tonight is to keep an eye on Brooklyn, and when the clock strikes twelve, drag her ass out of here. And I'm totally okay if it's kicking and screaming. Impatiently, I glance at my phone for the twentieth time in the last two hours.

It's only eleven.

This has officially become painful.

I'm snapped out of my dark thoughts on how I'll torture Brooklyn when a stray hand slides its way across my jean-covered butt.

Seriously?

Even though I try to control it, my heartbeat hitches before I spin around with tightened fists, ready to knock some unsuspecting jerk senseless.

"Excuse me," I snarl through clenched teeth, "get your damn hand off my ass before I break every single bone in your fingers!" Contrary to what you might think, it's not an idle threat.

I'll do it.

As I turn, my gaze slams into probably the widest, burliest chest I've ever had the misfortune to inspect this up close and personal.

A sigh of disgust leaves my lips before I can rein it back in.

Perfect.

Slowly, I crane my neck upward until I'm finally able to glare into his eyes. The freakishly large oaf now standing in front of me has the audacity to smile lazily, his gaze happily blurred. "Hey sexy, want to dance?"

The guy barely looks able to stand upright let alone move his gargantuan body on the dance floor. If he goes down, it'll be like a massive tree falling. And I don't even want to think about the huge mark he'll leave on his potential dance victim.

My brows draw together in aggravation before I shake my head. "No, I don't want to dance. What I'd like is for you to remove your hand from my ass."

Because—believe it or not—it's still there.

His grin widens before he squeezes my butt cheek in that massive paw of his. My eyes widen with shock as steam pours out of my ears.

Oh, hell no—that did *not* just happen.

Wiping the disgust from my face, I give him my best come-hither smile. Just because I never use these kinds of tactics doesn't mean I don't know how. His already dilated eyes widen like he just hit the jackpot. Stepping a bit closer to the knuckle-dragging Neanderthal, I crook my finger all sexy-like until he bends down. When our lips are close enough to touch, I drag my mouth to his ear. Before I can utter a word, I clamp my fingers around his balls—which are, in case you're wondering, oversized just like the rest of him—in a death grip. Just for good measure, I give them a little twist.

He hisses out a breath in response.

Now that I have his undivided attention, I growl, "If you don't get your damn hand off my ass immediately, I will continue squeezing until something pops. Do I make myself clear?"

"Perfectly," he squeaks, sounding almost faint.

Not a second later, he releases my offended butt cheek.

And I, in return, release his nuts. But not before I tighten my grip one last time to drive home the gravity of the predicament this moron now finds himself in. For about ten seconds we glare at each other before he carefully backs away from me and my nut-clenching fingers. As he does, his face gets all sad and mopey like I've done something wrong, which is seriously laughable.

Frankly, I'm still pissed as hell.

"You're not a very nice girl," he mutters like a cross child before taking a huge gulp, of what I assume to be beer, from a red plastic cup.

Unattractively, I snort in response "Nope. But hopefully you've learned a valuable lesson regarding the pitfalls of grabbing some unsuspecting girl's ass." Although, gauging from his unapologetic stance towards me, my guess is that he has not taken this lesson to heart. On second thought... "Just refrain from grabbing *any* girl's ass. Contrary to what you apparently think—we don't like it. *At all.*"

"Some girls do," he pipes up, still sporting an intense frowny face, which is probably supposed to make me feel bad.

It doesn't.

Eyes narrowing, I shake my head. "No, we don't. It's degrading and just plain rude."

He smirks before sneering. "No one's ever complained before."

Not only do I find that comment completely dubious, but I can almost feel my blood pressure skyrocketing. Yup, Brooklyn is definitely a dead woman because this party has moved beyond painful to full-out tortuous.

"What's your name?"

"Alex Mc—"

I hold up my hand and cut him off. "That's enough." For a moment, my gaze flies around the vicinity we're standing in. Luckily, as packed as this massive party is, it doesn't take long to find what I'm looking for.

"Excuse me," I shout over the pulsating music at a pretty girl walking past us. With a smile gracing her lips, she turns. The high wattage smile dims once she realizes she doesn't know who either one of us are.

Before she can make a hasty get away, I launch into my spiel. "Hi, what's your name?"

Her gaze, which is slightly blurry as well (*jeez...are there seriously no sober people at this party?*) bounces between me and Alex. I can tell she's hesitant to give me any information.

"Stacy."

I give her my most reassuring smile. "Hi, Stacy, I'm Cassidy and this is,," I point to the obnoxious buffoon standing next to me, "Alex. We're having a little disagreement that needs to be settled. Would you mind weighing in on the matter?"

Since Stacy still looks uncertain, I barrel on. "My friend here thinks it's perfectly acceptable to walk around a party grabbing the butts of girls he doesn't know. And furthermore, he's under the impression that we enjoy it. I'm wondering if you might have any thoughts on the matter."

Stacy no longer looks hesitant or uncertain as her heated gaze swings back to Alex. Then, in a big sweeping gesture, she jerks her hands out in front of her. "What makes you think *any* girl would enjoy being touched by some random dude she doesn't even know?"

Alex opens his mouth as if he might actually have a rebuttal in mind, but Stacy has other ideas. Like screeching at him in a very high, potentially eardrum shattering voice.

"Where do you get off thinking you can grope a girl simply because you're drunk at a party? Is there something seriously wrong with you? Do you have any concept that we're living in the twenty-first century?"

Alex snaps his mouth shut, and even though it's difficult, I do my best to suppress the smile that is desperately trying to spread across my face as she continues to berate him.

"That's called sexual harassment, buddy." Her hands fly to her hips as she continues to glare. "Do you know that I could call the police and have you ticketed? Or even arrested!"

Okay, I'm not sure if that's true but I'm going to roll with it.

As if finally realizing this teeny-tiny chick is about to go batshit crazy all over his dumb ass, Alex's wide brown eyes shift helplessly to mine as Stacy pokes a slender finger at his massive wall-like chest.

He looks like he might want me to intervene on his behalf. I almost laugh because that is *so* not going to happen. I'm viewing this whole thing as a *teachable moment*. I only hope Alex is teachable. Although, in all honesty, the jury is still out on that one.

From what I've seen tonight, my guess is probably *not*.

"How would you like it if a chick you didn't know started groping you at a club or a party?" Hostility flashes in her blue eyes. It wouldn't surprise me in the least if she started foaming at the mouth. My guess is that Stacy has been manhandled one too many times before.

Hopefully Alex isn't stupid enough to answer that question.

"I'd be totally down with it." For the first time in five minutes, he actually smirks.

Stacy's mouth drops open as her eyes widen in disbelief. A moment later, her hand shoots out. I'm half afraid she's going to bitch-slap Alex into next week when she grabs a girl walking past us and yanks her over. The girl, wearing a pair of four-inch heels, stumbles before recovering her balance. My hat off to her for remaining upright. It's not always easy to do in sky-high heels.

"Ally, this *guy*," she waves her hand in Alex's direction as if that term is debatable, "thinks it's perfectly acceptable to grab a girl's butt at a party."

If the frown is any indication, Ally is none-too-pleased by this information either. One hand settles on her hip as her lip curls in disgust. "Why do guys always think that's okay to do?" Even though this is posed as a question, it's more rhetorical in nature. "I am so damn sick and tired of that shit!"

Silently, I shake my head before shrugging. Alex's gaze darts with more unease between the two fuming girls who are all up in his face.

"Ahhh—"

He never gets a chance to finish that thought (I'm being overly generous with that assertion) before both Stacy and Ally steamroll over him. "It is definitely *not* okay! You can't just walk around touching women inappropriately!"

"Ahhh—" Alex's mouth gapes like a fish out of water. You can actually glimpse the moment he grasps the severity of his predicament.

"What's going on over here?"

A tall brunette shoves her way into the tight circle before glancing around at the four of us.

"Oh hey, Ashley. Can you believe this jerk thinks it's okay to sexually harass a woman?"

Now Ashley's brows are lowering as her gaze arrows straight to Alex. "No one in this day and age could possibly think that it's okay to touch a woman without asking first."

She waits for Alex to clear his good name. Unfortunately, Alex continues to stare at her. He looks perplexed and a little surprised that he's the object of three hot girls' interest.

Of course, that interest isn't the kind he's been trolling for this evening.

Alex takes a hasty step backward as all three girls crowd into his personal space. Every single one of them talking or shouting at the same time. Since Alex will be tied up for the foreseeable future, I decide my work is done here and take off in search of Brooklyn. I'm more than ready to go home before any more of these drunken louts decide that party time ass grabbing is a legitimate sport.

I'm no more than ten steps away from Alex and his irate entourage, who are currently, by the volume of their collective voices, giving him a major ass-chewing, when a male voice says near my ear, "I saw what you did back there."

Since I've filled my quota for inane conversations this evening, I ignore him and keep pushing my way through the thick press of bodies. I'm tired, a little bit cranky, and more than ready to take off. If I have to drag Brooklyn out of here, I'm more than willing to do it. And I certainly don't have the wherewithal—not to mention the patience—to deal with any more hammered, frat boy-asshole-types tonight. Alex squandered the very last of it.

Without bothering to turn, I throw the words over my shoulder and continue to weave my way around clumps of drunken college coeds. "I don't know what you're talking about."

"Sure, you do."

I can practically hear the laughter simmering in his rich, deep voice. Realizing this guy isn't going to leave me alone, I decide the best course of action is to stop and politely let him know that I'm not interested in anything he might be offering up this evening. Exasperated at getting held up when all I want to do is find Brooklyn and leave this out-of-control party, I wheel around toward the voice at my ear. As my eyes land on his face, I suck in a big breath of air before almost choking on it.

2

CASSIDY

don't know what's going on with me, but I can't stop staring. And when I say *staring*, I mean full-on checking him out. It's embarrassing. Although honestly, I don't think I've ever seen anyone as beautiful as the guy standing before me.

Okay, so maybe *beautiful* is the wrong word. I don't think guys really like being referred to as *beautiful*, but there isn't another word to adequately describe him.

He's completely beautiful.

It's tempting to stand here and stare at him for the rest of the night.

But I won't because, in my limited experience, beautiful guys are—more often than not—egotistical douchebags. Even though I'm only nineteen, I've already had my fill of those.

So thanks, but no thanks.

That being said, my fingers almost itch to slide their way through all that messy chocolate-colored hair. And don't even get me started on those golden-brown eyes of his. Yup, totally dreamy.

Er...if I were a dreamy sort of girl, that is.

Which, trust me, I'm not.

He's almost as tall as Alex but not quite as broad in the shoulders.

Athletic-looking with long, lean muscles that are showcased in jeans and a simple dark, T-shirt that hugs his chest and upper arms quite nicely.

And damn if that isn't my very own personal kryptonite.

This guy is way too gorgeous for his own good.

Mine too.

It takes effort to shake myself out of the stupor that has fallen over me, because I'm definitely not in the market for a boyfriend or a random hookup or even a friends-with-benefits situation.

I want nothing to do with guys, period.

End of story.

Then he goes and smiles this smooth, slow grin that spills its way dangerously across his strikingly handsome face.

Aw, crap.

The kicker is a pair of perfectly placed dimples that wink at me.

No doubt about it—*definitely* kryptonite material.

It's almost laughable the way my heart slams against my breast as I stare. I'm not the kind of girl who is susceptible to male eye candy. No matter how beautifully packaged it is.

So...whatever he wants, I'll be passing on. Now, if there happens to be a tiny pang of regret sliding its way through me at the notion of walking away, I shut it down before I can make any more disastrous decisions in my life. Because, trust me, I've already made more than my fair share of them.

"Nope, sorry." After the calamity that was last year, I'm only beginning to find my bearings. Self-preservation is now the name of the game. "I have no idea what you're talking about."

Unfortunately, he isn't so easily deterred. I almost sigh. The good-looking ones never are. "So, what did Alex do to deserve being chewed out by a pack of angry women?"

Without bothering to answer, because that's exactly how one gets sucked into these kinds of conversations, I swing away. The sudden need to escape surges its way through me. I push and shove with more impatience, searching for Brooklyn's blonde head in the crowd.

Even though I'm desperate to leave, I refuse to abandon Brooklyn.

We agreed early on to always use the buddy system when out at night which is partly how I got wrangled into this mess in the first place. If I'm not being forced to join her for a night of heavy drinking and possible hookups, I usually make sure she's with someone who won't flake out at two in the morning and leave her stranded at some off campus fraternity party.

Bad things happen to girls who think there is safety in a party of one.

I'm hoping if I ignore Mr. Beautiful long enough, he'll give up and go away. That's usually my go-to weapon of defense. And most of the time, it's effective.

"Hey, are you going to answer me?"

Again, his voice is distractingly at my ear. I can practically feel his warm breath ghosting over my flesh. Little shivers of pleasure laced with fear skitter their way down my spine. I grit my teeth in response, attempting to ignore him.

Good-looking or not, this is just annoying. Although, most of my irritation is directed at myself for the reaction he's able to pull so effortlessly from me. It's taken the better part of nine months to emotionally deaden myself. Somehow this guy has shot all my hard work to hell with two adorable dimples and a pair of gorgeous whiskey-colored eyes. Not to mention the rest of the package.

Yeah, it's best *not* to think about that right now.

Without a word of warning, I spin toward him again. I'm hoping the element of surprise will have him backing off. Except he's much closer than anticipated. With the shitty luck I'm having this evening, I crash into his muscular chest.

Did I happen to mention how hard all that chiseled strength is beneath my fingertips?

Or that I might actually enjoy running my hands over what I imagine to be amazing pecs?

This isn't good.

With lightning quick reflexes, he reaches out to steady me as my gaze clashes with his.

"No." Usually, if ignoring doesn't work, bitch-mode will get the job done rather nicely. That's my second go-to line of defense. And since I'm not naturally a bitch (I'm really not), it's not something I enjoy doing.

Once in a while, I'll actually get called a lesbian for not being interested. Why is it that the most persistent guys are always the ones who take rejection the hardest? And they certainly like to go right for the jugular when it becomes clear—to them anyway—that they won't be tapping anything of mine with anything of theirs.

Totally annoying.

Narrowing those gorgeous eyes of his, half his mouth lifts into a smile. My breath catches again. How can that be just as devastating as the full-blown smile he's already treated me to?

I almost have to shake my head to clear it of the spell he's weaving around me.

"No?" He tilts his head a bit to the side and continues to watch me. There's just a hint of a smirk hovering around the edges of his lips.

"No." Forcing myself to hold strong against all this gorgeousness crammed into one irresistible package, I repeat before elaborating, "I wasn't going to answer you."

Brows drawing together, he blinks as if I'm some sort of strange specimen smeared across a microscope slide. "What's your name?"

I shake my head.

Nope. We are definitely not going to play this game. There is no way in hell I'm getting dragged into a quasi-friendship with this guy. I can already feel it would be a mistake of epic proportions.

If, and that's a really big *if*, I have a type, this guy is it. Therefore, he must be avoided at all costs. That would be the smartest move to make and I'm all about being smart. I refuse to fuck up my life any more than I already have.

His brows, which are thick but not overly caterpillar-like, hike up his forehead in disbelief. "So, let me get this straight—you won't tell me what Alex did to upset you *and* you won't give me your name?" Laughter brims in his rich, deep voice as he shakes his head.

The slow scald of a blush burns its way across my cheeks. Nervously, I glance around the crammed, dimly lit room one last time, hoping Brooklyn will magically appear so I can grab her and bolt, but that apparently isn't meant to be.

There hasn't been a Brooklyn sighting in at least twenty minutes.

"I'm not upset." But I'm definitely getting there. And it has absolutely nothing to do with the gigantic ass who groped me and everything to do with the gorgeous, tawny-eyed, dimpled Adonis who won't leave me alone.

"But you did sic those three girls on him, right?" He nods his head to the left, and my gaze naturally slides in that direction. We're both able to see the incredibly tall and brawny Alex along with the three girls who are still in the process of ripping him a new one. Focusing on that for a moment lightens my mood considerably, because you can just tell those girls have totally committed themselves to their mission. It's doubtful Alex will be going anywhere for a while. And if he does manage to escape their clutches, they'll probably follow him, picking up more girls along the way.

Technically speaking, I only pulled one girl into our conversation. That being said, I'm not going to lie, it's kind of a proud moment for me. I really hope Alex has learned his ass grabbing lesson tonight.

"He got what he deserved," I say.

I consider that entire incident a public service to all women who attend Western University.

You're welcome.

Not to be thrown off course, he persists. "So just tell me what he did to deserve it." He looks genuinely interested. But still...

I narrow my eyes because this little back and forth is exactly what I didn't want to get sucked into.

Hmm...ignoring him didn't work.

And bitchiness hasn't deterred him either.

Maybe if I just give him the answers he's after, he'll get bored and wander off in search of easier prey.

Huffing out an aggravated breath, I mumble, "He grabbed my ass."

Those golden eyes darken as the corners of his mouth sink into a deep frown. "I'm sorry he did that to you. I think Alex is pretty wasted."

I scowl. "Being drunk isn't an excuse for sexually harassing me. What he did was wrong." I stab a finger in Alex's direction. "That dude got what he deserved. Actually, he's lucky I didn't knock his front teeth out."

Eyes flaring, he holds up both hands. "I never claimed it was an acceptable justification for touching you." He looks upset that I think he's making excuses for his meathead friend, but I don't care. I want him gone. His very presence unnerves me, and I don't like it.

Even though I know he means well, I carry on with my plan to drive him away. "Actually," I cut in, "that's *exactly* what you said."

His thick brows jerk together as he shakes his head. "But it's not what I meant. I just wanted you to understand that he drank a few too many and isn't using good judgment. Alex is a harmless guy. But yeah, I guess he thought you were pretty and was looking for a way to approach you."

This conversation has gone from bad to worse.

My mouth falls open. "So, you're telling me," I say with a shitload of disbelief, "that this is my fault because he thinks I'm *pretty?*"

Is this guy for real?

His eyes widen at the insinuation. "No," he snaps with a bit of heat, "that's not what I meant at all." His expression turns to one of frustration as he runs a hand through his messy brown hair.

I'm momentarily distracted by those rich, chocolate-colored strands. Yup, totally dangerous.

"But that's what you said."

Thankfully, this conversation is going exactly where I need it to—and that's right down the tubes. Like I said before—gorgeous guy, total asshole behavior. Guess I'm not as far off the mark as I'd originally suspected. But this is exactly what I want—for him to expose himself as a douche, and for me to move on without a second thought.

What doesn't make sense is why I'm left with a vague feeling of disappointment. I force that thought away before I can examine it too closely.

Looking exasperated, which yeah, is a totally adorable look on him as well, he snaps, "Damn it, I know that's what I said. All I wanted to do was apologize for Alex pissing you off." He glares at me with those amazing golden eyes of his. "I'm apologizing on behalf of my friend. That's it. Okay?"

Uncertain where we go from here, I shrug. "Fine. Apology accepted."

It's definitely time to leave. If this guy has any self-preservation skills whatsoever, he'll let me go about my business without trying to detain me.

"Bye." I give him a half wave and swing around to search the thick press of bodies for my roommate.

Make that my former roommate...

"Hold up!"

Holy crap!

All I want to do is shake this guy loose.

Why can't he take a hint?

I'm not interested!

I don't want to be interested.

I don't need the distraction.

And he's definitely a distraction.

"I need to find Brooklyn so I can get the hell out of here," I mutter.

"What?" His breath feathers along the back of my neck, making goosebumps ripple across my arms. I grit my teeth, attempting to suppress my body's natural reaction to him.

Heat flares in my narrowed eyes as I careen toward him for a third time. "Are you following me?" My gaze locks on his. As annoyed as I am right now, I still find him completely dreamy, which only exacerbates all those feelings of frustration and annoyance that are roiling through me.

"Um...yes?"

He sounds none too sure. His gaze holds mine, and even though I don't want him melting the thick sheath of ice protecting me, he is.

I inhale a deep breath before slowly blowing it out and trying to calm the raging mess inside me once and for all.

"Look, you seem like a nice guy." Well, as nice of a guy as I'm going find at an ass grabbing kegger. "But this isn't going to happen."

His brows slide together and it's kind of...argh, it's kind of adorable.

Aw hell, it's completely adorable. Damn him for being completely gorgeous and adorable. That is such a lethal combination. I'm sure he has all the girls at Western swooning at his feet.

But I'm not one of those girls.

"What's not going to happen?" His confusion only adds to his adorableness.

Seriously, I cannot catch a break here.

I waggle my finger between us. I have to stifle a groan because he's so damn close. And yes, I probably should have known he would smell amazing. Like the ocean on a perfectly sunny day with just a hint of a breeze. I want to inhale a big breath of him. I don't dare because he's much too dangerous for the likes of me.

"This."

"I just want to know your name," he replies quietly as if he actually means it.

I can't deny that a tiny part of me wants to tell him.

Holding firm against all that cuteness packaged neatly in front of me, I force myself to give him a patronizing look. "*Right.*" I roll my eyes. "Sure, you do." Then I go for the kill. "Look, I'm not going to fuck you. Not tonight. Or tomorrow night. Or ever."

I point to all the scantily clad girls that surround us.

Of which there are many.

"There are a lot easier marks around here than me. Go find one of them to play with."

I spin back around but don't get far. Surprised by the sudden grip on my upper arm, he swings me to him. His brows are scrunched and low over his eyes as he glares.

"I'm not interested in getting laid, and it's a shitty assumption for thinking that's the only reason I'd want to talk with you."

Eyes wide, I freeze beneath his touch as my heart jackhammers painfully. A sudden release of adrenaline careens through my veins as sweat pops out across my brow and my chest tightens. Even though his grip isn't punishing, it has every cell in my body seizing with panic.

I don't like being touched. Or grabbed. Or manhandled.

In all honesty, I'd been nice to Alex and had let him off easy.

But this...*this* isn't okay.

"Take your hand off me!" I growl, unable to stop the fine tremble from sliding through my body.

His eyes widen as he drops my arm as if I've burned him with the heat of my words. Silently, we stare for a long, painful heartbeat. Or maybe it's twenty. The rowdy laughter and pulsing music that surrounds us fades to the background.

My ragged breath hitches as I suck in oxygen before forcing it slowly out.

Even though he's dropped my arm, I'm still gripped by a tidal wave of anxiety as it crashes over me, threatening to drag me under. The slight trembling turns into bone-shaking tremors. My chest feels like it is being squeezed by a vise.

I can't breathe.

I have to get out of here.

A few more seconds and I'll be choking on my panic. I can feel the familiar tendrils coiling inside me. The last thing I need is to lose my shit in front of all these drunken strangers.

Silently, I spin on my heels before shoving my way through the thick press of bodies until I reach the front door. As soon as I get to the porch, the brisk night air slaps at my cheeks, and I inhale deep gulps of fresh air before stumbling my way down the sidewalk like a drunken idiot. I need to put as much distance as I can between myself and that party. Even though I try to settle the frantic thoughts rolling through my head, it's impossible.

It's too late to rein in all my out-of-control emotions.

Bending over, I vomit my dinner onto someone's overgrown front yard. The only bright side I can find in this mess is that my pile of puke probably won't be the only one gracing the lawn come morning.

3

___

CASSIDY

A low groan rumbles its way from deep within the mountain of pillows and blankets.

"I don't feel good," the voice croaks. "I think I have the flu."

I snort with about as much derision as I can muster. "What you technically have is called the twenty-four-hour booze flu," I singsong gleefully before yanking open the thick, ugly blue curtains covering our dorm room window and allowing bright sunlight to filter in.

It's impossible to summon one ounce of pity for someone who knowingly inflicts this kind of pain onto themselves.

Brooklyn whimpers before attempting to burrow further into the abyss of blankets and pillows piled high on her dorm-issued twin bed.

"Come on, up and at 'em, sunshine. You've got class in forty." I pretend to wince as I add with false pity, "Oh, and don't you have Calculus this bright and fine Friday morning with Professor Ling? Yeah…that's going to suck for you."

"No," she moans. "No class. Can't go. Not today. Too sick. Head pounding. Might throw up. Must sleep."

"Didn't you tell me that your partying wouldn't get in the way of attending classes? I made you promise before agreeing to live together."

And yes, I really had secured a verbal agreement from my bestie regarding this kind of situation. After last year, I'm not interested in partying. My sole objective is my classes. But moving in with Brooklyn, who I've known forever, seemed like a far better choice than playing Russian roulette with a random roommate assignment.

"No," she mumbles before smashing another pillow over her face, "I never promised any such thing."

"Sure, you did. I've got it in writing somewhere around here." I move loudly around the room, preparing for my nine o'clock class. Grabbing a protein bar, I open the wrapper and take a big, crunchy bite.

"Bitch," she mutters from under the covers.

Well, I think that's what she mutters.

I grin at the mound of pillows and blankets. "But I'm a lovable bitch, right?"

Most of the time.

Probably...

She grumbles something unintelligible I can't quite decipher. I'm not sure if she agrees or disagrees with that statement. But since she's experiencing a killer hangover, I'm going to guess she's in disagreement.

"You're down to thirty minutes now. Tick tock, tick tock." I set a glass of water and two acetaminophen tablets on the table beside her bed. "Take the pills and guzzle the water. It'll help." Honestly, it can't hurt at this point.

The only good thing I have to say about Brooklyn this morning is that the girl can definitely hold her liquor. I thought for sure when I'd texted last night to meet me outside the house, and then carried her drunk ass home, she would be puking all over the place.

Much to my pleasant surprise, that hadn't turned out to be the case. Nor had she died of alcohol poisoning either.

So, win-win in my book.

She ignores me and mutters, "I think you'd be a much happier person if you got laid once in a while. Just something to consider."

"I'm already a perfectly happy person." My sunny disposition nose-dives at the suggestion.

I tried that trick last year…it hadn't worked out so well.

After ten more minutes of cajoling Brooklyn from bed, she reluctantly pulls the pillows and blankets off her face before blinking at the harsh sunlight pouring in through the large bank of east-facing windows. She covers her eyes with a hand as if the bright light might scorch her retinas. "You're a horrible person for forcing me to get up when I feel like such crap."

My gaze slides over the little bit of her I can see. Her long blonde hair is in total disarray and her skin is waxy looking. Actually, she looks a little green around the gills.

"If it's any consolation, you look just as bad as you feel."

"Bitch," she grumbles.

Unaffected by her new pet name for me, I shrug. "Alright then, I'm off." I wrap a turquoise scarf around my neck before grabbing my oversized messenger bag and sunglasses as I head out. "See you later, alligator."

Just as I'm about to close the door, I whip it open and poke my head back inside.

"Get your lazy ass out of bed right now," I bellow at the top of my lungs.

In answer, she hurtles one of her hot pink pillows at the door. It falls pathetically short of its mark. I shake my head at such an embarrassingly sad attempt.

"Has anyone ever told you that you have really shitty aim?" A future softball competitor, she is not. It's doubtful she'd even do well in an over forty beer league.

Her second attempt almost hits its intended target. "Better."

I smile as one of her hands snakes out from the thick pile of blankets to flip me off.

With a snicker, I shut the door before hustling my way across campus for my nine o'clock class which—thanks to Brooklyn—I'm running late for. I try to multitask on the fly as I read a text sent by one of my professors. Even though this bad habit is always ill-advised when trying to maneuver through a herd of students who are also attempting to haul ass across campus, I do it anyway.

I certainly can't deny my own stupidity as I smack into a wall. With a grunt, I stagger back a few steps before strong arms reach out to steady me.

To the best of my knowledge, walls don't have arms.

It only takes a moment for my belly to hollow out because I think I recognize that muscular chest.

Crap.

Could life seriously be cruel enough to throw this guy into my oblivious path within twelve short hours of our previous meeting?

The answer to that question is a resounding *yes*.

My gaze arrows to his smiling, golden-brown eyes. A slight wind ruffles his gorgeous hair as we stand in the middle of the cement walking path that snakes its way through campus.

"Oh, you've got to be kidding me," I mutter, feeling off kilter.

One of his dark brows lifts at my disgruntled greeting. "Let me guess," he says, "now you think I'm stalking you."

My eyes widen before narrowing in consideration.

Hmmm. I suppose that's a possibility.

"Are you?"

He snorts before shaking his head. He shifts his weight, looking as if he might be settling in for a long conversation. "I don't even know your name, remember? You wouldn't give it to me last night."

"It's a good thing I didn't, because apparently, there's an excellent chance you might be stalking me," I quip while trying to think of a hasty exit strategy.

He runs his tongue across the front of his teeth.

I feel the effect of it straight down to my traitorous core.

Somehow, this guy has triggered more responses within me in the past twelve hours than any other guy has in the previous nine months.

"I'm not saying this to sound like a conceited jack—"

"But that's exactly what you'll sound like if you continue with that train of thought," I finish sweetly, hoping to cut him off so I can bale on this conversation.

"—ass, but most girls would be delighted to have my attention."

My gaze slides reluctantly over him again.

All right, I'll secretly admit that statement is probably accurate. With all that messy dark hair, golden-brown eyes, and handsomely chiseled face…

And let's not forgot about his muscular body. I'm willing to bet there's a six-pack hidden under that grey Henley.

My mouth dries at the thought.

What the hell am I doing?

I give myself a quick mental slap before rolling my eyes. "You're right, that *totally* makes you sound like a conceited jackass."

His eyes narrow.

I can almost feel the heat of them moving over me, singeing me in the process. Even though the morning air has a slight chill to it, I'm starting to feel hot all over.

"What did you say your name was again?"

A smile spreads slyly across my face. "I didn't, and because I don't want to encourage someone who I might have to take out a restraining order against, I'm not giving it to you either." Rather pointedly, I glance down at the phone in my hand. "Not that this conversation isn't scintillating, but I need to get going or I'll be late for my nine o'clock."

"Seeing as we're both heading the same way, I'll join you," he says smugly.

I groan.

Loudly.

Being coy has never been one of my fortes.

"No, that's okay. I'm in a hurry." I give him a bit of side-eye to see if he's gotten the hint that I'm not interested in him or his company.

If the grin gracing his lips is any indication, he hasn't. Or he just doesn't care. I'm going with the whole *doesn't care* theory.

Have I mentioned how aggravating I find this guy?

My feet grind to a halt as I glare at him.

He's tanking my morning mojo. Maybe if I make him uncomfortable enough, it'll penetrate his thick skull that I'm not interested.

He stops before eyeing me quizzically. After a few silent moments slide by he asks, "Are we going to stand around all day or head to class? 'Cuz I'm up for either."

Grrrr.

"Fine," I huff, figuring I'll only have to walk with him for a block or so before we go our separate ways. If I'm lucky, I'll never lay eyes on him again.

Thank god I don't know his name. It'll hopefully make forgetting him that much easier. I won't be able to put a name to that gorgeous face.

I internally wince at my own unfiltered thoughts.

Because I still think he's beautiful.

Ridiculously so.

And that's really saying something with the harsh morning sunlight pouring down on us. Anyone can look like a ten in dim party lighting. Somehow this guy manages to pull off being an eleven in bright sunlight at nine in the morning. And it wouldn't surprise me to learn that he just rolled out of bed looking like that either. The way the sun highlights all the different shades of mahogany color in his hair has something hot arrowing straight down to my core.

For the love of god and all that's holy, I still want to drag my traitorous fingers through his hair. I want to muss it up even more than it already is. He has one of those artfully messy hairstyles that not many guys can pull off so effortlessly. I, on the other hand, feel as if I've barely scraped myself together with a high ponytail and a scarf...

I seriously need to get away from this guy before I do something completely crazy and actually start to like him.

His deep voice breaks into the chaotic whirl of my thoughts. "So, where you headed?"

I sigh, reluctant to give him any more info than he's already been able to gather. I don't want whatever this is between us to become a habit.

"Psychology."

"Huh." A smile spreads across his face. "201?" He looks way too happy as he poses the question. It only shreds the last of my frayed nerves.

My guarded gaze swings to his as we continue walking. "That's right."

His grin broadens, and those damnable dimples flash and wink. "What a coincidence. Me, too."

Perfect.

But that doesn't necessarily mean we have to sit next to each other, does it?

I'll ditch him as soon as we enter the lecture hall. After all, it seats well over two hundred people, so there's plenty of room to put some much-needed distance between us. But now I'll have to see him three times a week for the remainder of the semester.

Talk about crummy luck.

"Hey, Cole," simpers a skinny blonde from out of nowhere.

Cole.

Crap.

I kind of like that name. And somehow, even though I don't know him, it fits perfectly. Now I have a name to go along with his striking face.

Double crap.

He offers a friendly smile along with a chin lift. From the corner of my eye, I can't help but watch their interaction. I want him to be flirty or maybe even stop and talk with her.

He doesn't.

"Hey, Jules, how's it going?"

A smile lights up her pretty face just before her eyes rove over him, eating the guy up alive. Jules isn't trying to hide the fact that she'd like nothing more than to take a big bite out of him. Even though I'm walking beside him and it's fairly obvious we're together—although not together, if you know what I mean—she doesn't spare me a glance.

Which is seriously fine with me…

But rude just the same.

"Are we gonna see you at the Alpha Sig party tonight?" Her voice lowers, becoming all sexy and sultry. At this point I want to roll my eyes. Doesn't this girl realize that it isn't even nine o'clock in the morning?

"Probably."

"Then I'll *definitely* look for you there." She bats her thick, mascara-laden lashes at him, and it takes everything I have inside not to bust out laughing.

I'm almost embarrassed for her.

She skewers him with an intense look. Kind of like she's attempting to use Jedi mind tricks or subliminal messaging, or something along those lines. I think she might be trying to convey that when she finds him tonight, there'll be an extra special treat in it for him.

Of a sexual nature…wink-wink.

It's entirely possible the protein bar I wolfed down might make an unexpected reappearance if I don't get out of here pronto. I'm unsure how much of Jules I can take this early in the morning without becoming violently ill.

Maybe I'd be more tolerant if I'd had my morning cup of coffee…but then again, probably not. Rather than watch the pair of them make googly eyes at one another—all right, so maybe the googly eyes are fairly one-sided—I hasten my step, thinking this might be the perfect opportunity to execute an escape plan. I don't like the way Cole makes the nerves in my belly tremble.

It's disconcerting.

"Okay, well, I'll catch you later." I speed up as we reach Dorin Hall, the social sciences building. Actually, I have absolutely no intention of catching him later.

Just when I think I've shaken him loose, kind of like a sticky burr, he's once again at my side as I push my way through the wide set of doors.

I do a double take before frowning.

Son of a—

4

———————

CASSIDY

"*D*id you really think you could ditch me that easily?" His whispered words send a shiver skating down my spine as something hot unfurls in the pit of my belly.

Or possibly lower.

Crap.

"It was more of a hope on my part," I reply lightly, searching for an empty seat in the already crowded room.

One empty seat is all I need.

Bingo.

As I scan the lecture hall, I find a girl with long blonde hair waving erratically at Cole. Just in case he doesn't notice her wild gesturing, I point out the frantic female. These girls are seriously ridiculous. Not to mention, desperate. But hey, I can totally help a sister out. Especially when it benefits me in return.

"You seem to have a fan over there who'd very much enjoy the pleasure of your company."

He flicks a casual wave in her direction as I start down the thinly carpeted steps. I like sitting front and center in all my classes. It feels as if the students buried in the back of the lecture halls are too busy talking, sleeping, or texting to pay attention.

Just as I step away, Cole slings a muscled arm across my shoulders, steering me toward his friend as he points in her direction.

"Look, there are two open seats. How perfect is that?"

My body tenses at the physical contact as I attempt to shrug him off. "No thanks. I like sitting near the front."

Apparently, he isn't as picky about seating as I am because he says, "Okay, lead the way. We'll sit where you want today."

Today?

I don't think so.

This has me skidding to a halt as my brows lower. Probably not the most attractive expression, but I don't give a shit at the moment.

"Cole," I say with far more patience than I'm feeling, "there's obviously a girl over there who would love to sit with you. And just in case you're confused," I shake my head before pointing to myself, "I'm not that girl."

Having said that, I stalk down the stairs toward the front of the lecture hall. Professor Mullens is already standing at the podium, ready to begin. I want to get to my seat and forget all about Cole whatever-the-hell-his-name-is.

Unfortunately, I have a sneaking suspicion I'm going to have a hard time doing that.

This pushy guy brings out the worst in me.

And I don't like it.

I don't like the way I react to him.

I don't like losing control over my emotions.

It's just one more reason to steer clear of him in the future. I already have more than enough reasons to shoot him to the tippy top of my *avoid like the plague* list. Actually, he's the only one occupying that list.

As far as I'm concerned, the guy already has three strikes against him, which is three too many.

He's way too good-looking (strike one).

He's too easy going (strike two).

And he didn't flirt, not even a little bit, with that girl (strike three, damn him).

Warning bells are already ringing inside my head, and I didn't even know the guy existed before last night. That seems like a bad sign.

We'll just make that strike four.

I slip into a seat parked between a guy and a girl. Neither of whom I know. I can't help but huff out a relieved breath that whatever little dance was happening with Cole is over. I'll just have to be careful to avoid him in the future. It shouldn't be difficult with a campus of twenty thousand students.

Just as I slide my computer from my bag, Cole taps the guy next to me. My fingers still as I wait for his next move. Because he can't possibly have one. I won this round.

I—

"Hey Garret, would you mind sliding over so I can sit next to my girlfriend?"

Gasping, my mouth tumbles open. And it just hangs there before I have the good sense to snap it shut.

He did not just say that!

But yeah, he did. Cole just told a complete stranger that he's my boyfriend.

"No problem." Garret grins as his gaze travels over me before gathering up his stuff and moving one desk over.

With an amused smirk, Cole settles next to me before closing the distance between us.

"Checkmate," he whispers.

"You've got some serious mental health issues, you know that, right?" I hiss, feeling completely at a loss and out of control.

That's the one thing I can't handle.

Emptying his backpack, he leans over again. "Shhh, the lecture is about to begin, and I really want to hear this."

Gnashing my teeth together, I jerk forward as Professor Mullens launches into the topic of current research methods within the field of psychology.

"We're going to start today's lecture by discussing the differences between qualitative and quantitative research methods. Everyone should have read chapters four and five from the book already, so let's delve in by exploring some of the finer points regarding each method."

I open my computer and begin typing notes, but can't seem to focus. Not with Cole sitting next to me. Every once in a while, his muscular leg brushes against mine, jerking me out of whatever research method she's discussing. Before I can stop myself, my gaze flickers to him.

It's almost surprising when he refrains from saying a word for the entire duration of the class. He simply takes notes on his computer, and yet I'm completely distracted by his presence. I'm barely able to follow along as the professor outlines when and why we use each method.

It doesn't take long for the fifty-minute class to turn tortuous.

Why am I so affected by him?

He's nothing special...not really. All right, fine. That's a lie. He's gorgeous and easy going. Argh...I need to get out of here before I self-combust.

As soon as the lecture ends, I bolt from my seat like my ass is on fire. I need to get away from him.

"Excuse me." I bounce on the tips of my toes before snapping, "I need to go, or I'll be late."

This isn't exactly true, but that doesn't really matter, does it?

When he doesn't immediately move out of my way, I push past him.

"Hold on and I'll walk out with you." He quickly stuffs his computer into his backpack before taking off after me.

As soon as we're out of the social sciences building, I spin around toward him. I'm pretty sure there's a mixture of fire and fear glowing in my eyes. "You know I'm one step away from taking out a restraining order, right?"

Instead of getting annoyed the way I expect, he grins. Those damn dimples flash, making his face more handsome than before. What's clear is that I'm not as indifferent as I'm pretending to be. And that scares me. A lot.

Within fifteen minutes of meeting him, he triggered an anxiety attack.

That's bad news.

I want to laugh. Or maybe cry because I'd thought they were getting better. I'd transitioned almost seamlessly to Western this fall. And there's no way in hell I'll allow myself to backpedal. Cole sparks something unwanted within me. Something I'm irresistibly drawn to all the while making me feel distinctly out of control and frightened.

That's one hell of a lethal combination.

For me, anyway.

I need to run him off before everything gets more complicated.

"Good, then at least I'll be able to figure out your name."

Hmm. I don't have a snappy come back for that. I can only shake my head and snort.

This guy is impossible.

Impossibly good-looking.

Impossibly persistent.

Impossibly charming.

Just plain impossible!

It kind of makes me wish I'd met him before...well, before my life imploded.

I shove the thought away before it can take root. The fact of the matter is that I didn't. Cole is in the here and now, and I'm...*broken*. The sooner he realizes that, the better off we'll both be.

"Holy shit." His hand flies to his mouth as his golden eyes widen with exaggeration. "I think you might have chuckled."

The way his gaze roves over my face only makes the edges of my lips twitch even more. He really is impossible. Being the smart-ass he apparently is (that's strike five), he gasps in mock astonishment. "And a smile. An honest-to-goodness smile. I wasn't sure it was possible."

I roll my eyes, all the while trying to get my facial muscles under control. It's not as easy as it should be.

"See, you like me." He winks before adding with just a hint of arrogance, "You want to date me."

My brows snap together. "Oh, that reminds me, please refrain from telling people I'm your girlfriend." There. The smile has been completely wiped away.

"You will be." He looks smug and way too self-confident about his prediction. It's perplexing and…oddly attractive.

Damn.

Damn.

Damn.

Disconcerted by how this conversation is unraveling, I shake my head. "No, sorry. I don't date."

"That's good, because I don't want my girlfriend dating other guys. It sets a bad precedent."

I draw in a steady breath before reiterating, "I'm not your girlfriend. And I have no intention of becoming your girlfriend." I have no intention of becoming anyone's girlfriend. That's when it hits me. "Oh, I get it. You think this is a game and I'm playing hard to get. Let me disabuse you of that notion."

Why is it always this way?

Whatever Cole thinks is happening here needs to end. It's getting out of control. I'm not interested. All right, maybe I'm a little interested, but that's beside the point. I'm not here to find a man.

"I think I know how to solve this."

Before he can ask any questions, I push into his space until my body is aligned against his. Little tingles of awareness dance across my flesh as my breasts press against the solid wall of his…oh my…powerfully built chest.

I almost lose focus as my breath hitches.

Gazing up into those tawny-colored eyes, I pour all the hunger I can't allow myself to feel into that one lustful look. Unable to resist the opportunity, I stroke my hands over his pecs until they're sliding up and over the broad set of his shoulders.

Jeez. This guy is hard all over.

I gulp as that thought rings unwantedly throughout my head and tingles of awareness shoot down to my core in response.

What becomes obvious is that I'm not the only one affected here.

He draws in a ragged breath as we silently hold each other's gazes. Heat and hunger fill his eyes as my legs nearly buckle.

"I love you," I whisper. "Let's move in together. I want to quit college, marry you, and have lots of babies. At least four. Maybe five. How does that sound?" I trail my fingers over his chest, enjoying the play of hard sinewy muscle.

His arms snake around my body, hauling me impossibly close. My nipples pebble against his strength and my brain become a little hazy from the intimate contact. My eyes widen because his chest isn't the only hard thing I'm feeling...

Oh my...

"I think that sounds pretty damn fantastic. Let's do it," he murmurs seconds before his mouth crashes onto mine. I expect the slide of his lips to feel forceful, almost punishing, but they're not. In fact, the caress is soft and—

Before it can go any further, I jerk away from him and bark, "What the hell do you think you're doing?"

Heads snap in our direction as my heart pounds and skin prickles with awareness. And my lower regions...

They've snapped to attention as well.

Crap.

His lips quirk at the corners as his eyes crinkle with humor. "Um, I was kissing the girl I'm going to marry. Why? What did it feel like I was doing?"

He's way too cool and collected.

And I am so not...

This is the part where I act like a child by screeching in annoyance before stomping away. "We are *not* dating, and we are certainly *not* getting married!" Guess that one backfired. My breasts are still tingling and feel achy from being pressed against all that delicious strength.

And that kiss...holy hell.

My fingers fly to my lips as his laughter follows me.

The bastard.

"I'll be seeing you around!" He shouts as I vacate the area as fast as possible.

I don't bother to glance back before flipping him the bird. This has not been one of my finest hours. As I stalk away, embarrassment slides through me. Why does this guy have such a knack for bringing out the worst in me?

Better question—what am I going to do about it?

I have the sinking feeling that avoiding him will be impossible.

Somehow, I think that kiss sealed my fate.

5

CASSIDY

"Cassidy, your four o'clock is here."

With my nose buried deep in a calculus book, I murmur, "Great Lisa, send him back."

Lisa, our sort-of-receptionist, hovers in the doorway for a few moments until I'm forced to glance up and meet her wide gaze.

Only then does she mouth, "He's *soooo* hot." As if to add emphasis, she rolls her eyes.

I roll mine in response before shaking my head. Also for emphasis. Lisa thinks most guys are *soooo* hot. I'll admit, sometimes she's right. And sometimes she's wrong.

Very, very wrong.

But I suppose beauty is in the beer goggles of the beholder...or something like that. Not that Lisa usually drinks on the job. Although, sometimes I seriously have to wonder.

I plaster a smile across my lips and wait for my next appointment, interested to see how far off base she is today. A few seconds later, the smile falls off my face as Cole strolls into the room. As soon as he sees me, he stops, obviously just as surprised as I am. But that doesn't stop the wide smile from settling across his handsome face.

There's that shit luck again.

I can't seem to catch a break where he's concerned.

My eyebrows lower as I glare. "You keep turning up like a bad penny."

The kiss we shared the other day is, at this very moment, rolling through my brain and I can't make it stop.

Brooklyn is probably right. I need to get laid if I can't stop thinking about one tiny, insignificant kiss that shouldn't even be on my radar.

But yeah, it is so on my radar.

Cole steps into the small room we use for math tutoring before lowering himself down across from me. His tall frame makes the room shrink around us. His golden gaze doesn't relinquish mine, which only heightens my awareness of him, along with my discomfort. That's all it takes for my nerves to hum.

"And here I was thinking this was more serendipitous than anything else."

That has me snorting.

Serendipitous my ass…

But I can't actually say that to him. This is my place of employment. Even if it is just a few hours a week, it's important I maintain a professional manner. Eyeing him, I realize that's going to be impossible and wonder if a potential firing looms in the near future. The problem is that I need the small amount of money this job brings in.

It's the thought of being let go from my position that has me saying, "Maybe it would be best if you work with a different tutor."

His brows slide together in genuine confusion, as if he doesn't remember the stalker accusations I recently hurtled in his direction. Or that I flipped him the bird.

"Why would I want to do that? Don't you know Calculus II?"

"Of course, I do," I shoot back before thinking better of it, "I took it in high school."

He stares for a moment. "You took Calc II in high school? Wow. I'm impressed. You're obviously a math genius. I only made it through pre-Calc. And I pretty much wanted to shoot myself the entire year."

I shrug, not liking how this conversation has backfired on me. It's becoming a pattern.

When I remain silent, he asks, "What year are you?"

I bite down on my lower lip before reluctantly admitting, "Freshman."

It's technically true. What I don't bother to mention is that I should really be a sophomore. It's none of his business.

"You're a freshman taking Calculus III?"

The question makes me fidget on my hard plastic seat as a slow grin tugs the corners of his lips upward. The way his dimples wink from across the small table that separates us, sets off a little flurry of excitement, which is impossible to stomp out, within the confines of my belly.

"Yes," I mutter, giving him my best *I'm-trying-to-make-you-uncomfortable-so-that-you-leave-me-alone-and-never-come-back* stare.

He whistles, oblivious to the subliminal messages I'm directing his way. "And you understand Calculus II?"

Is he for real?

Of course, I understand Calc II. I could probably do it in my sleep.

"I passed with a ninety-eight percent."

"In high school?" His brows shoot up.

"Yes," I ground out uncomfortably. Leaving and never coming back doesn't seem to be uppermost in his mind.

He grins. "After careful consideration and interviewing several potential candidates, I believe you're the best tutor for me."

His words have me biting down on my lower lip. It would seem like I'm not much of a *genius* after all.

"Fine, let's just get started." So we can get this over with as quickly and painlessly as possible.

"Great." A satisfied smile trembles around the corners of his lips as he pulls out his calculus book and notepad. It's enough to make my belly hollow out. Honestly, you'd think I'd be used to the feeling by now. Instead, it throws me off every time it happens.

"Your name is Cassidy, huh?"

Since we both know it is, I don't bother dignifying the question with a response.

I clear my throat. "Why don't you show me what you're having trouble with." I need to get this show on the road and him out the door, not to mention out of my life.

Is that even possible anymore?

Unconsciously, my gaze falls to his lips as that kiss tumbles its way through my head for probably the hundredth time. It takes everything I have inside to force it away.

Unaware of my discomfort, he flips open his book, thumbing through a few pages before turning it around until I'm able to see the problems. After a few moments, he gets up and resettles on the chair next to me so we're both able study the page together. "I can't wrap my brain around the unit on parametric equations."

Distracted by his nearness, I nod, attempting to focus on the concepts, which is a challenge because he smells damn near edible. It's a potent concoction of the ocean and citrusy sunshine. I hate how intoxicating it is.

It takes a few attempts to forget about his delicious scent and slip into tutor mode, as I do my best to re-explain parametric equations in a way that makes sense. By the time sixty minutes have slipped by, Cole has plowed his way through four challenging problems.

What this hour has taught me is that Cole is smart and focused. He grasps complicated concepts easily when they're broken down into manageable chunks and explained properly.

Ugh.

Like I need anything else to like about him.

Once the last problem has been tackled, we both sit back in our plastic chairs before stretching out cramped muscles.

He rubs the back of his neck, shifting it one way and then the other. "Thanks. That makes so much more sense now. I wish Professor Ling could have explained it like that the first time."

Cole has him for Calc II this semester, and I have him for Calc III. Luckily, math has always come easily, so I don't struggle. I don't need to attend the lectures to understand the concepts. I could easily get through the book on my own. But most people don't grasp mathematics like I do, which is why tutoring in my spare time works well for me. I can set my own schedule, and in the two weeks I've been working in the tutoring lab, there have been no shortage of students to help.

With his golden-brown gaze locked on mine, Cole asks, "Are you done for the day?"

"Yup." I roll my aching shoulders, trying to work out all the kinks. I've been tutoring for three straight hours. Not only am I tired, but I have my own studies to get through. When his knee brushes against mine, my thoughts arrow straight back to him and those pesky butterflies in the pit of my belly wing their way back to life again. I'm left feeling both uncomfortable and slightly shaken. No one has ever affected me this way.

He makes everything worse by leaning into my personal space. Now I'm able to see the ridiculous amount of gold flecks churning in his whiskey-colored depths.

Nope. I definitely don't like the effect he has on me.

"Want to grab something to eat? All this calculus has made me work up an appetite. I'm starving."

My stomach takes this opportunity to embarrass me by rumbling in agreement.

One side of his mouth lifts into a knowing grin. "Should I take that as a yes?"

I shake my head. The fragile comradery we've carefully forged over the previous hour dissolves as I draw my protective armor around myself.

"Sorry, can't. I have a protein bar in my backpack. I need to head over to the library and study for a few hours."

"Come on, Cassidy," he cajoles, dimples flashing enticingly.

I'd be lying if I didn't admit, at least privately to myself, that the sound of my name rolling off his lips does funny things to my insides. As far as I'm concerned, it's one more reason to stay far away from Cole.

The word *danger* continues to flash like a bright neon sign in my brain. I'm smart enough not to ignore a warning when I see one.

I shake my head. "I don't think that would be a good idea." In fact, spending more time alone with Cole is a disastrous idea. My fight or flight instincts have kicked in.

Too bad they kicked in a year too late.

"Give me one good reason why it isn't a fantastic idea." He sits back, crossing his arms over his wide chest as if it's a challenge. Which it's not. I have nothing to prove to this guy. My gaze unconsciously drops to his well-defined pecs. Even through a tight-fitting T-shirt, I'm able to make out their contour. It takes a moment to realize I'm staring before yanking my gaze back to his.

What greets me is a knowing smirk.

I clear my dry throat, needing a distraction. "Now that we have a working relationship, I shouldn't be hanging out with you." I wave my hand in the air. "I'm sure there are rules or something about it."

"So, you're telling me there are policies written down that state this? If that's the case, I'd like to see them."

When I remain stubbornly silent, he presses onward.

Jerk.

"I'm curious, did they make you recite a tutoring oath regarding your fraternization with the students when you began working here?"

My lips flatten, because now he's just making fun of me.

"Okay," I snap, "why don't you try this answer on for size—I don't want to encourage someone who might be stalking me. Does that answer work better for you?"

"At least it's a more legitimate reason for not grabbing food with me. But still, we both know I'm not stalking you." His expression turns thoughtful. "I like to think of it more as actively pursuing you."

Fear spikes through my veins. "And what if I don't want to be pursued?" I whisper.

The smile falls from his face as our gazes stay locked.

A heartbeat ticks by before he reaches out, his larger hand covering mine.

My attention drops to our clasped fingers. Normally, I don't like being touched. When he'd grabbed my arm at the party, everything in me had seized up. But his hand lying gently over mine doesn't trigger a response. Actually, that's a lie. It does do something to me…something I'm unwilling to acknowledge.

"You don't know me." And I don't want him to know me either. Not the real me. Not the one who made such a mess out of her life last year.

I hold my breath and wait for the familiar knives of panic to slice me up inside.

It's a surprise when they don't.

He squeezes my hand, and my gaze bounces up to his. "Is it so difficult to believe that what I already know makes me want to find out more?"

I gulp, breaking eye contact before carefully slipping my hand from his. "I don't date."

That's non-negotiable. There are rules I've set in place for myself this year. And from what I've learned, the biggest problem with rules is when you start bending or breaking them. After that happens, there's nothing to stop you from totally disregarding them and careening out of control.

And I can't afford to careen out of control.

Not again.

When I had started at Western, I'd been fully prepared for the panic attacks to roar back with a vengeance. Surprisingly, they hadn't. In the two weeks I've been on campus, the only one I've suffered from was when Cole grabbed my arm. That debilitating feeling had been enough to give me serious pause where he's concerned.

"How about a non-date then?"

Lost in the whirl of my thoughts, I repeat, "A non-date?"

That sounds suspiciously like a way of sneaking around the rules.

"Yeah. You know, just two friends grabbing something to eat." One of his brows hikes up across his forehead. "You hang out with friends, right?"

"Of course."

Just not very often. I've just transferred in and I'm not the type of girl who goes out of her way to make new friends. Sure, I hang out with Brooklyn. And I reluctantly go out when she needs a wingman… or wingwoman, as the case may be.

As for hitting up all the fraternity and off campus parties…or, in other words—hanging out, drinking myself silly with a crowd of strangers, and screwing around with random guys I'll never speak with again?

Nope. I don't do that.

Not anymore.

I blink, attempting to shake off the icy cold memories that are slyly wrapping themselves around me.

That's not a road I'm willing to go down again.

"Cassidy?" Cole reaches out, tentatively stroking my hand with gentle fingers. "Are you all right?" I stiffen, waiting for the thin threads of panic to suffocate me.

When I realize it's not going to happen, I force the stiff corners of my lips to rise. "I'm fine."

For a second time, I slip my hand from his and focus on gathering up my books before shoving them into my brown leather bag. Refusing to make eye contact, I shoot to my feet. "Dinner sounds great, but I really need to get moving. Sorry. Maybe next time."

Little does he realize there will never be a next time.

For someone so large, he's surprisingly agile as he rises to his feet and towers over me.

"You need more than a protein bar if you're going to get any work done at the library. You'll probably end up with a killer headache if you don't eat a decent meal. I promise we'll find something fast so you can hit the books."

Indecision floods through me as I bite down on my lower lip. My gaze slides to him as I silently weigh the consequences of spending more time alone with him.

He's dangerous.

He makes you feel things you aren't ready for.

"Okay." The word is out of my mouth before I can stop it. "But this is not a date," I add. "It's just like you said, we're two people grabbing something to eat."

It doesn't mean anything.

My belly rumbles again as if re-solidifying my decision.

A satisfied smile curves his lips upward. "You're finally admitting that we're friends?"

I glare but can't summon any real anger toward him. "Don't push it," I mutter.

With a grin, he holds the door open for me. "Right."

As we walk out of the math tutoring center, I say goodnight to Lisa. She waves back, her eyes crawling all over Cole. I give him a little side-eye, wondering if he's aware of the effect he has on the opposite sex. I remember the girl we ran into last Friday while walking to class, and the other one who'd waved frantically at him in Psychology.

Cole seems to be a fan favorite with the girls at Western.

They can have him as far as I'm concerned, because I have zero interest in starting anything with him. Even if he's dreamy in the looks department, smells delicious, and has dimples that make my panties flood with heat.

I almost wince.

He smiles at Lisa, giving her a polite nod but nothing more. There is absolutely nothing flirtatious about his manner. No appreciative or lingering looks. In fact, there's no checking out of any kind going on, which is strange because Lisa is super cute with long dark hair, blue eyes, and gravity-defying boobs.

And Cole doesn't even blink in her direction.

From the slight frown marring Lisa's pretty face, she doesn't understand his reaction either.

I almost wish he'd checked her out in front of my face. It would make everything so much easier. When it comes down to it, I don't want to like Cole. There's already way too much to like about him. I can practically feel myself getting sucked in by him and I'm still trying to fight against the lure of it.

Hopefully, this dinner will be short and sweet because I'm already regretting this decision. Instead of turning toward Union like I expect, Cole walks towards the parking lot.

"Where are we going?"

"My car is parked right over here. I thought we could grab something from Leno's."

This has me stopping in my tracks. "We're not going to the Union?"

"Leno's is only a few blocks away, and the sandwiches are fantastic. Not to mention fast. Much better than anything we'll find at the Union."

As if the subject has already been settled, he walks through the parking lot.

Twilight has just started to fall, making the shadows stretch and lengthen on the ground.

"Come on, Cassidy. I promise, forty minutes tops and then I'll drop you off at the library. If we go to the Union, you'd have to walk all the way across campus. Either way, it'll end up taking the same amount of time. And the food is way better at Leno's."

Unconsciously, I trail after him.

What he says makes sense...sort of.

As soon as I'm at his side, he reaches out, nabbing my fingers with his own. I glance down at our clasped hands before glancing at him in confusion. Of course, there's a smile tipping the corners of his lips upward. Something unwanted pings at the bottom of my belly.

I wish I could get used to the feelings he dredges up inside me. They would be so much easier to ignore if that were the case.

"This isn't a date," I repeat in a voice that sounds high-pitched and twitchy.

"Whatever you say."

His response only makes me twitchier.

Regret swamps me as he tows me through the parking lot until we arrive at a sports car.

My gaze licks over it before one brow rises. "You own a Shelby Mustang?"

Surprise flares in his eyes as a slow smile spreads across his face. "Pure Detroit muscle, baby."

He strokes a hand gently over the exterior. Clearly there is a real love affair going on between them. I almost smirk. Maybe I don't have anything to be worried about after all.

A smile touches my lips as my attention gets pulled back to the vehicle. She really is a beauty. Electric blue, with two thick white racing stripes down the middle.

"2008?" I ask, completely taken in by the gleaming Mustang.

Inspecting the rims, I wait for an answer. Honestly, I'd be surprised if I was wrong. When he remains silent, I glance over at him. I've seen enough muscle cars to identify the make and model. My dad and I used to attend classic car shows.

Corvettes and Mustangs. Those were his favorites.

Don't get me wrong, I like Mustangs too. But I really love Camaros. It's been over a year since I've been to a car show.

The smile slips from my lips.

When my gaze locks on his, he says, "I think I might love you, Cassidy."

I snort. Guys are so like that. Anytime a chick knows even the slightest detail about a muscle car, or cars in general for that matter, their minds literally explode. It's ridiculous, not to mention sexist, but I'd be lying if I didn't admit that I get off on it a teeny-tiny bit.

Ignoring the declaration, I run my hand over her sleek polished lines. And yeah, even I refer to them as *hers*. Weird, I know, but there's just something beautiful and sexy about muscle cars. So, I completely understand why guys refer to them as females.

"Five hundred and forty horses with a V-8 engine. She's gorgeous." I glare. "You're an idiot for keeping her at school."

He blinks. Twice. "Say it again," he murmurs. His voice is all thick and gravelly.

"Gladly." Then I repeat with more emphasis, "You're an idiot."

He waves at me. "No, the other part. Just whisper it real slow-like. Maybe lick your lips a bit." Raising his brows, he waits expectantly.

All right, I can't help it. Laughter bubbles up from me as I shake my head. "Come on, let's go. I've got a lot of studying to get through tonight. I can't stand around all-night gawking at your precious car."

Before I can grab the handle, Cole is there, popping open the door for me. Just as I slide onto the soft-as-butter leather seat, he reaches across my body to fasten the belt. As our gazes collide, I can almost feel the electricity snap and sizzle between us.

"That's twice now, Cassidy. You better watch out because I'm on a roll."

"Twice?" I echo.

With deft fingers, he clicks the belt into place as his attention stays pinned to mine. "That I've made you laugh."

As difficult as it feels, I drag my gaze from his to stare out the windshield before inhaling a gulp of air. Because he's right.

That's twice.

Two more than usual.

Dangerous.

Completely dangerous.

6

CASSIDY

"Okay, Cassidy, you can go back now. Dr. Thompson is ready to see you." The receptionist smiles as she shuffles around a few papers on her perfectly tidy desk.

I give her a brief smile in return before walking through the door and into the office of the psychologist I've been meeting with. After I'd received my acceptance at Western this summer, I'd realized I would need to continue with my sessions. Dr. Thompson has turned out to be a perfect fit.

Her office is decorated in soothing tans and whites, with splashes of blues and oranges that catch the eye. There's actually a couch, but there are also comfy chairs. Since I'm a creature of habit, I always gravitate to the same chair. I'm sure that says something about my personality. Dr. Thompson usually sits directly across from me with a notebook close at hand in case she wants to jot down a few notes. In the beginning, I found it disconcerting and wanted to take a quick peek to see what she'd written down. Now it seems normal.

All right...I still want to peek at the notebook.

Once we're settled, Dr. Thompson starts off our session just like she always does. There's a measure of comfort in our established routine that calms my frayed nerves.

"Tell me how this week is going for you." She has kind eyes, and they hold mine as if genuinely interested in my answer.

I inhale a deep breath before quietly pushing out the dreaded words. "I had an anxiety attack last Thursday night."

I can tell my response catches her off guard by the way her narrow brows draw together before carefully smoothing out. She knows this is the first episode I've experienced at school. It's actually the first one I've had in months. Another wave of unease crashes over me. I'm terrified of backsliding.

Terrified of tumbling back down into that yawning pit of despair I've only recently crawled out of.

"All right. Tell me exactly what happened, Cassidy." Her words are calm and soothing. In response, my muscles loosen as I sink into the chair.

If there's someone who can help me through this, it's Dr. Thompson.

I blow out a breath and recount everything that occurred Thursday night. I tell her about my interaction with Alex and then Cole.

"Had you been drinking at all? Even a sip?" The question isn't censorious, merely curious. Like me, she's trying to get to the bottom of what triggered the attack.

"Nope, just a diet cola." I haven't had a sip of alcohol in more than nine months. Not since that night.

She gives me a slight smile before jotting down a few notes. "All right."

The anxiety of that night threads its way through my body before crashing over me like a massive wave. As much as I don't want to let it suck me under again, I don't know how to stop it from happening.

"He grabbed your upper arm from behind and spun you toward him," she clarifies.

"Yes." Hearing her describe the incident that way makes me feel as if my throat is closing up and I'm being strangled from the inside out. My eyes widen as my fingers claw at my neck as if that will loosen the pressure.

"Cassidy, I want you to look at me." Her words are firm but comforting. My gaze flies to hers. "You're safe in this office. We're going to work through this together, all right?"

Unable to verbalize a response, I nod.

"I want you to close your eyes and relax into the chair."

When I don't immediately comply, she says, "We're going to engage in some breathing exercises to help calm you."

I jerk my head and settle against the chair before squeezing my eyes shut as the soothing timbre of Dr. Thompson's voice washes over me. Any moment I'll hyperventilate and totally lose it.

"I want you to focus on drawing in slow, deep breaths. Inhale through your nose and then breathe out through your mouth. In and out. Good. You're doing wonderfully."

I concentrate on the sound of her voice. On breathing in before slowly pushing it out. Little by little, my muscles relax. First the tips of my fingers and then my toes. My arms and legs. After a while, everything feels limp as a noodle while she continues to instruct me. When she falls silent, I peel open my eyes, realizing that I no longer feel as if I'm being suffocated.

"Better?" she asks before sitting back and watching me closely.

"Yes, much better." No longer does my body feel strung tight, riddled with anxiety and icy cold panic.

"Good." She asks gently, "Do you feel like you might need a prescription at this point?"

Drawing in a deep breath, I turn the question over in my mind. I don't have anything against taking pills if they're needed, but... "No. It only happened once, and I don't want to start taking anything again."

I've been down that road before and want to handle this on my own.

"I understand your feelings and I respect them, but you need to promise that if you experience another attack, you'll call the office right away. Even though you're reluctant, we may need to revisit the subject again."

"I promise that I will." My hope is that it won't be necessary.

"Good. Why don't you tell me how your classes are going? It's been a little over three weeks since the semester began. Are you over-whelmed by the workload?"

Something within me settles, because academics are the easy part. With the exception of last year, I've always excelled scholastically. Especially in math and science. Steering the conversation away from what caused my panic attack to school feels like safe terrain. There's no racing heartbeat, frantic thoughts, or panicking.

I can handle this.

"My classes are going really well." After the disaster of last fall, it feels good to be doing well.

"And working in the tutoring center hasn't added too much stress?"

"No." My thoughts immediately turn to Cole and the probability that he'll be popping in from time to time. "I really like tutoring. It fits in my schedule and I'm enjoying it more than I thought I would."

"I'm glad to hear that. It sounds like you've got a good handle on your courses and your job. Other than the anxiety attack, everything else seems to be going well." She smiles before jotting down a few more notes. "That has to feel good."

I draw in another deep breath before releasing it. "It does feel good."

Not only am I excelling, I'm enjoying my classes. It's a complete contrast from last year when I felt like I was drowning in my course-work almost from day one. Being at Western feels like a second chance, and this time, I refuse to blow it.

With a glance at the clock, Dr. Thompson wraps up our session. "We have about ten minutes, is there anything else you'd like to discuss before you leave today?"

"The guy who grabbed me…" my voice trails off as awareness skit-ters through me. Even thinking about Cole has my insides prickling. It isn't necessarily a bad thing, but he affects me more than I want him to.

More than I'm comfortable with.

Spending that hour tutoring him, and then grabbing dinner afterward, only made me like him more. He's ridiculously easy to be around.

She leans toward me before pressing the issue when I fall silent. "What about him?"

"He's in one of my classes and showed up at the tutoring center the other day."

Why am I even bringing this up? I wish it were possible to backtrack or snatch the words from the air. I don't want to discuss Cole.

"Does he make you uncomfortable?" Concern threads its way through her voice that this guy might be harassing me. He isn't, of course.

While Cole makes me feel uncomfortable, it's not for the reasons she thinks. "No, he's not bothering me like that. And I haven't felt like I was going to have another anxiety attack when we've been together either."

She tilts her head. "How do you feel about him then?"

I shrug, almost afraid to admit that he's the first guy in a long time to make me feel anything remotely sexual. After last year, I just kind of shut down. For reasons I don't understand, Cole is different. I haven't been able to run him off. Even though that felt threatening at first, it no longer does.

"I'm not sure," I admit. "Scared. Nervous."

But sort of excited too.

As that realization flits through my head, I decide to keep it to myself for the time being.

Cole forces me to feel things I'm not quite ready to explore. I can't deny there's something about him that attracts me. And it's not just his looks either. The more time I spend with him, the more I like him. For someone like me who is fairly anti-relationship, it's kind of a problem. I don't want to like him anymore than I already do.

I don't want to like him at all.

Dr. Thompson pauses before pulling off her thin, black framed glasses. "Do you think it's a good idea to get involved with someone right now?"

I sigh, unsurprised that she's hit the nail on the head so quickly.

Even though this is only our third week working together, she's really good at what she does. Astute. Intuitive.

"Probably not." Actually, it's the worst possible idea. I know it. And Dr. Thompson knows it as well. The only one who doesn't know it is Cole.

"How come?"

Of course, she realizes why it's a terrible idea, but she wants me to verbalize the thoughts out loud. It's a cheap counseling trick. But it's one that works.

"Because it's important that I focus my energies on school, and pull my life together so I can get healthy."

"I think those are valid reasons to take a break from relationships. Just remember, it's not forever. The fact that this boy has triggered an anxiety attack is concerning. Getting healthy is your first priority and then, when you feel better equipped to handle stressful situations, you can think about relationships again. You're finding success at Western, and we don't want to do anything that will derail it."

She's right.

In all honesty, I didn't need her to confirm that getting involved with Cole will more than likely end in disaster for me, but it's probably good that she did.

7

CASSIDY

"This is going to be so much fun! Thanks again for coming with me tonight." Snuggling into her jacket, Brooklyn bounces excitedly on the bleacher seat as her gaze tracks the hockey players skating by the Plexiglas that surrounds the ice. "That's him, number fifty-five."

A dreamy look fills her large green eyes. As she sighs, her warm breath escapes into the frigid air of the rink. I roll my eyes even though she isn't paying me the slightest bit of attention.

Nope.

Her focus is trained on her brand-new crush.

Number fifty-five.

I shift in my seat and watch the players skate past. Not that I would admit this to Brooklyn, but this is surprisingly more painful than I'd imagined it would be. I haven't skated in more than nine months. At this very moment, my fingers are almost itching to wrap themselves around my old fiberglass hockey stick. As I stare at the ice, my mind tumbles back, trying to recall a time when I've been off skates for more than four or five days in row, let alone almost an entire year. This is the first time since leaving school last year that I've stepped foot inside an ice arena.

Blinking back to the present, my gaze travels around the space. The sights and sounds—even the smells, are the same. My breathing hitches as I fight to suck in air.

Up until last fall, I'd played hockey my entire life. House teams and then travel teams. All of which led me to a scholarship playing at a Division I college. But last year, I'd imploded under the stress and pressure. I'd been forced to leave in disgrace before the first semester ended.

Sitting in the stands and watching Western's men's hockey team has it all rushing back. Old wounds, I'd assumed had scabbed over, have been made surprisingly fresh again. It takes effort to shake off the web of memories trying to tangle themselves around me.

I clear my throat and pick up the thread of our previous conversation. "No problem." Although, at the moment, it does feel like a problem. One that's eating me up alive.

I refocus my attention on the guys as they run through their warm-up routine of stretching and passing drills before taking shots on goal. It's like a well-choreographed dance. One I miss. The ache in my heart flares back to life. It's almost shocking to realize how painful it is to sit here and watch them.

After the bottom fell out last December, I shut down and refused to think about hockey. And for a long time, it worked. Now...

Not so much.

It's pushing in at the edges.

It's a relief when the players take their positions on the ice and the horn is blown. The puck is dropped, and the action starts. The game is so fast-paced that I'm able to forget about the past and focus on watching the players move the puck up and down the ice. The game ends up being an exciting one, with the score tied or separated by just one goal. There are so many times when Brooklyn and I jump to our feet and scream at the top of our lungs. We're certainly not the only ones. Western's fans are rabidly loyal.

And I love it.

I love a fanatic crowd. It ups the energy level in the arena. What I love most is that I'm able to lose myself in the fast-paced action of the game. I don't have to think about the past or how I crumbled under the pressure. Brooklyn doesn't know anything about hockey, but she is, as usual, her exuberant self.

I seriously love that about her.

"Go the other way!" she yells before adding, "Hurry! Faster!"

I almost laugh at how silly she sounds. A couple of people in the seats surrounding us turn their heads as well, but she looks like she's having so much fun that they end up smiling before turning back to the game.

Every time a whistle is blown, Brooklyn looks at me for a quick explanation.

"Offsides," I tell her.

Another whistle.

Her questioning gaze shoots to mine.

"Penalty for high sticking," I mutter with a roll of my eyes. At this point, these players should know better.

Whistle.

Brooklyn quirks a brow, waiting for a reason as to why the action has stopped.

"Icing." Again, should know better than to slap it all the way across the ice. Dumb.

Whistle.

"Penalty for holding." I grumble before bellowing, "That was a crap call, ref. Open your eyes for a change! Here, I think I've got a spare pair of glasses for you!"

Brooklyn bursts out laughing before yelling, "Yeah, crap call, ref! Totally crappy call!"

We grin at each other before dropping onto our seats and reaching for our shared box of popcorn.

Whistle.

That one I don't have to answer because it's obvious.

Fighting.

"Crap call, ref!" Brooklyn yells again.

I shake my head. "No, it was actually a good call. Not in our favor, but it was the right one to make." I sip my diet cola and watch as one of our players skates over to the penalty box. He's still mouthing off to the player he'd been brawling with.

"Exactly whose team are you on?" she asks as if she knows a damn thing about the sport.

What Brooklyn likes about hockey are the hot guys who look even more strapping with all their padding and gear. And...well...she's not wrong about that.

I roll my eyes in answer.

When the game finally ends, the crowd goes wild because the Timber Wolves have managed to pull off a win. From what I can tell, their team looks solid. They have a lightning quick offense and a solid, not to mention huge, defense. This is where the strapping comment comes into play. And the goalie was pretty talented as well. Not much slid past him tonight. Even though it was bittersweet to watch, I can definitely see myself coming back to catch a few more games during the season.

"We're all heading over to a little bar after this to celebrate, are you in?" The unexpected rush of adrenalin from tonight's win has Brooklyn bouncing on the edge of her seat with even more energy than usual.

"You never mentioned going out after the game," I groan.

Brooklyn knows I'm not much of a partier, but she doesn't understand the reasons for it. I haven't wanted to talk about last year.

She smiles brightly before stating the obvious. "If I had told you, you wouldn't have agreed to come with me tonight."

I narrow my eyes because she's right. As painful as the memories are, I'm glad Brooklyn talked me into coming with her. I haven't had this much fun in a long time. Until tonight, I hadn't realized how much I missed hockey.

Interrupting my thoughts, she gives me sad puppy dog eyes and steeples her hands together as if in prayer. "Please, please, please," she begs prettily. Already I can feel myself weakening. "We'll have so much fun!"

Argh...I don't want to go.

I don't want to give in.

I don't…

"All right, fine. I'll go."

Ugh.

I hate when she talks me into these kinds of situations because I usually end up regretting them. "But I'm not staying long." One hour, tops. Then I'm heading back to the dorms.

Brooklyn beams with satisfaction. "Yay! Now you can meet Austin. He's *sooo* cute and *sooo* nice. I really like him, Cass." She gives me a meaningful look. "He could totally be the one."

I almost snort.

The one for what?

Today?

Tomorrow?

This week?

Next week?

Yeah, sure. We'll see about that. Brooklyn is well-known for hopping from one guy to another at the speed of light. In the three weeks we've been rooming together, she's been out with four different guys. Number fifty-five is forth in that line up. Needless to say, the other three guys are still texting and calling, but she's already moved on. So, do I really expect this one to last any longer than the others?

Nope.

After most of the fans empty from the stands, Brooklyn and I meander our way to the lobby to wait for Brooklyn's new flavor of the week. All I can say is that the girl definitely has a type—hot, athletic, and likes to have a good time.

Just like she does.

It takes about twenty minutes for the guys to filter out of the locker room. The coach will usually talk to the team (or yell if they lose), discuss what went right (or wrong), and then they shower and change.

Brooklyn squeals as her guy saunters out of the locker room with a smile lighting up his handsome face. Just like I suspected, he's hot and athletic. In true Brooklyn fashion, she runs and jumps into his outstretched arms before wrapping her legs around his waist. A number of his teammates hoot and holler in response. Unaffected by the catcalls, she kisses the hell right out of him.

Unfortunately, watching them is like staring at a horrific traffic accident. You don't necessarily want to watch, but you're helpless to rip your gaze away.

"Guess the tables have turned and you're the one stalking me now."

My heart skips a beat as I spin toward the deep male voice. Before I turn, I know exactly who I'll find.

Cole.

"Well, damn. I guess you caught me." I almost cringe as the words fly out of my mouth. My heart pounds painfully into overdrive. The last thing I want is for him to think I've turned into a fangirl.

It's obvious from his chuckle that he doesn't take me seriously. And right on cue, his gorgeous dimples come out to play.

"You know you kind of suck as a stalker, right?"

"Sorry, I'm still trying to get the hang of it. Remind me to ask you for some helpful tips. You seem to be a real pro at it."

My belly dips as he grins at me. I almost wince, realizing that this banter is totally counterproductive to what I need to happen.

He shifts his stance. "For one, you're supposed to stay out of sight. You know, hide in the bushes, peek around corners, wear disguises, follow discreetly from a distance. That kind of thing. Maybe we can get together later and I can give you a stalker one-oh-one crash course. Stalking for dummies or something like that. Totally free of charge, of course."

Dimples.

Again with those damn dimples.

If he's trying to wear me down, those dimples are doing an excellent job. He must realize it because he flashes them at me every chance he gets.

I blink, attempting to shake myself free of the thick fog that always seems to descend when he's near. "No, I don't think that'll be necessary. You've given me quite enough to go on already."

He steps a bit closer, invading my space. My heart stutters at his nearness.

"I don't want to brag or anything but I'm one of the best."

"Good to know." I point to an area about twenty feet away. "I'll just go stand over there for the time being."

His gaze stays focused on mine as he changes the subject. "Did you enjoy the game?"

That's the moment it hits me like a ton of bricks.

"Oh," I gasp in surprise, "you were out there!" I shake my head, feeling like an idiot. I mean, duh…of course, he was out there. His hair is all shiny and damp. And he smells amazing.

All masculine and…

I shutdown that line of thinking. I'm supposed to be distancing myself from him, not trying to inhale him.

Unaware of the dangerous thoughts running through my head, he winks. "See, you're better at this stalker-thing than you give yourself credit for."

My eyes widen as I shake my head. The last thing I need is for him to think I'm into him.

"I didn't come here to see you," I blurt, pointing to Brooklyn who is still wrapped around number fifty-five like a python. "That's my roommate. I came with her." My cheeks heat as I make one last ditch effort to convince him of my innocence. "I didn't even know you played hockey."

His brows rise as he barks out a laugh. "Wow. All right, I got it. You didn't come here to watch me play tonight. You're not interested, and you barely know I breathe. FYI—my ego has been completely anni-hilated."

Even though the last part is highly doubtful, I close my eyes, imagining my face going up in flames.

"You know what I mean," I mutter.

Almost gently, he knocks his broad shoulder into my narrower one before saying softly, "I'm just giving you crap, Cassidy. Calm down."

Sheesh…if only I could.

I open my eyes and glare. "You're such a jerk." The truth of the matter is that he isn't...

With a grin, he shakes his head. "No, I'm not."

"Yes, you are." Unable to help myself, I chuckle before giving him a considering look. My mind rewinds to the game as I assess him. "You're number five. Defense. Two goals and two assists. And your last goal was really sweet. Right in the five-hole."

He gapes at me for a solid minute. I'm seconds away from waving a hand in front of his face when he drops to his knees.

His gaze holds mine as he says solemnly, "It would truly be an honor if you would consider stalking me."

The edges of my lips tremble. If I'm not careful, this guy will be my complete undoing. At the moment, I just want him off his knees. His antics are drawing too much attention from his teammates. Even Brooklyn is staring at us with interest. And that, I don't need.

"Get up and I'll give it some thought."

Cole pops easily to his feet before grabbing my hand. Part of me wants to yank it away, but a bigger part wants to leave it safely secured within his larger one.

"You know hockey." There's a fair amount of surprise riddled throughout his voice.

"Die-hard fan."

It's not *technically* a lie.

Although it isn't precisely the truth either. It does, however, seem like the easiest way to explain my knowledge without...well, actually explaining it.

"Let me get this straight, you know about muscle cars, hockey, and are pretty smart because you took college level calculus in high school."

I blink. "Is there a question wrapped up somewhere in there?"

He smiles. "I guess not. You're smart, beautiful, and know about cars and hockey. If I'm lucky, you'll start stalking me."

Breaking eye contact, I shake my head. "I'm not those things." Sooner or later, he'll realize the mistake he's made, and then disappointment will set in. My happiness dims as those thoughts take root inside me.

His fingers slip under my chin before lifting it until I have no other choice but to meet his eyes. His gaze locks on mine, holding it captive. My heart picks up speed, making me wish I could be the girl he thinks I am.

"Yeah, you are. And I get the feeling I've only just begun to scratch beneath the surface."

Those quietly spoken words have me jerking out of the trance that had fallen over me. The last thing I need is for Cole to scratch beneath the surface. I don't want him delving any deeper into who I am or getting to know the real me.

Half the time, I don't even want to know the real me.

Not anymore.

I glance away before tugging my hand free and scrambling back in retreat. He silently studies me like I'm a puzzle that needs solving.

I don't like it.

And I certainly don't like the way it makes me feel.

I need to go. I can't do this.

My gaze darts to Brooklyn. She'll be fine on her own. Hell, her legs are still wrapped around…damn, I can't remember what his name is. Whoever he is, he'll take good care of her. He'll make sure she gets back to the dorms. Or, at the very least, he'll make sure she goes home with him.

"You ready to go, Cass?" Brooklyn—who is finally standing on her own two feet— gives me a curious stare as she loops her arm through number fifty-five's. "I'm going to catch a ride with Austin." Her gaze shifts speculatively to Cole before she smirks. "Do you want to ride with us or do you want—"

I shake my head. At this point, all I want is to head back to the safety of the dorms. Back to where my heart doesn't feel like it's going to jackhammer right out of my chest.

Cole waves them off as everyone splinters apart, leaving the arena. "Don't worry about Cassidy, I'll make sure she gets there."

Nerves spark along my skin as I spin toward him. "But I don't want to go to the bar," I whisper. Thick tendrils of anxiety are already wrapping themselves around me. "I'm going to head home." I need to get out of here before I lose my shit and embarrass myself.

"Okay," he says easily, "I'll take you home." He doesn't attempt to talk me out of my decision, and for some reason, that only makes matters worse. I don't want Cole to give me a ride home. I don't want to spend any more time with him.

I'm starting to like him.

Too much.

I realize that Dr. Thompson is right. I'm not ready for this.

I almost laugh. I'm nowhere near ready for this. Look at me, I'm a complete mess. Even if he doesn't see it yet...I am.

He reaches up, his hand settling under my chin before tipping it so he can study my eyes. My muscles stiffen at the contact.

My throat works as I try to tamp down my rising anxiety. Already my body is humming with nerves. My chest feels as if someone is crushing it in their fist. Needing to block out my surroundings, I screw my eyes tightly shut and inhale an unsteady breath through my nose before exhaling slowly from my mouth. I keep this up until the vise squeezing my chest slowly loosens and I can breathe again.

When I finally open my eyes again, I realize the lights in the arena have dimmed and we're standing alone in the lobby. The sound of our combined breathing echoes off the cement walls. My face flames with hot licks of embarrassment. His hand still grips my chin as his gaze remains locked on mine. He breaks the physical connection between us by taking a step in retreat.

God, I am such a freak.

Even worse than that?

Cole has to realize it by now. Just look at me...I'm a fucking mess. I want to die of humiliation as I stand ramrod straight in the empty lobby. Well, I certainly won't have to worry about him flirting with me anymore. Maybe that's for the best.

What am I saying?

Of course, it is.

"Are you ready to go?" His voice is soft, which only makes me feel like more of loser. Why does he have to be so damn nice?

"Yeah." I need to get out of here before I completely fall apart.

"Come on." This time, he's careful not to touch me.

I have no idea what is going through his brain, but I'm relieved he doesn't try to hold my hand or throw an arm casually around my shoulders. And I'm grateful he doesn't probe me with questions, because it's doubtful I'd be able to answer them.

"I'll take you home now."

I nod as we leave the darkened arena behind us. The parking lot is deserted as we walk in silence to his car. He opens the door for me before leaning over and sliding the seatbelt carefully across my chest. After he snaps it firmly in place, he remains hunkered on the pavement next to me so that we're eye level. His gaze searches mine in the darkness, as if he's somehow able to sift through the thoughts I'm not strong enough to give voice to.

After what feels like an eternity, he whispers, "I won't hurt you, Cassidy."

Even though his words have something desperate twisting inside my chest, I say, "I'm sorry, I just can't."

He inhales a steady breath, filling his lungs completely, before exhaling it back into the atmosphere. Instead of arguing, he closes the door and walks around to the driver's side before sliding in beside me. The ten-minute drive to the dorms is made in excruciating silence.

8

———

COLE

"**W**hat's your problem, dude? We won!" Austin shouts from across the table in the noisy bar. "Fucking act like it."

Before I can respond, his attention becomes ensnared by the curvy blonde perched on his lap. I'm surprised he even noticed me sitting across from him in the first place.

With a grunt, I nurse my beer instead of replying, because what am I supposed to say to that?

That I'm stuck on a gorgeous chick with the most beautiful ebony-colored hair I've ever seen. Or the biggest, clearest blue eyes I've had the sad misfortune of gazing into.

Fuck.

I'd get the shit kicked out of me if I said something like that.

And you know what?

I'd totally deserve it.

Hell, I probably deserve it for even thinking along those lines.

I'm so screwed.

Even worse than that?

I'm not sure if there's anything I can do to salvage whatever Cassidy and I have going between us. Maybe I've only known her for a week, but she's all I think about. That's not a good sign.

She'd jokingly accused me of stalking her.

Well, she's not too far from the truth.

I mean…no, I'm not *actually* making a conscious effort to follow her around campus. Luckily, we run into each other regularly, which helps to feed this fixation I have with her.

At the party last Thursday, I hadn't given much thought to her reaction when I'd grabbed her arm. After tonight and the way she'd shutdown, I realize that more is going on.

It's like she'd been frightened.

Of me.

Of me.

Which doesn't make a damn bit of sense.

Clearly this girl has issues, but she surprises me at every turn. I'd thought it was hot that she was into muscle cars. Her knowledge of hockey has totally upped her hotness factor.

I haven't been this interested in someone in a long time.

Unfortunately, every time I attempt inching closer, she throws up more roadblocks. A few days ago, I'd thought I was making a little bit of headway. Especially after I cajoled her into grabbing dinner.

Turns out that's not the case.

Tonight, she totally froze up on me.

I don't know what to make of her.

Frustration pounds through me as I run my hand through my hair. No matter how hard I try, I can't wrap my mind around this girl. She wouldn't have revealed her name if I hadn't run into her at the tutoring center, which brings me to how damn smart she is.

I sported an uncomfortable boner in the tutoring center while she explained whatever the hell it was she'd taken her time to reteach me.

And you know what?

Her explanation had made more sense than the professor's.

I take another long swig of beer and stare across the table we have to ourselves in the back corner of Zep's, a local dive bar close to campus. The owner always reserves about five or six tables on game nights for the team. It's tradition, and what I've learned from hockey is that you don't mess with tradition.

Ever.

My gaze flickers to Cassidy's roommate who is wriggling around on Austin's lap. They look moments away from putting on an X-rated show right in front of me.

What's her name again?

Beth?

Brenda?

Brin?

Damn if I can remember.

I close the distance between us because this is a person who can fill in some of the blanks for me. I just have to get Austin to stop sucking her face long enough to pry some information from her.

"Hey, Beth." I pause and wait for her to make eye contact. "What's the deal with your roommate?"

When she turns toward me, Austin cooperates by licking and sucking on her neck. Can't say the guy doesn't always have my back.

"It's Brooklyn," she corrects.

"Oh, right. Sorry, Brooklyn." At this point, I can't see any reason not to delve straight in. With my luck, she'll lose focus. "So, what's up with Cassidy?"

Her eyelids feather closed as Austin nibbles away at her earlobe. "Ummm, what do you mean?"

Do I seriously need to spell it out for this girl?

I want details.

And lots of them.

Anything.

Everything.

I want to understand what I'm working with here. If I wait around for Cassidy to finally open up, I'll be waiting around forever.

She's like sand. Already I feel her slipping through my fingers, which is starting to make me desperate. I'll be honest, desperate isn't my usual style.

Here's the most important question…

"Is she seeing anyone right now?"

Her roommate giggles as if that's the funniest thing she's ever heard. Or maybe Austin has just found her ticklish spot. This feels like pulling teeth. I need this girl to concentrate for five damn minutes.

"No," she says when her laughter subsides, "Cassidy doesn't date."

Hmmm. She admitted that to me.

I'd just assumed she was blowing smoke up my ass. I mean, come on, the girl is totally hot. She's gorgeous, with a nice body. And super smart. Not to mention, quick-witted. She's the total package.

So, what's her deal?

Why isn't she dating?

My attention is pulled back to Brooklyn when she adds, "Cassidy is really focused on school."

I lean closer before gesturing for her to continue. "What else can you tell me?"

"Umm…" Brooklyn's eyelids drift shut again as Austin sucks the flesh of her neck into his mouth. She tilts her head, allowing him greater access.

I almost roll my eyes. "Uh huh."

Jeez, just spit it out. I need something here. So far, she hadn't told me anything I didn't already know.

"There's not much to tell."

I frown, wondering if this girl is purposely being evasive. I'm beginning to suspect she is.

After a few silent moments, she opens her eyes and pins me with her green gaze. She doesn't look nearly as wasted as I first suspected. "Why are you asking?"

Her expression changes, and she looks more like a mama bear protecting her cub.

I lean back in my seat before taking another pull from my beer. It's probably a little too late to play it cool. "Just curious, that's all."

It's so much more than that. I wasn't kidding when I admitted to being kinda sorta obsessed with her.

Trust me, this isn't a proud moment for me.

Brooklyn nibbles on her lower lip before confessing, "Cassidy wouldn't like it if she knew you were asking questions."

Before I can stop myself from nose diving headfirst into pathetic, the words shoot out of my mouth. "Has she mentioned me at all?"

Brooklyn squints before asking, "What's your name again?"

Ouch.

Austin, being the asshole that he is, vibrates with laughter. "Cole Mathews."

"Nope." She shakes her head before twisting the knife further into my heart. "She hasn't mentioned you at all." Giggles erupt from her. Looks like Austin found that ticklish spot again. "Don't feel bad, she never talks about guys. Even if she liked one, she probably wouldn't say anything about it. That's just Cassidy."

"Don't feel bad, she says…" I grumble the words to myself before taking another drink from my bottle. Easier said than done.

I don't realize that I've become tangled up in my thoughts until a slender hand settles on my chest. When I glance up, my gaze collides with smoky-colored eyes. Mandi. She's one of those girls who shows up for all the hockey games and hangs around with the team when we party, hopping from one player to another. There are a number of guys who greatly enjoy the benefits of having groupies.

I'm just not one of them.

"Hi, Cole." She flashes a smile as her red nails stroke across my chest.

My gaze slides from the top of her sleek auburn bob to the tips of her ridiculously high heeled shoes. And, because I'm a guy, I can't help but notice exactly what's in between. A low-cut shirt that emphasizes her breasts and a short skirt that barely covers her ass, all the while showcasing long, toned legs. It's not that this girl isn't gorgeous, but there's something about the knowledge that she has no problem fucking you along with all your teammates.

No matter how good-looking this girl is, I'm just not into that.

Even though I have zero interest in her, my lips lift into a smile. "Hey, Mandi. How you doing tonight?"

For some reason, I can't help but compare Mandi to Cassidy—with her long black hair, clear blue eyes, and sweet curves. Every time I see Cassidy, she's dressed in jeans and a soft looking sweater. I like that her style is low-key. She doesn't seem like the type to showoff everything she owns, or sleep with an entire shift of hockey players simply because they're part of the roster.

"Much better now that I've ran into you." There's a sexy curve to her lips as she toys with her thick auburn hair.

"Mind if I sit down?"

Well, why the hell not?

Apparently, I've got nothing better going on.

"Nope, pull up a chair."

She giggles before dropping down onto my lap and tangling her arms around my neck. "Or I could just sit right here." Her mouth is inches from my own.

"Yeah, I guess that works too."

The way her ass wriggles against my junk should have something stirring south of the boarder, but it doesn't.

As she murmurs in my ear, I allow my eyelids to drift shut. In my mind, it's Cassidy I'm imagining on my lap, whispering sweet promises about all the dirty little things she'd like to do to me.

It's those thoughts that have me stiffening right up.

Which is when I realize how screwed I am.

And not in a good way.

9

CASSIDY

"Where'd you disappear to last night? I thought we were going to hang out at the bar after the game."

Even though Brooklyn looks as though she didn't get a wink of sleep last night, her voice is chipper and brimming with curiosity.

I glance up from the bowl of oatmeal I'm trailing my spoon through as we sit in the cafeteria with its walls of floor to ceiling windows. Brilliant sunshine pours down on us. Even this early in the morning, students are bustling past with trays full of food before their days get underway.

"I decided to head home after the game instead."

"Well, you missed an awesome time last night. We had a blast." She grins before digging into her scrambled eggs, toast, and fruit. She waggles her perfectly plucked brows before dropping her voice. "And what happened after the bar was even more fun, if you know what I mean."

I roll my eyes because yeah, I know *exactly* what she means. Instead of taking the bait, I clear my throat. "Austin seemed nice."

"He's a real sweetheart. Did you have fun at the game? I have to admit that I never realized how exciting hockey could be. Maybe we can check out a few more games this season," Brooklyn adds before popping a chunk of cantaloupe into her mouth.

Actually, I had a blast at the game. The realization that I still loved hockey had been like a punch to the gut.

But seeing Cole...

It's obvious he's someone I need to steer clear of.

For him to cause one anxiety attack could be chalked up to coincidence.

But two?

That's harder to dismiss.

The breathing exercises helped to calm me, but I can't stop thinking about how pensive he'd been on the ride back to the dorms. I'd racked my brain for something to say. A million different things had come to mind. In the end, I'd chickened out. All of it would lead to conversations about my past, and I wasn't ready to open that can of worms.

The moment he'd pulled in front of the dorms, I'd mumbled a quick thank you before jumping out of the car as if it had been engulfed in flames. I probably don't need to worry about staying away from Cole, he'll avoid me like a particularly nasty case of crabs.

Not bothered by my lack of response, Brooklyn inhales her eggs and toast as she continues to chatter about the bar. Thank goodness for Brooklyn and her obliviousness.

"The guy who gave you a ride home last night, his name is Cole, right?" she asks in between bites.

I glance up from my tepid bowl of oatmeal that has long since lost its appeal. "Yeah."

He's the last person I want to talk about. Especially with her. I don't need my roommate making a big deal out of this.

And she will.

It just so happens to be her MO.

"I think he might be interested." She grins around another bite before giving me a wink as if this is good news.

A pit settles at the bottom of my gut.

After last night, that's probably the furthest thing from the truth. I'm sure he thinks I'm a total head case.

And…he's not wrong.

"He was asking about you. I'd totally consider getting with that if I were you." Brooklyn waves to a few girls from our floor as they walk past, looking for an empty table.

Ignoring the last comment, I frown before leaning forward and attempting to reclaim Brooklyn's distracted attention. "What kind of questions?"

"Oh, I can't really remember. Just about, you know, normal stuff."

That's not good.

I gulp. The small amount of oatmeal I've managed to force down churns dangerously in my belly. Anxiety bubbles up inside me as I gather up my bag and shoot out of my seat. I need to put a little distance between myself and this conversation. "I need to speak with one of my professors before class starts."

That's a lie, but I can't sit here any longer and listen to Brooklyn talk about Cole as if we're going to get together, because it's not happening.

Brooklyn's dark blonde brows slide together in confusion before she grumbles, "Hold on, hold on. Jeez. I'm not even done eating yet." Rather impressively, she shovels the rest of her breakfast into her mouth before setting her tray down by the garbage can.

As we push through the cafeteria doors, she says, "I'm seeing Austin again tonight." A giddy smile overtakes her face. "I like him so much." She grabs my arm, squeezing it in a death grip as we walk along one of the cement pathways. Even though the weather has grown cool, bright sunlight cuts through some of the early September chill. "Just in case you were wondering—yes, he's amazing in bed and knows exactly what to do with his tongue. Which, I'm not going to lie, is a huge plus in his favor."

"Ummm, I wasn't wondering about that at all." I laugh and shake my head. "But thanks for the overshare."

"Which part was over share? The sleeping together part or the inventive way he uses his tongue?"

I wince, attempting to keep the visual at bay. "All of it."

She rolls her eyes before huffing out a breath. "Oh, come on, that's hardly too much information."

"It's actually the definition of TMI."

"It's not like I told you about how he—"

This time, I slap a hand over her mouth to stop her from speaking. "TMI, Brook, TMI."

After a few seconds, I remove my hand from her pouting face.

"You're such a buzzkill."

"If not wanting to hear all the gory details of your sexcapades makes me a buzzkill, then so be it."

I can't help the slight smile that tugs at the corners of my lips. This is one of the things I like about Brooklyn. No, not hearing about her overactive sex life, which she is always eager to share in vivid detail, but that she's so light, sunny, and full of energy. I enjoy being around her even though she's always in perpetual motion. It can be exhausting, but it's a good kind of exhausting. Most of the time, it allows me to escape from myself, and that's almost always a positive.

"He seemed nice," I tell her. Although, I can't exactly say I spoke with him, because Brooklyn had been sucking the life out of his face the entire time we'd been in the lobby.

She clenches my arm again. "I have an idea. Maybe we can all go out some time." Her gaze slides to mine in excitement.

"All go out?" I repeat. All who?

I blink, and that's when the *all who* hits me.

"You know—you, me, Austin, and Cole," she says as if I'm too dense for words.

This has me stopping dead in my tracks before I swing toward her. The people walking directly behind us grumble as they weave their way around us.

"No." My belly dips as I shake my head. "That's not a good idea."

In fact, after last night, it's a terrible idea. I don't need a pity date. I don't need a date at all. My life had been far less complicated before Cole shoved his way into it.

"Why not?" She hooks an arm around my shoulder as we continue walking. "You need more of a social life, and I'm going to help you out with that."

"Who says I need more of a social life?" I yank my sunglasses off the top of my head and settle them on my face.

"Umm, me. That's who. Seriously, Cass, you can loosen up without getting completely shitfaced and dancing naked on top of the table. It's okay to let your guard down every once in a while and enjoy yourself. Go out with a couple of guys, have some fun." She grins before waggling her brows. "Experiment. Play the field a bit." Her expression turns devious. "Find someone with a really great tongue."

When Cole's handsome face pops up in my brain, I groan and whack her arm.

Other than the whole tongue comment, maybe Brooklyn has a point about letting my guard down, but that doesn't make it any easier to do. I have so much to prove this year. To myself. To my family. Even thinking about them makes me cringe. Their disappointment last year had been palpable.

"Okay." I finally give in because one— maybe I do need to loosen up a tiny bit, and two—I want to end this conversation as quickly as humanly possible. And agreeing with Brooklyn is the easiest way to accomplish that objective. "Maybe you're right."

She beams just like I knew she would.

From the corner of my eye, I watch as a guy passing by us almost stumbles while staring at her.

My lips lift in amusement. That's the effect Brooklyn has on the male species.

"Good. A lot of the guys on the hockey team live off campus, and there's a party happening next weekend. You can start by loosening up there."

Well, hell.

My shoulders collapse at that bit of news.

"You can't just go with Austin?"

If we go to a hockey party, Cole will probably be there and I'm not ready to see him again.

"Cassidy," she says in a tone full of warning.

"I'll think about it, okay?" That's the best she's going to get from me. Everything that happened last night is too fresh in my mind for me to consider hanging out with Cole anytime soon.

10

CASSIDY

It's not quite seven in the morning as I run through the sleeping streets of the small-town Western University calls home. The sun is just beginning to peek over the horizon, washing everything in a soft pink glow. The air is crisp, the leaves overhead vibrant in their orange, red, and yellow colors.

After the hockey game last week, I made the decision to slowly start incorporating exercise back into my routine again. In high school, I'd spent a ton of time working out and skating. After failing out last year, that had been another thing that had fallen by the wayside. I've decided to run three times a week. Okay, so maybe it's more of a jogging/speed walking type of thing but still…I'm out there, doing it.

I'm pretty sure that counts for something.

Not working out six days a week for the last nine months has taken a toll on my waistline. I used to be muscular and toned all over. Now, not so much. I'm a lot softer than I once was.

One side benefit to working out is that it helps clear my head. I'd spent so much of my high school years exercising that this feels like a little piece of normal clicking back into place. Today, I haven't stopped once to walk, and I'm already twenty-five minutes into my run. I push myself a bit more and turn onto Elm Street for my usual loop.

Just as I round the corner, another jogger comes into view. He has a long-legged stride that eats up the sidewalk between us. I veer to the right so we can pass each other. When he's about thirty feet from me, my belly hollows and I realize that it's Cole. He looks more delicious than any sweaty guy has a right to. I, on the other hand, know that my face is beet red as if I could stroke out at any moment. When our gazes collide, he slows his pace before stopping about five feet away. I have no choice but to do the same. Nerves scamper across my exposed flesh.

His smile is tentative as his eyes drift over me. "Hi."

He doesn't even sound winded.

"Hi," I huff, trying to catch my breath. Even though my heart is racing, I doubt it's from the physical exertion. That's the kind of effect Cole has on me.

I half expect him to jokingly throw out a stalker comment, but he doesn't. Guess we've moved on from that. It should make me happy, instead it leaves me feeling oddly bereaved. It's like I can't have a normal relationship with someone because I'm too screwed up.

His eyes hold mine; their golden intensity arrowing straight through the heart of me, and I shiver in the early morning sunlight.

"Hey, how's it going?" he asks.

"Great." *Lie.* "How about you?"

In all honesty, I'm not sure if I want to know. I'm half afraid he's already moved on to a nice, normal girl. One who doesn't fall apart when he touches her.

Awkwardness descends like a heavy blanket, until it feels as if I could choke on it. What sucks most is that all of the other times we've been together, our banter felt effortless. This is anything but. All I can think about is escaping before this situation jackhammers to an all new low.

"I've been busy with school and practice," he says. His eyes are focused intently on mine as if he's trying to figure out what's going on between us.

When he opens his mouth to say more, I cut him off, needing to pull the plug on this disastrous conversation. "I bet. Well, I'd better get back to it."

His lips lift at the edges, but it's nowhere near a full-fledged smile. Not like the ones he showered on me before he realized I was a nutjob. There are definitely no dimples in sight.

I wince.

Why does that even matter?

I'm frustrated with myself for feeling hurt by this awkward interaction. Clearly, I'm in no frame of mind to be anything more than a friend to Cole. On second thought, maybe not even that.

Just as I'm about to take off, he slides over, blocking my path. He reaches out but at the last second, drops his arms to his sides. My wide gaze tracks the movement before they swing up to his again.

He must sense the questions burning in my eyes because he clears his throat. "I've noticed that you don't like to be touched."

Neither of us move. I barely feel as if I'm breathing.

It takes effort to suck in a deep breath before forcing it out again. I'm not panicking. I'm more embarrassed that he's figured me out so easily. Now that he's spoken the words out loud, there's no way to ignore my behavior or pretend it doesn't exist. And that's hard. It leaves me feeling vulnerable and exposed, like I need to explain myself to him.

"No," I say quietly, "I don't." As difficult as it is, I leave it at that.

He takes a tentative step toward me. When I don't retreat, he takes another, and then a third until I have to crane my neck to hold his steady gaze. He's so close that I can feel the heat radiating off his body. It's as if he's the sun and I'm drawn to the warmth.

"I can't stop thinking about you, Cassidy," he whispers. He pauses, gaze searching mine. "I've tried to," he admits, with more honesty than I've given him, "but I can't."

Air gets trapped in my lungs as my mind spins. I guess we have that in common. As much as I want to push him to a place where I no longer think about him, I haven't been able to do it. I've never felt so conflicted in my life. I'm not ready for what he forces me to feel.

It scares me.

He scares me.

"Breathe," he says. The moment he murmurs the words, I realize I've been holding my breath. Very slowly I release it back into the atmosphere. "I'm going to touch your shoulders, okay?" His words are calm, soothing.

I can breathe.

I'm not panicking.

My chest doesn't feel tight or achy.

"Okay."

Almost in slow-motion, he brings his hands up until they're able to rest lightly on my shoulders.

"What are we going to do about this?"

His words are like a calm stream washing over me. Somewhere deep inside me, they spark a flicker of hope that maybe he sees more in me than I'm capable of seeing in myself.

Confused and unsure, I shake my head. "I don't know." I really don't. There are a thousand reasons why this is a terrible idea. A thousand reasons why a relationship between us is doomed to fail.

Before I can think better of it, I whisper, "I'm a little bit broken." Probably more than just a little.

For a long silent moment, he holds my gaze with his golden one. "You don't have to tell me anything right now, but if we're going to do this, you'll have to trust me enough to let me in."

My teeth scrape against my bottom lip. "What if I can't?" It's hard to imagine forcing out the words.

Especially to Cole.

"We'll take it slow, Cassidy. So slow that it won't even feel like we're moving." The edges of his lips tip upward as his fingers press into my shoulders.

"Why?" How can he be this patient?

I shake my head, still scared, but feeling a tiny bit of hope as well. "Why are you bothering with this? With me?" He has to realize there's something wrong with me. He has to know that a relationship won't be easy.

Because I'm not easy.

Not anymore.

He cocks his head, and for the first time in more than a week, I watch as a genuine smile curves his lips. I'd be lying if I didn't admit that my heart flutters at the sight of his dimples.

He chuckles as if the reason should be obvious. "Because you're all I've been able to think about since I met you. Whatever secrets you're keeping, you can trust me with them." The smile fades as a serious expression replaces it. "I won't hurt you."

Here's the thing…I can't jump blindly off the cliff with him. Even if he makes me feel like I want to. "I need some time."

He pulls me a bit closer. It's nowhere near close enough to be flush against his body, only enough to tease me with the heat of him. "I can give you that."

The corners of my lips tentatively slide upward.

Here's a guy who has seen me lose it and isn't running for the hills. It makes me wonder if I can really trust him.

"Are you coming to our party Friday night?"

"I think so. Brooklyn has only mentioned it a few dozen times." Probably more. If I have to hear one more word about Austin, I'm going to be sick.

He grins. "I'm sure she has since I asked Austin to make sure his new girl brought her roommate along."

I chuckle as his fingers squeeze the tops of my shoulders again. An arrow of heat shoots through me.

I glance away, watching as a car speeds past us. "I should probably get back to the dorms." I need to shower and get ready for class.

"How about I run back with you?"

I shake my head. "You don't have to do that."

The sun shines down on us, warming our skin. People from neighboring houses are sliding into their cars and leaving for work or school. It's perfectly safe for me to be out running by myself.

One side of his mouth quirks. "I want to."

That's when I realize it's not a safety issue for him. He wants to spend more time with me.

"Okay," I concede, knowing I'll enjoy the feel of him at my side.

We take off, jogging back to my dorm, which is about a mile and a half away. I'm sure he has to slow his pace, even though I try to quicken mine. Neither of us speak, instead we listen to our iPods. When we finally arrive in front of Washington Hall, the girls' dorm, I turn to him, my chest heaving.

When I'm finally able to form words, I say, "I've just started running again. I'm a little out of shape." It's almost embarrassing that I used to run five miles in less than fifty minutes, three times a week, to keep my stamina high.

"You don't look out of shape." His gaze slides over my body.

If my cheeks hadn't already been heated from our physical exertion, he would have seen the hot blush scorching them.

"How often do you run now?"

I suck in another breath as my heart continues to jackhammer. "Three times a week. Usually Monday, Wednesday, and Friday around six thirty." I actually want to double over, but there's no way I'm doing that in front of him.

He nods, stretching his calf muscles. "Would you like some company?"

I'd love to spend more time with him…

"I won't be able to keep up with you," I admit, "I'm not fast enough." My brows draw together as I take a good look at him. "You're not even breathing hard," I accuse.

That is so unfair. I'm practically ready to keel over and he looks as if he's been out for a Sunday stroll. Even worse than that—it was only a mile and a half.

So pathetic.

He flashes a grin, showing off his dimples. And just like it always does, something warm slides through me at the sight of them.

"I run and lift weights four times a week. Plus, we're on the ice every day but Sunday," he chuckles. "I'd better be in good shape, or my hockey career would be over with pretty damn fast."

Still unsure, I warn, "You won't get much of a workout if we run together."

He places his hands on my shoulders before giving them a gentle squeeze. He doesn't ask permission, but moves slowly enough that I could stop him if I wanted. For some reason, that makes me feel better. More in control of the situation. Cole isn't going to rush me into something I'm not ready for.

He holds my gaze. "I'm not looking for a challenge. I want to spend time with you doing something we both enjoy."

A wide smile spills across my face as I nod. "Okay."

I like the idea of waking up and running with him three times a week.

He squeezes my shoulders one last time. "Save me a seat in Psych?"

"I will." Another flutter erupts in my belly. I enjoy my Psychology class, but now I'm looking forward to it even more.

When he leans toward me, I think that maybe he'll kiss me. I draw in a deep breath and wait as a strange concoction of longing and fear spiral through me. Instead, he presses a soft kiss against my forehead before pulling away and searching my eyes.

He smiles as if he can feel the disappointment flooding through me. "Slow, right?"

Heat rushes to my cheeks as I suck my lower lip between my teeth and nod.

In that moment, I realize just how much I wanted to feel the warm pressure of his lips coasting over mine.

With a wave, Cole takes off, heading back to his house at a much faster clip. As I watch him, I feel surprisingly happier than I've been in a long time.

11

CASSIDY

With our arms linked, Brooklyn and I get absorbed into a herd of students heading to the same party. My brows rise as I stare up at the large Victorian that looms in front of us. It looks as if it's bursting at the seams with people. Even though it's only nine o'clock on a Friday night, drunken revelers are spilling out onto the darkened lawn, plastic beer cups in hand, laughing and hollering as music pulses from inside.

I give Brooklyn at bit of side-eye. "Jeez. It looks like the entire campus is here."

"Didn't you see the flyers plastered all over school? I think it's a," she uses her fingers to make air quotes "fundraiser."

I can only imagine what will be bought with the money they make tonight.

Probably more red plastic cups and beer.

It takes effort to push through the throng of people and make our way inside the house. My gaze darts around, overwhelmed by the sheer number of partiers crammed inside the living room. Every square inch of space is occupied. And if I'd thought the music was pumping outside, it's much louder once you're inside the space. I have no idea how we'll ever find Cole or Austin in this mess.

Just as that thought flits through my head, there's a tap on my shoulder. I turn, because honestly, if this is going to be another party where my ass is constantly being grabbed, I'm out of here. Blaring music and a bunch of drunken strangers looking for a hookup isn't exactly my scene. Instead, I find Cole staring down at me with that trademark sexy smile lighting up his face.

Wait a minute…did I just think that?

Unconsciously, my gaze drops from his eyes to his lips.

He really does have a sexy smile. Actually, if I'm being honest with myself, Cole is just plain sexy.

Crap.

I am so over my head with him.

Closing the distance between us, he whispers in my ear, "Remember, we're taking this slow." He draws back enough to stare at my face. "You keep looking at me like that, and I'm not sure how slow I'll be able to keep things."

That's all it takes for me to rip my gaze from his. A couple of seconds tick by before I feel the slide of his fingers beneath my chin. He lifts it until I have no other choice but to meet his penetrating stare. I suck in a breath as he pins me in place with his scorching hot gaze.

"I'm not saying I don't like it," he says. "I just want you to know that it affects me." His fingers stroke the delicate flesh beneath my chin before sliding upward to cradle my cheek.

Nerves explode in the pit of my belly as I glance around the packed room, searching for a new topic. "I can't believe how many people are here."

I have to clear my throat when it unexpectedly cracks.

A knowing smile tugs at the corners of his lips as he allows our previous conversation to drop before taking a look around and nodding. "There's a band playing in the backyard. Let's grab something to drink and we can head back there for a while. You want a beer?"

I shake my head.

I'm not against drinking, it's just not something I do anymore. I like to be clearheaded and in control. Especially around Cole. He scrambles my brain more than alcohol.

"How about a bottle of water or cola instead?"

Already my throat feels parched. "I'll take water, please."

I turn to ask if Brooklyn wants something, but she's no longer behind me. I blink at the space she'd been occupying only minutes ago. So much for sticking together.

"I guess it's just me," I add.

"Well, I'm happy to see *just* you." His fingers wrap around mine. He watches me for a moment as if to gauge my reaction.

I release a sigh when nothing happens.

All right, maybe that's not exactly true. There's a little shiver of pleasure snaking its way through me. Because Cole is usually so smooth with his lines, I can't resist teasing, "Just so you know, that was really lame."

He laughs as if pleased by my comment. "Maybe, but it's absolutely true." Then he jerks his head toward the back of the house. "I'll bet Austin and Brooklyn are already there."

With that, he tugs me through the thick crowd of people standing inside the living room. As we weave our way around groups of students, I notice how Cole catches the attention of several girls we move past.

As we pass through the kitchen, Cole snags two bottles of water before handing one to me.

"Thanks." I twist off the cap and take a long drink.

"No problem."

With his hand wrapped around mine, he tows me toward the back door. Even though there are just as many people jam-packed into the large, fenced-in yard, there's a lot more room to spread out. The band is already set up in one corner of the yard, tuning their instruments.

"Dude, there are so many hot girls here!"

I turn in the direction of that booming voice until my gaze slams into a barrel-like chest before gradually climbing upward until I can see his face.

It's one I, unfortunately, recognize.

The corners of my mouth tug down at the corners as I stare at Alex. I haven't had the pleasure of running into him since the night we got into it at that party. Equally silent, he stares back at me as if trying to place where he knows me from. It only takes a few seconds before he makes the connection.

"Hey." His eyes widen before narrowing. "I remember you!" His gaze slides accusingly to Cole who stands at my side. "That's the girl who got all those crazy chicks mad at me." Gone is all his jovial disposition. "Do you know that they yelled at me for at least forty minutes? It was a total buzzkill. And they wouldn't stop following me around for the rest of the night either. There wasn't a single girl who would talk to me after that." He thrusts out his lower lip like a sullen toddler. It's difficult to take him seriously when he's pouting and glaring like that.

The temptation to laugh is almost impossible to resist. Instead, I smile sweetly. "Hi Alex, good to see you again."

His expression turns pinched. "Why are you here?"

Before I can respond— because trust me, there's one on the tip of my tongue and it wasn't going to be nice—Cole cuts me off.

"She's with me." This is followed up with, "Do you have a problem with that?"

I blink. I have yet to witness Cole get all hard-assed.

It's shocking just how sexy it is. I want to throw my hands up in disgust because everything the guy does is attractive.

Alex's deep brown gaze swings from Cole to me and then back again before he lifts his hands in a gesture of surrender. "There's no problem."

Cole's voice is still tough as nails when he adds, "Maybe you shouldn't go around ass grabbing, if you don't want to have a pack of angry chicks bitching you out all night."

Alex's eyes narrow as his lips thin. "Maybe." He gives me a glowering stare before stalking toward the house.

An apology sits on the tip of my tongue as I swing toward Cole, but he beats me to the punch.

"I'm sorry about Alex. Believe it or not, he's actually a decent guy."

"Clearly," I agree with a laugh. The jury is out on that one. That's now two crappy interactions I've had with the guy.

His lips tremble around the corners. "I'm serious, he really is. He can just be a little dense sometimes. He'll come around." There's a beat of silence before he tacks on, "Eventually."

"I'm sure he will." I won't, however, hold my breath.

For the next couple of hours, we listen to the band. They're a local group who play at a lot of bars around town. They also perform exclusively at the hockey parties, since the lead singer knows one of Cole's teammates. Before I realize it, I'm dancing with Cole, Austin, and Brooklyn. After a while, Alex joins in. In a shocking twist, he turns out to be smooth on his feet.

A few drinks later, he sidles up to me like a puppy dog with its tail tucked between his legs and apologizes for grabbing me a couple of weeks ago. Even though I'm pleasantly surprised by the olive branch, I can't help but wonder if Cole put him up to it.

Once we've exhausted ourselves from dancing, we stand near the front of the makeshift stage, listening as the band finishes up their last set. By now, the crowd has thinned, and the atmosphere is mellower. I stifle a yawn. As awesome as tonight has been, it feels like it's time to head home.

My gaze coasts over the crowd, searching for Brooklyn or Austin, but I don't see them.

Cole leans down and whispers, "I think they disappeared upstairs about twenty minutes ago. Do you want me to see if she's staying over?"

I shake my head, already knowing that I'll be walking back without her. "No."

She's been crashing here with Austin quite a bit. I assume it's a pattern that will only increase in frequency. Brooklyn is past her usual expiration date when it comes to settling down with one guy. I think she must really like him.

Cole is quiet for a few moments. "I can drive you home or, if you want—" uncertainty flicks across his expression "—you can crash here tonight."

I suck in a breath.

Before I can shake my head, he forces out the rest in a rush of words. "We'd just sleep, I swear. Or you can stay in my room, and I'll bunk somewhere else. Whatever you're comfortable with."

He steps toward me, drawing me into the warm circle of his arms until I'm able to feel the heat of his body. "I know you need to take this slow, and I don't want to push you into something that makes you uncomfortable. So, if it does, I'll grab my keys and take you home."

Surprised by his thoughtful offer, I chew my lower lip.

Do I want to spend the night?

With Cole.

My mouth turns bone-dry as that thought rolls around in my head. Sleeping is the only thing we'd be doing. There's no way I'm ready for anything more. Even though Cole kind of makes me want more.

"And you would be okay with that?" I ask cautiously. The last thing I want is to put myself in another bad situation.

"Absolutely."

His expression is so sincere that I can't help but believe him. Searching his whiskey-colored eyes, I realize how much I want to spend the night with him. I want to experience that closeness with him.

"Okay."

Before I can rethink my decision, Cole wraps his hand around mine and tows me through the small pockets of people who are still standing around and drinking, even though it's after two in the morning. Nerves scamper across my flesh with each step that brings us closer to his bedroom. Cole leads me up the wooden staircase and then down a long hallway until we stop at a locked door. He pulls a key out of his pocket before opening the door and ushering me inside.

The muscles in my belly contract as I grind to a halt in the middle of his room and take everything in. A queen-sized bed with a navy comforter is pushed back against the far wall. There's a desk situated near the door with neat stack of books piled on top of it. The backpack I always see him carrying around campus lies on the floor next to it.

My gaze slides to Cole who is rifling through a large, dark wood dresser that matches the desk. An overstuffed chair has been crammed into the corner.

Not that I'm surprised, but his room is neat and clean. Sure, there's a pile of clothing stacked on the dresser along with some hockey gear lying around, but that's about it.

He pulls out a light gray T-shirt and a pair of athletic shorts before handing them to me. More tension gathers inside me. I've never spent the night in a guy's room before.

I shift, pointing toward the hallway. "I'm, ah, going to use the bathroom."

Butterflies have winged their way to life and are fluttering around madly in the pit of my belly as I take a hasty step toward the door.

"Yeah, sure, but don't change in there. All right?" His lips lift into a crooked smile. "Wait until you get back here to do that."

My eyes flare as I carefully set the clothing down on the bed as if it's a bomb that could detonate at any moment before fleeing to the bathroom down the hall. I shut the door and click the lock into place before leaning heavily against it. My heart slams almost painfully against my ribcage.

Only now do I wonder what I've gotten myself into.

Maybe this wasn't such a good idea after all.

I gnaw my bottom lip until it feels pulpy before squeezing my eyes tightly closed and doing a quick self-check. Inhaling a deep steady breath, I hold it captive in my lungs before slowly forcing it out again.

Nope, I'm not having any breathing issues.

My chest isn't tight and achy.

I don't feel nauseous, even though my belly is a jittery mess.

I'm…okay.

I'm not on the verge of freaking out.

Half a dozen deep breaths later, I feel more in control of myself and the situation.

When I return from the bathroom, Cole is sitting in the armchair tucked into the corner. He leans forward so that his elbows rest on bent knees. His long, muscular legs are bare and sprinkled with fine hair. When he hears me walk in, he glances up and meets my gaze. He's already changed into a faded T-shirt and athletic shorts that are similar to the ones he gave me. My shirt and shorts are still sitting neatly folded at the end of the bed.

His steady gaze holds mine as he rises to his feet. "I'll turn around so you can change."

I release a nervous breath as he crosses his arms over his chest before turning his back to me. For a heartbeat, I stand there, strangely paralyzed before shaking myself out of the mental stupor and grabbing the soft T-shirt. I hold it up and take a better look at it.

Western Wolves Hockey.

My fingers trail over the navy embossed letters. I peek at him to make sure his back is still turned before bringing the shirt to my nose and inhaling.

Cole.

The fragrance is purely him. It's a mix of the ocean and something that's masculine in nature. The thought of wearing his clothes and cocooning myself in his scent has my belly hollowing out.

Even though the broad expanse of his back faces me, I still turn away before stripping out of my shirt and bra. A fine tremble racks my fingers as I slide the jeans down my hips and legs before whipping on Cole's faded gray T-shirt and athletic shorts. The shorts are a few sizes too big and refuse to stay at my waist.

My head is bent as I try to tighten the drawstring. I'm startled when his fingers brush mine aside and pull the string tight, tying it in a knot that rests below my belly button. When his knuckles drift over the bare skin of my stomach, I suck in a deep breath.

His gaze slices to mine as he straightens, backing away until there's once again distance between us. "Better?"

"Yes." Those butterflies in my belly feel as if they are trying to escape. I'm not sure how much more of this I can take. A small part of me wants to do more than just sleep in his bed. But the other part— the more cautious part—knows I'm not ready.

I'm probably pushing the boundaries of what I can handle without having a small—or god forbid, *huge*—freak-out. I don't want Cole to see me like that. He's already witnessed enough.

As I stand motionless, I realize that everything has quieted down-stairs. My gaze slides from his to the queen-sized bed. My nerves ratchet up a couple hundred notches. I've spent the last nine months pushing people away and yet, somehow, Cole has managed to sneak past all my defenses.

The last thing I want to do is put myself in a situation that ends badly. I force my gaze back to Cole who silently watches me.

It's as if he can read my thoughts, which is disconcerting on an entirely different level.

"I could pile pillows in the middle of the bed like a wall if that would make you feel better." He pauses. "Or I could sleep in the chair. I don't want you to be uncomfortable."

His earnest gaze holds mine before he offers a lopsided smile. "I promise, nothing will happen. We've totally slow-tracked this rela-tionship."

I can't help but believe him. Against my better judgment, his calm words dissolve the tension bubbling up inside me.

Feeling foolish, I give my head a little shake. "No, it's fine." I reem-phasize, "*I'm* fine with this." I don't want him to think I'm some weird chick who constantly loses her shit.

We move at the same time, lifting the covers before settling on our respective sides. When we're both settled, Cole snaps off the light on his bedside table, plunging the room into darkness. There's a low hum of activity from the first floor, but for the most part, it has calmed considerably.

After a couple of minutes of holding myself perfectly rigid, I turn toward him. He does the same until we're face-to-face. There's about twelve inches of space separating us and I'm good with that. It feels safe. Even though I'm tempted to run my fingers over the sharp angles and planes of his face, I don't dare.

He remains still, not making a move toward me. Maybe it's foolish to trust him so soon, but I can't deny that I do.

I like Cole. I desperately want to believe he's a good guy.

He makes me feel things I've never experienced before. Sometimes that scares me, tempting me to retreat, but it also excites me, which is confusing.

"What are you thinking about?" His hushes voice slides over me in the darkness like warmed honey.

I draw in a breath before gradually forcing it out again. "That I don't want to make any more mistakes."

"Do you think this is a mistake?" He doesn't sound offended, just curious. As if he's willing to prove that trusting him isn't one.

Tension settles in my shoulders as I shrug. "I don't know." I hope not. "I screwed up last year. I don't want to continue down that path." I'm trying to be as truthful as I can without vomiting the whole sordid story.

"This isn't a mistake."

His confidence is a turn-on.

What I've discovered about Cole is that there is no end to his sexiness. It's so much more than his good looks. He's such a nice guy and so completely self-assured in who he is. It's almost enough to make me believe, that whatever this is between us, can't be misconstrued as anything other than right.

I want, almost desperately, to believe him.

To believe *in* him.

I want that more than I've wanted anything in a long time. I suddenly crave the intimacy he's making me believe I can have with him.

"You sound so sure," I whisper.

"That's because I am." There's a pause. "I'm going to touch your face, okay?"

I draw in a quick breath before nodding just once. In the darkness that has settled around us, it's enough.

Almost as if in slow-motion, his hand rises before carefully stroking over my cheek. That's all it takes for my eyelids to drift shut.

His touch feels so good.

Right.

The way he caresses my face sends a million shivers galloping across my skin.

"Cassidy."

My eyelids flutter open before my gaze locks on his.

"If you can't believe in you, then believe in me. Because I *am* sure about this. You just have to trust me not to hurt you. Tonight I have the only girl I want in my bed and I'm not going to mess that up. I'm not going to rush you into something you're not ready for. You're the one in control here. It's all up to you."

A soft sigh escapes as his touch awakens so many dormant emotions within me. I've never had a guy say something like that to me. There are times when Cole seems almost too good to be true.

Our gazes stay locked as he inches closer. My breathing stays even as I enjoy the sensation of his fingers stealing over my flesh. When I don't protest, he scoots just a fraction closer until I can feel his minty breath feathering across my lips.

My attention falls to the perfect bow-shaped curve of his mouth. Memories of what it felt like to have his lips sliding over mine flood through me.

Even in the darkness that swirls around us, it's like he can read my mind.

"I want to kiss you." There's a beat of silence as my heart thunders against my breast. "If you tell me not to kiss you, I won't."

My gaze bounces from his lips to his eyes. Somehow, I know he isn't the kind of guy who will force himself on me. He's asking for permission, and he'll be fine with whatever my decision is. It gives me a sense of control even though I don't necessarily feel in control of the feelings careening through my body.

It's almost a surprise when I hear the scrape of my own voice fill the stillness of the room. "I want you to kiss me."

One side of his mouth lifts at the corner.

Drawing closer, his lips settle over mine. He caresses them gently, coaxing mine to open under the light pressure. His touch isn't tentative or unsure, but it's not overbearing either. The care he takes only makes me want him more. Something that feels suspiciously like warmed honey slides through me as he continues to play havoc with my mouth. He doesn't shove his tongue down my throat or get carried away.

He nibbles at my lips, all the while using light, teasing strokes that feather across mine. A whimper escapes from me as he continues the torment. There is nothing demanding or punishing about the kiss.

If there had been, I'd start panicking. Instead, what he's doing makes me want to move closer. I'm tempted to run my tongue along the seam of his lips and explore his mouth the way I've secretly dreamed of doing since our first meeting.

I have no idea how long we lay there, wrapped up in each other. Our bodies pressed so close that I feel every hard line and taut muscle. Our lips continue to touch, stroking over the another until I'm drunk with the taste of him.

When I don't think I can stand another moment, his tongue flicks the corner of my mouth and I moan. The sound that escapes is low, achy, and full of need. Cole groans in response. He nips at my bottom lip, sucking the fullness into his mouth. His hands cradle my face, never straying.

It's his restraint that propels me into rubbing my body against his, craving both the closeness and friction.

He continues to nibble and lick at my lips until I want to scream with the tension that has settled in every muscle. Even though I'm nervous, my tongue darts out to lick at his lips. Arousal bursts to life in my core as I dip inside his mouth. It doesn't take long before our teeth are scraping against each other.

The way he makes me feel is almost a revelation. I haven't been interested in guys, or sex, in a long time. Almost a year. Since the desire hasn't been there, I haven't bothered with…well, let's just say, I haven't felt the need to take matters into my own hands, and leave it at that.

As quickly as those thoughts enter my mind, they scatter to the wind as Cole teases my senses by sucking my tongue into his mouth. Silently, I admit that maybe he's right. Maybe this isn't a mistake. How could anything that's wrong feel this amazing?

I'm not sure how long we explore each other's mouth. All I know is that the first fingers of light begin to stretch across the horizon when I finally fall asleep in Cole's arms. I can't deny the odd contentment that settles over me.

Unwilling to question it, I do the only thing I can and snuggle up against him, allowing myself to relax before drifting off to sleep.

12

—————

CASSIDY

My brows are knit tightly together as I glance suspiciously around before asking, "What are we doing here?"

It's a few minutes before five o'clock in the morning, and the ice arena is closed. The lights are off, the concession stand is locked up tight, there's not even a maintenance guy on duty to question our presence.

Even though this isn't the first time I've posed the question, Cole remains tight-lipped. The only thing he said is that it's a surprise.

The first wave of questions fell from my lips as we stood outside the arena, and I realized it wasn't open. That's when Cole had produced a key. I'm not going to lie, it had struck me as a little bit sketchy. The last thing I need is a police record to go along with the other crap I put my parents through. They'd probably disown me.

Officially.

But I trust Cole.

I do.

He doesn't strike me as a guy who engages in criminal activity. Right now, I can only hope I'm not wrong about that. Then again, he's never done anything to warrant my mistrust.

My mind tumbles back to Friday night.

And all the time we spent kissing.

The time spent in his bed had been—for lack of a better word—hot.

Arousal coils tight in my core just thinking about it. I've never spent that much time kissing someone. Even though it had been tempting to take it further, I'm glad we hadn't.

One thing is for sure—Cole knows how to kiss. His lips are soft, yet firm. Who knew that just licking and nipping at someone's mouth could be so erotic?

Even more amazing than that, I hadn't felt a moment of panic. No anxiety or chest tightening.

Nothing.

I'd felt safe, and more importantly, in control of the situation. It was as if Cole had known exactly what I needed and how to give it to me.

"Cassidy?"

I'm snapped out of those thoughts when he waves a hand in front of my face.

My gaze snaps to his. "Yeah?"

A slow smile spreads across his face as if he knows exactly what had been running through my mind. He steps closer before wrapping his arms around me.

"Whatcha thinking about that has such a sexy little smile lighting up your face?"

My eyes widen as my cheeks fill with heat. It takes effort to clear my throat. "Just wondering if this little surprise of yours will end with a ride in the back of a police cruiser."

A chuckle escapes from him before he tugs me closer and nips at my lips. "Aw damn, how'd you guess?"

His eyes flare with heat as liquid warmth floods through me.

I am in so much trouble with this guy.

The tendrils of need that had been curling at the bottom of my belly dissipate as I elbow him in the ribs. With a quick kiss, he leads me through the deserted lobby to the counter where they keep the rental skates.

Disappearing through the side door, he asks, "What size are you?"

"Eight," I answer, still wondering what he's up to.

A few moments later he returns with an ugly pair of brown rental skates, which he holds by the blades in one hand. "Okay, let's go."

"We're seriously going to skate?" I guess I shouldn't be too surprised. We are, after all, at a skating rink. But it's an empty, closed skating rink.

Misunderstanding the question, a smile tumbles across his face as he teases, "What, you don't know how?" He reaches out, gently stroking the curve of my cheek. "Don't worry, I'll teach you. It's not that hard."

One of my brows quirks, but I remain silent. He thinks I don't know how to skate, huh?

Well, this should be amusing.

"Come on, it'll be fun," he says, as if trying to convince me, which is kind of hilarious. "I promise."

"Oh, it'll definitely be fun," I agree.

"I've been teaching skating lessons since I was in high school. If I can teach five- and six-year-olds, then I can teach you in no time."

That comment almost has me skidding to a halt.

Instead of giving myself away, I bite back the sharp retort about my skating abilities. This guy is definitely in trouble now. I grab the skates before forcing my lips into a tight smile.

"I can't wait."

Cole turns on the lights while I drop down on a bench inside the frigid rink before unlacing the boots and shoving my foot inside each brown skate. These are the ugliest things I've ever seen. I'll probably be falling all over the place. Silently, I inspect each blade. They might be crappy skates, but at least the blades appear to be freshly sharpened, which should help.

Hopefully.

Then again, I haven't skated since last December. It's entirely possible I'll end up on my ass no matter what. I can't believe how strange it feels to lace these things up. Especially since they aren't mine. A year ago, I wouldn't have been caught dead in crappy skates like these. In the past, I've always had the newest and best equipment on the market. Each pair of skates molded to the contours of my feet for a perfect fit.

This situation is so rife with irony, I'm almost choking on it.

Instead of playing Division I hockey, I'm with a guy who doesn't think I can skate.

How on earth had I fallen so far in life?

Irritated with myself for dwelling on the past, I shake the thoughts away.

As I rise to my feet, I'm inundated with so many memories that I almost stagger under the heavy weight of them.

Cole sits to tie his own skates. He must keep all of his equipment here in a private locker room for the team, because he's now wearing a black warm-up suit with the team emblem and a pair of gloves. He told me to bring a jacket, gloves, and a hat, which is what I'm wearing since it's cold in the rink.

As I wait for Cole to lace up his skates, I'm suddenly antsy to get out on the ice. The urge to stretch my legs pounds through me like a steady drumbeat. I can't believe how much I've missed it. Even in crappy rental skates, I just want to feel that first glide across a fresh sheet of ice.

I watch as my warm breath puffs out in the chilled air. The scent of the ice and the feel of the rink overload my senses.

A lifetime of memories crowd the inside of my brain until I become lost within them. I grew up at our local ice arena. I've lost track of how many times Mom rolled her eyes before telling Dad and me that we should have our mail forwarded to the rink because we spend more time there than at home. Like everything else, it's a bittersweet memory.

Once his skates have been laced up, Cole rises to his feet before holding out his hand to me. I take his gloved hands as he props his stick against the Plexiglas wall. He opens the heavy metal door and steps out onto the ice before flipping around to wait for me.

I have to bite my lip to keep from smiling. He's adorable when he thinks he needs to coddle me. It almost makes me feel bad for tricking him.

Almost.

"Don't worry, I'll catch you if you fall." He waits patiently for me to close the distance that separates us.

Maybe I'm a terrible person for doing this, but I can't resist.

"Are you sure?" I grip the wall as if terrified, gingerly hobbling out onto the smooth sheet of ice, wobbling a bit as I go. My arms flail as Cole swiftly grabs hold of me before towing me toward him. I allow Cole to do all the work while I glide without moving my feet.

"See? You're doing so awesome!"

He gives me an encouraging smile as if he's proud that I haven't fallen on my ass. It takes everything I have inside not to burst out laughing. He's too damn sweet. That being said, he shouldn't have made assumptions about my skating abilities. That's where he screwed up.

"Do you want to try gliding now? I promise, it's really easy. You won't have any problems." He releases my hands before demon-strating how to take long, smooth strokes with my skates.

I bite down on my lower lip to keep the smile from dancing across my face. This is way too much fun and I'm nowhere near done toying with him.

Eyes wide, I wobble a bit and flail my arms before taking a few short, choppy strokes.

He beams, circling around me with ease. "You're a natural. We'll have you skating like a professional in no time." He transitions smoothly from forwards to backwards as if floating across the ice. If anyone is a natural, it's him. He is incredibly fluid. I could stand here and watch him for hours.

"Oh, I don't know about that." My skates move rapidly beneath me as I pretend to lose my balance.

Within seconds, he eats up the distance between us before pulling me into his arms and holding me close. His attention drops to my parted lips. Time stands still as my heartbeat speeds up. His gaze returns to mine, looking more heated than before.

"I'm going to kiss you, Cassidy," he murmurs, voice sounding like crushed gravel. "If you don't want me to, you'd better tell me now."

My breath hitches as need floods through me, igniting a firestorm in its path.

"I want you to kiss me."

I tip my face toward his and wait for his lips to settle over mine. He caresses them gently, making me forget where we are. Just as I sink further into the warm embrace, he draws away before untangling himself from me, leaving my body to pulse and throb with need.

"Okay, let's try that again." He motions for me to skate toward him. Slightly disorientated from that kiss, I pick up each skate as if clumsily trying to walk across the ice.

"No, not like that," he patiently instructs. "You have to glide. Just remember, long smooth strokes."

Long smooth strokes.

Now that's a distracting thought. Maybe even more so than his kisses.

It doesn't take long before I'm imagining Cole caressing my insides with long smooth strokes. God, I bet he's good at it. I mean, come on, of course he is. His kisses are literally mind-blowing. Even thinking about them has me clenching my inner thighs together, which is something I've never felt compelled to do.

"Cassidy?"

I blink and refocus my attention on Cole. I can't believe I was just thinking about that. Here I am, practically fantasizing about him when all we've done up to this point is kiss. But they were some seriously super-hot kisses, if that counts for anything. Mentally, I'm nowhere near ready for more. And yet, it seems like my body is begging for it.

I give my head a little shake to clear it. This charade has gone on long enough. It's time to end it. For a moment, I wonder if he'll be pissed that I played him. I hope not, but I guess we're about to find out.

I take one long, perfect stroke, and then a second.

"Cassidy!" He beams. "You're doing awesome! Keep it up, baby!"

My eyes widen and I almost stumble at the endearment.

"Careful!" He looks ready to race over and catch me if needed. The funny thing is that I wasn't even trying to stumble. I take another long stride and then another until I'm flying across the ice.

"Holy fuck," he shouts in amazement as I leave him behind.

At this point, I can't contain myself. A few chuckles slip free as I pick up more speed. I crouch low, finally doing what I've been dying to and push myself faster. It feels so good to stretch my legs and use muscles I haven't exercised in almost a year. Even as I speed across the smooth ice, it feels like second nature. I peek over my shoulder only to find Cole standing where I left him. His mouth is hanging open as he continues to track me. I round the corner, racing up the other side of the ice until I whip past him, flipping around so I can wave as I skate backwards around another curve. With our gazes locked, I criss-cross my skates, picking up more speed in a series of complicated strokes.

I see the moment understanding dawns across his face. "You," he bellows, "knew how to skate the entire time!"

I can't help the gurgle of laughter that falls from my lips at his stupefied tone. The expression on his face is priceless.

"No, you're just a really great teacher," I yell back. "Didn't all those five- and six-year-olds take off like this?"

My snappy response spurs him into motion as he digs his blades into the ice and takes off after me. Because he's fast, I know he'll catch me in a matter of moments. I flip back around before forcing my legs to pick up more speed.

When he finally catches up, he jerks me into his arms as we continue to circle crazily across the ice. I shriek, afraid that we're going to fall. When we slow, I'm laughing so hard that tears are streaming down my cheeks and my belly hurts.

He bands his arms around me as his eyes narrow with disbelief. "I can't believe you lied to me!"

A smile lights up my face as I shake my head. "Technically, I didn't lie. I never actually *told* you I couldn't skate. You just *assumed* I couldn't." I giggle before adding, "You know what they say when you assume. It makes an ass out of both you and me."

His arms tighten even more until I find myself pressed up against his body. A heartbeat later, his lips crash onto mine in a kiss that almost makes me forget my own name. Even though this kiss is more forceful than the others we've shared, it still doesn't scare me. Instead, it turns me on. Just as that realization hits me, he backs off.

"Sorry." Breathing hard from our race across the ice, he leans his forehead against mine.

"It's okay." I hold his gaze before adding softly, "I liked it."

A slow smile spreads across his face. "Is that so?" One brow arches as he searches my gaze.

"Yup."

And I want more of them.

More of him.

"Noted."

He leans in, slanting his lips gently across mine. After a few seconds, he draws away. "Figure or hockey?"

A patronizing smile curves my lips. As a female hockey player, I'd always looked down on all that figure skating crap. My forced retirement from the sport hadn't changed that. "Hockey, of course."

"Unbelievable." He untangles his arms from around me before taking off toward the door that leads off the ice.

For the first time, anxiety slices through me as I hug my arms around my middle. "Where are you going?" Even though I found this little prank amusing, maybe he didn't.

"To get another stick," he shouts as if it should be obvious.

I suck in a deep breath before pushing it out again and force my muscles to relax.

A few minutes later, he returns with some equipment before tossing me a pair of gloves with a shake of his head. "Un-freaking-believable."

Unable to help myself, I raise a brow. "Un-freaking-believable that a girl can play hockey?"

In the years I spent skating, I came across my fair share of pompous asshats who thought a girl had no business being out on the ice. Especially with them. Not necessarily my teammates, but definitely ones we played against. Instead of getting frustrated or quitting, it forced me to elevate my game and prove I was a worthy opponent. I learned to skate faster, play smarter, and be tougher.

His brows draw together. "No, just that you played hockey and didn't tell me."

"Oh." I feel ridiculous for overreacting. Heat fills my face as I glance down at the white leather gloves and flex my fingers. They're a bit big but they'll do.

Cole tosses me a stick. It's been a while since I've held one in my hands. Without waiting, I take off again. I fly forward before seamlessly switching to skate backwards. He grabs three black rubber pucks from his pocket and drops them onto the ice.

When he passes one to me, I dribble it with my stick blade, moving the puck faster across the ice.

Cole watches me for a while before murmuring, "You've got really soft hands."

I glance up and meet his inquisitive gaze before giving him a slight smile. "That's what my dad always said."

"How long did you play for?"

Even though it's a casually asked question, I suspect it's more than just curiosity that has him delving carefully into my background.

I'll tell him, but that doesn't mean I plan on giving him the uncensored version. As much as I'm starting to trust Cole, that doesn't mean it's easy to lower my guard and bare my soul.

"I began skating when I was three, and played on the boys' house team until I was eleven before making a girls' Triple AAA team until college."

Questions flicker across his expression as he digests what I've said. His gaze drops to my stick as he watches me handle the puck.

"Pass it to me." With a tap, it slides right to the end of his stick as he moves across the ice. "What made you decide not to play in college?"

He snaps the puck back to me. Instead of responding, I race up the ice before hitting it top shelf. In the middle, near the top of the metal bar is where it ends up. I can't deny the satisfaction that slides through me as the puck lands exactly where I placed it.

As I circle the net, Cole skates over.

"You didn't answer the question." He shakes his head, a small smile curving his lips. "You're really good." A chuckle falls from his lips. "You know that, right?"

I smile tightly, no longer wanting to discuss hockey.

"Cassidy, why aren't you playing college hockey?" His words are softly spoken as if he understands that he's treading on shaky ground. "You must have been scouted."

Without answering, I take off backwards, once again creating distance between us. It's not just physical. It's emotional as well. The further away I get, the more in control of my emotions I feel.

"Do you mind if we just skate?"

With every question he voiced, I could feel my chest tightening up. I don't want the amazing time we've had to be ruined by another anxiety attack. I want to forget about everything except the feel of the ice as I glide over it.

His gaze follows me until I reach center ice. Just as I wonder if my silence has pissed him off, he fishes the puck out of the net and passes it before blowing past me.

"Don't think I'm going to take it easy on you because you're a girl."

I inhale a deep breath before releasing it as my muscles loosen. True to his word, he doesn't push me.

A sly smile lifts my lips. "Be prepared to get your ass handed to you by this girl."

That's all it takes for the thick tension to dissolve.

"Big talk," he says with a grin. "Now I'm really scared."

"You should be."

For the next hour, we scrimmage. Even though I'm wearing crappy brown rental skates, I can't think of a time when I've had more fun on the ice.

13

CASSIDY

"It's nice to see you looking so happy. Things must be going well," Dr. Thompson says with a smile as she continues to study me.

Her thin black framed glasses are perched on the bridge of her nose. Every hair of her blonde, shoulder-length bob is in perfect place. Her beige suit is carefully tailored and form-fitting. A thick strand of creamy pearls clasped around her slender neck completes the picture. She sits back, looking pleased with my progress.

I have to admit, I'm happy with it as well.

Her comment has a small smile blooming across my face. I can't remember the last time I've felt this good. Even thinking back to before my life imploded, I'm not sure I was happy. I spent my high school years stressed out. There was always another game to excel at. Another test to ace. Scouts sitting in the stands that I needed to perform for like I was a circus act.

There's no longer the same pressure to succeed.

But it's more than that. A lot of my happiness has to do with Cole. I can't believe what an amazing guy he is. It makes me laugh that I'd tried so hard in the beginning to blow him off.

"Tell me what's been going on to put such a smile on your face."

I decide to start with a safe topic because I'm unsure what Dr. Thompson will think about me getting involved with someone. The whole no-boys-rule has been chucked out the window.

Even though Cole and I haven't made anything official, we've been spending a lot of time together, and I've been known to, occasionally, spend the night at his house. We're still taking our relationship slow. But it works for me.

For us.

"School is great. I have A's in all my subjects, and I'm not feeling overloaded by the workload either." That's different from last year when I'd been drowning in my classes.

Dr. Thompson smiles before nodding. "I'm not surprised. You're very bright, Cassidy. I suspect these courses aren't challenging enough for you."

I shrug, even though I privately agree with her. I don't feel especially challenged, but that's okay. After my disastrous first semester last year, I wasn't ready to dive headfirst into the deep end of the pool. I've been dipping my toe in the shallow end of the baby pool. Now that we're nearing the end of September and I'm still doing well, I've considered speaking with a few of my professors to see if they can make recommendations for second semester.

"And your tutoring is still working out?"

"Yeah, I love it," I say enthusiastically. "I've been able to pick up a few more hours each week. And I have a steady load of students who are requesting to work with me."

She settles back in her chair. "Okay. I'm happy to hear that school and tutoring are going well." There's a pause. "What about your anxiety attacks? Have you experienced any since we last met?"

I search my mind even though I know the answer. "No, none."

It's a huge relief.

I finally feel like I'm moving forward and making steady progress. The anxiety attacks were so frightening. Debilitating. The fact that I don't have any idea when one will strike only ramps up my fear. I'm constantly on edge, waiting for something to trigger one.

"Hmmm. That's interesting. Are you using your breathing techniques when you begin to feel anxious?"

"I do, and it helps calm me down. I'm always careful to stop when I start to feel agitated and mentally self-check. Lately, I've been feeling really good."

Great, even.

I'm not used to feeling like this. As much as I hate to admit it, it feels like I'm waiting for the bottom to fall out. Life seems to be going a little too perfect.

She breaks into my thoughts with another question.

"And you're continuing to run?"

"Yup. Three times a week."

Not only am I running with Cole three times a week, but I also meet up with him twice a week to work out on the ice. We usually get to the rink around five in the morning before the place opens. It's amazing to have a full sheet of perfectly smooth ice all to ourselves. Those early morning sessions with Cole are the best part of my day.

"Do you think that's contributing to the way you've been feeling lately?" She studies me before jotting down a few notes.

"Yes." Although it's not the only reason. "Definitely."

Unease blooms in my belly as I nibble at my lower lip. I need to be honest with her. Keeping secrets from your therapist defeats the purpose of having one.

Dr. Thompson continues to study me in that quiet way of hers. "Is there something else I should know about?"

Over the course of the last month, I've grown to value Dr. Thompson's input and advice. Without a doubt, I realize that she has my best interest in mind, and it helps to hear an objective perspective on some of the issues I've been struggling with.

"There is something else."

More like someone else.

"All right." With a raised brow, she patiently waits for me to continue.

It takes everything inside me to push those two little words out into the atmosphere. "A guy."

Her expression remains neutral. "A new one? Or the one from before?"

I gulp, remembering how Cole triggered two anxiety attacks. Well, a full-fledged one and a sort-of one. I'm fairly certain that's splitting hairs.

"The one from before," I quietly admit, unable to stop myself from fidgeting under her steady gaze.

Air gets trapped in my lungs as I steel myself, waiting for the censure I'm sure that will follow.

Instead, she nods before jotting down a few more notes. "Have you been spending a lot of time together?"

I hesitate, terrified she'll tell me that it's in my best interest to break things off with him, and that I need to focus on myself and school instead of a new relationship.

"Yes."

"And there haven't been any anxiety attacks?"

I shake my head. "None at all." I can't imagine having another attack with Cole. I find his presence so calming and feel so at ease with him.

She falls into another silence before asking, "Are you sleeping together?"

Heat rushes to the surface of my cheeks as I shake my head. "No, but I've spent the night with him. We're taking this relationship slow, and he's okay with that."

A kernel of hope flares to life when she doesn't immediately suggest I stop seeing him. I like Cole more than I've ever liked anyone before. Even though we've both agreed not to rush this, I know where it's heading, and I don't want it to end.

"It certainly sounds like this relationship is serious."

I release a steady breath before a smile curves my lips. "I think it might be." Until this very moment, I didn't realize how much I wanted it to be.

"Have you shared your past with him?"

Even though the question is asked lightly, it sits heavily between us. And just like that, a huge weight settles in the middle of my chest, making it difficult to breathe.

"No." Barely can I force out the response.

We're taking this slowly, I remind myself. He's all right not knowing everything about me. At some point I'll have to tell him, but we're not there yet.

With a nod, she asks more specifically, "Have you told him anything about the last year?" Her gaze is direct and unwavering.

"No."

I just need more time before I confide in him. Before I expect him to swallow and accept how much of a trainwreck I was.

She pulls off her glasses before carefully setting them on the table next to her chair. "If you're going to have a real and genuine connection with someone, then you need to be honest with them. Is there a reason you haven't been?"

Every last drop of happiness I'd been brimming with ten short minutes ago drains from my body, leaving me to feel weighted down and restless.

I squeeze my eyes tightly shut before shaking my head and shrugging helplessly. "I don't know. I guess I'm afraid his opinion of me will change."

She nods. "Opening yourself up and being vulnerable with someone who matters can be scary. But it's important that you're honest with him and yourself. You can't have an authentic relationship if you're keeping parts of yourself hidden. He needs to accept all of you, not just the pieces you choose to show him."

My fingers flutter to the collar of my shirt, tugging on it as my chest tightens up. "He understands that I'm not ready to open up just yet. We've talked about it. I just want to give him more time to get to know the person I am now."

A heavy silence falls over us.

"Then maybe you aren't ready for this just yet. Perhaps your focus needs to remain on you right now." Her gaze searches mine. "I understand that's difficult to hear but I think you need to give it serious consideration."

Even though I was expecting her to voice these concerns, it still hits me like a punch to the gut, and my shoulders collapse. Deep down, in a place I haven't wanted to acknowledge, I've secretly been wondering the same thing. Now that Dr. Thompson has brought up my own fears, it means I need to consider the merit of them.

Maybe I'm not as ready as I thought I was.

14

CASSIDY

Cole eases his Mustang over to the side of the familiar tree-lined street before cutting the engine. For a moment we both stare at the red brick, two-story house situated on a pretty corner lot.

My breath hitches as I contemplate my childhood home.

I'm having some serious second thoughts about what I'm intent on doing. And, truth be told, I feel guilty for dragging Cole into it with me. He's aware that there's tension with my parents, but has no idea how bad the situation is.

"Ready?" The softly spoken question slices through the thick silence of the car.

I straighten my shoulders before turning to meet his gaze.

At this time of the day, both my parents should be at work, leaving the house empty. I've spent the previous week going round and round with myself about this. What I keep coming back to is that it's my hockey gear and I want it. I'm tired of wearing crappy rental skates.

What I don't know is if my equipment is still here or if Dad got rid of it. Ten months ago, that's exactly what he threatened to do. If that's the case, then I'm shit out of luck because I can't afford new equipment.

It takes effort to shake off the nerves that are dancing their way across my skin. "Yeah, let's get this over with."

I pop open the door and stalk up the driveway to the front door. My mom used to hide a key under the terracotta planter for emergencies. I'm really hoping that hasn't changed.

If it has, then this mission will come to an end as quickly as it started, and I'll be stuck with rental skates for the foreseeable future.

I breathe a sigh of relief when my fingers close around a slender piece of metal. "It's here."

My fingers tremble as I pull it out from under the large pot before sliding it into the lock. As I push open the front door, the air from within the house hits me like an unexpected blow.

When I'd been forced to leave college last December, my father had been so disgusted that he could barely stand to look at me. They'd arranged for me to live with my grandparents for nine months before I moved to Western in late August. I haven't seen or spoken to Dad in all that time. My mom and two younger sisters had visited occasionally, but it wasn't very often. Those visits had usually ended up being stilted and uncomfortable.

I stumble to a halt in the entryway of the house I'd grown up in, and yet had not been able to return to after the debacle that was my first freshman semester. It's just another devastating consequence from the fallout. Unconsciously, I rub my chest as it tightens with thick tendrils of emotion that feel like jungle vines trying to squeeze the life from me.

I nearly jump out of my skin as Cole lays a hand on my shoulder before giving it a gentle squeeze.

"Are you okay?" His gaze carefully searches mine.

He's beginning to recognize the signs of my anxiety, the ones that lead to an attack. It should embarrass me. Instead, it makes me fall a little harder for him.

I suck in an unsteady breath.

Am I okay?

I almost laugh.

No, I'm not. I want to get out of here and never return. My heart is galloping, racing as if it'll pound right out of my chest. The ache is building. Intensifying as it spreads, infecting more of my body.

I squeeze my eyes tightly shut and silently recite the words in my head.

Deep breath in. Slowly exhale out.

Deep breath in. Slowly exhale out.

Cole stays silent. His hand remains anchored on my shoulder as if tethering me to the earth. After a few minutes, the tightness in my chest loosens, receding like the tide.

I need to find my gear and hightail it back to school where I can breathe again.

As a child, I never imagined the day would come when this house wouldn't be my refuge. Now, this is just another place where I don't belong. A wave of sadness crashes over me, threatening to drag me to the bottom of the ocean.

"Yeah, I'm fine." I try to keep the strain from seeping into my voice. "Let's check the basement."

What I don't add is that if my gear isn't there, then my dad got rid of it the same way he got rid of me.

As we move silently through the first floor toward the staircase that leads to the basement, Cole finds my fingers before enveloping them in his larger ones. When I glance over my shoulder, he gives me a reassuring smile. I force myself to give him one in return. Without him by my side, I would have never been brave enough to make the trip. I don't think I could have faced the silent ghosts of my family.

Even though I'm taking gear that's mine, it feels like I'm doing something wrong. Like stealing stuff that doesn't belong to me. As much as I try to shake off the unsettling feeling, I can't.

Once we make our way to the basement, I move to the furnace room where the storage area is located. Our family has always jokingly referred to this room as a mini hockey store. My sisters dance and cheer, so other than shoes and costumes, they don't have equipment to store.

This room has always been for me and my dad. He grew up playing hockey, and played juniors straight out of high school. Two years after that, he was forced to quit when he broke his leg in three different places. He loved hockey way too much to give it up and continued playing in beer leagues. When I started skating, he coached me until I made a girls' travel team.

I think that's why my failure hit him so hard. He was totally invested in my hockey career. But still...even though he was disappointed, he should have been there for me.

I needed him.

I needed my entire family.

Even though I fucked up, I needed all of them to help pick me up again.

Unfortunately, that's not what happened.

I inhale a deep breath and squeeze my eyes shut again. I'm irritated at myself for allowing all this garbage back inside my head. Maybe I disappointed my family, but they let me down me too. When I needed them to stand by me, they'd taken the easy way out and shipped me off, leaving me to deal with the fallout by myself.

My eyelids fly open when Cole wraps his arms around my shoulders and pulls me against his hard body. He doesn't ask any questions. He simply holds me until I'm strong enough to move forward again. I don't understand what it is about Cole that makes me feel so safe.

"If they kept my gear, it would be here."

As we step into the back room, Cole looks around the shelving units my father built to house all of our old equipment. It's crammed full of clear bins that contain skates, socks, gloves, pants, shoulder pads, and jerseys. Fiberglass sticks take up a whole shelf as do the oversized bags.

"Holy crap, it's like a hockey store in here." There's a touch of awe tinging his voice as his gaze flies around the room.

One side of my mouth lifts. "Yup." I glance at him. "My dad owns a hockey and lacrosse store in town."

"Wow," he mutters before rifling through the sticks. He pulls out one before running his fingers across the shaft. "Do you know how expensive this is?"

His question is more rhetorical in nature because we both know how costly that brand of stick is.

"Do you see any of your old stuff?" he asks, helping me to search through the bins.

I take another deep breath before rifling through another plastic container, looking for the equipment I'd taken to school last year.

"Not yet," I mutter, realizing that maybe Dad really had pitched everything.

I wouldn't put it past him. He'd been pissed.

"If that turns out to be the case, I think you could probably piecemeal some of this stuff together and then we could look online for the rest. That would be the cheapest way to go." He gives me a wink. "Worst comes to worst, we can raid the lost and found at the rink."

I scrunch my face in disgust before realizing I might not have a choice in the matter.

"Yeah," I finally admit. "I guess."

The problem is that I want my stuff. Everything fit me perfectly.

Sure, I could probably find a pair of old gloves and definitely a stick in here, but skates?

No way.

I'd outgrown all of my old ones. Hockey skates could run at least three hundred dollars a pair. And those are the cheap ones. Plus, I don't really want to take anything that doesn't belong to me. That would only piss my dad off.

Just as I'm about to give up, Cole shoves aside a few old hockey bags and there it is, my pink and black bag. It's a little dusty but no worse for the wear. My heart skips a beat as he unzips it.

It's all there, looking exactly like the last time I saw it.

Cole meets my gaze with a smile. He zips it back up again before hauling it over his shoulder. "Do you have a stick?"

I rifle through a dozen sticks until I find my favorite and then grab one of my backups. I can't help but run my hand lovingly over the shaft. Both the grip and the blade are still wrapped in bright pink tape.

Cole shakes his head. "You are such a girl."

"Just remember that I'm a girl who can kick your ass out on the ice."

That probably isn't true, but the comment lightens the mood, which is exactly what I need.

He smirks. "That remains to be seen but we're definitely on for a rematch."

Just as we shut off the basement lights, the front door opens before getting slammed shut. The entire house shakes with the vibration of it as my stomach plummets to my toes. My feet grind to a halt as my gaze flies to Cole. By the sound of the heavy footfalls above us, it's my dad.

Shit.

Fresh waves of icy cold panic crash over me. My chest constricts, making it difficult to suck air into my lungs.

"I can't face him." I shake my head before whispering in a choked voice, "I can't face him right now."

Cole shifts his weight. Confusion is written all over his face as if he doesn't understand what the big deal is. "Is that your dad?"

"Yeah." My mouth has turned bone-dry. Any moment, my heart is going to explode from my chest.

He studies me carefully before understanding dawns. "Is he going to be mad that we're here?"

By the expression on his face, he already knows the answer.

My silence only reconfirms it.

I probably should have mentioned that my family and I aren't exactly on speaking terms. Then he could have made his own choice about whether to get involved in this. I'd really thought we could sneak in and out under the radar while my dad and mom were at work.

Cole has no idea what kind of minefield he's walked into. As I stand there, listening to Dad stomp across the wood flooring above us, I realize there isn't time to explain it to him. It's doubtful I could find the words even if there was.

"Cassidy," he says carefully, "everything will be fine. Let's go upstairs."

I want to laugh.

No…not laugh.

I want to run and hide. My dad is the last person I want to face.

Unfortunately, there isn't a choice in the matter.

Cole reaches out and grabs my fingers before securing them firmly in his hand. My gaze locks on his. "You're not alone. I'm here with you."

"Cassidy?"

I flinch as my dad's deep voice cuts through the air.

It takes effort to clear my throat and find my voice. "I-I'm in the basement." There's no denying the thin waver that snakes its way through my words.

My father doesn't respond as we make our way up the stairs to the kitchen where we find him leaning stiffly against the granite counter, his thickly-muscled arms crossed over his chest.

His eyes narrow on Cole and the hockey bag slung over his shoulder. After a long silent moment, his attention shifts to me. There is no warmth within his eyes as they lock on mine.

From the time I was a small child, people have commented on how much I resemble my dad. We have the same blue eyes and jet-black hair. But that's where the physical similarities end, because my dad is a hulking man who stands over six feet tall. He's solid. Built for defense. I'm petite like my mother. More finely-boned. Built for speed.

Without any pleasantries, Dad starts in on me just like I feared he would. The last thing I need is for Cole to have a front row seat to our family dysfunction. And I certainly don't want him to hear my father's version of what transpired last year. The picture he'll paint will undoubtedly be ugly.

"The neighbors called to let me know someone was breaking into the house. You're damn lucky they contacted me first instead of the police."

It's doubtful this situation will turn out to be a blessing for me. Being picked up for a little B&E would be preferable to the confrontation my dad is set on having. Although, I'm smart enough to keep those thoughts to myself.

"We didn't break in," I murmur, hoping he won't lose his shit and start foaming at the mouth.

"Why didn't you call and let us know you'd be stopping by? Why slink in here when you know perfectly well that we'd be at work?"

I'm fairly certain the answer to that question is painfully obvious to all three of us.

Instead of admitting truth, I say, "This was the only time we had between classes, and it was a spur of the moment decision." It's doubtful that I'm fooling anyone.

Including Cole.

Having him witness this exchange makes me want to cringe.

Dad's hard gaze shifts before silently scrutinizing Cole. My father doesn't say a word as his attention jerks back to mine.

He shakes his head as if I've managed to disappoint him all over again. "I thought you would have learned your lesson after last year, Cassidy. It's obvious that you haven't."

I turn to Cole before Dad can get any more wound up and murmur, "Could you wait for me in the car?"

I want him out of this house and away from my father. This is humiliating enough without him witnessing anything more.

Cole's concerned gaze bounces between my father and me. "I'll stay if you want me to."

Even though I normally find Cole's presence comforting, I shake my head. "No, it's fine. I'll be out in a minute." I silently plead for him not to argue. "All right?"

Tension fills every line of his face as he jerks his head into a tight nod before hesitantly backing out of the large, sun-filled kitchen. My dad and I remain silent until we hear the front door close quietly behind him.

His furious gaze never relinquishes mine. Any moment, I'll squirm like a six-year-old caught making mischief.

My father has always been blunt, and he cuts right to the heart of the matter as he stabs a finger at me. "That's no longer your equipment to take. You forfeited it when you got kicked off the team and flunked out of college."

The razor-sharp comments leave me wincing, but I keep my face an emotionless mask. I'll be damned if he sees how much his words and attitude are still able to inflict damage. Sometimes it's difficult to believe we were ever close. I'm his eldest and the only daughter who followed him into hockey. He used to be so proud of me and my accomplishments.

Both on and off the ice.

Miranda and Lexie had refused from the beginning to take skating lessons. He didn't bother trying to get them to play hockey. I, on the other hand, had loved it from the very first lesson. Sometimes I wonder if the reason I'd loved it so much was because we were the only two who shared it. Hockey was a bond that neither my mom nor my sisters could penetrate.

Seven o'clock practices on Saturday and Sunday mornings. Weekend tournaments spent out-of-town. College camps and recruiting trips. And then we'd hit a few classic car shows. It was always the two of us.

Me and my dad.

Last year ripped our relationship to shreds.

And now, we were nothing more than strangers. Actually, we were much worse than strangers because his anger and disgust were palpable and cut me to the quick.

My shoulders collapse. "Do you want the equipment back?"

"No, just take it." He shoves his hands deep into the pockets of his pants before walking over to the picture window overlooking the tree line at the back of the yard. There's a thick layer of vibrantly-colored leaves carpeting the ground.

"Who's the guy?" There is so much accusation riddled throughout the barked-out question. Without glancing at me, he shakes his head in disapproval. "Guess I should have known better than to expect you to pull your shit together."

My chest grows tight as I force out a response. "It isn't like that, Dad. Cole is just a friend."

Lie.

Cole is way more than a friend.

He wheels around, his furious gaze searing mine. "You fail out again and you're on your own. We won't give you any more money, and neither will your grandparents. There comes a time when you have to grow up and make adult decisions, and that time is now, Cassidy." He drags a hand through his thick black hair. "I don't understand where we went so wrong with you, I really don't."

Why can't he see that I made a mistake?

All right, a lot of them.

But still…that doesn't mean they raised me wrong, or I can't learn and grow from the experience and somehow, eventually, come out better because of it. He refuses to consider that possibility. He doesn't want to see that I'm trying to undo the damage I inflicted on all of us. His anger and disgust hurt more than I want to admit.

"I'm not going to fail out," I whisper.

There's no way I'll allow that to happen again.

He scrubs a hand over his face as if he doesn't know what to do with himself. "Yeah, well, you'll excuse me if I have a difficult time believing anything that comes out of your mouth."

I chew my lower lip. It's the physical discomfort that stops me from focusing on the pain he's so intent on inflicting.

"It's not like that. I'm doing really well." Why am I bothering to explain? He doesn't want to hear me. But I can't seem to stop myself. "And I'm tutoring other students at the tutoring center to make extra cash." It's on the tip of my tongue to tell him that Dr. Thompson thinks I'm improving, but he doesn't know I've been seeing a shrink, and I'm not about to let that particular cat out of the bag. It would only fan the flames of his fury.

"I guess we'll see what your grades look like in December," he grunts.

Everything inside me deflates. I can't believe how poorly this interaction has gone. "Yeah, I guess so." I just want to get the hell out of here. Neither of us seem ready for a civil conversation.

Maybe we never will be.

"Okay. Well…" I can't do this anymore. I just…*can't.*

My chest has tightened with the thick tendrils of anxiety weaving their way around it. Slowly, I inch my way toward the front door. Toward Cole and the Mustang parked out front. Toward the freedom of school, and away from the claustrophobia attempting to suffocate the life out of me.

Just as I slink into the hallway, he fires off another question.

"Why did you want your hockey gear? Are you playing again?" His thick brows are knit tightly together as if he can't believe I would have the audacity to step foot on the ice again.

I shake my head, all the while continuing to put more distance between us. "Cole plays for the Western Timber Wolves, and sometimes we skate together. I wanted to use my own equipment. It's been a while…" My voice trails off awkwardly.

He makes a noncommittal sound from deep in his throat. "Hmmm."

Thankfully, I've become pleasantly numb to his disapproval.

I point to the front door. "Cole's waiting, and I need to get back to school."

"Yeah, fine." He adds just the right amount of derision to make me cringe. "Thanks for stopping by."

There's nothing I can say, since we both know this wasn't a visit. I did exactly what he accused me of earlier. I crept into the house when I'd thought no one would be around. And I'd been caught red-handed.

I should have realized it wouldn't go smoothly.

"Okay." With that last mumbled word, I race from the house as if I'm fleeing the scene of a heinous crime. The front door slams shut behind me as I barrel down the drive, hurtling myself into the Mustang idling alongside the curb.

The moment I sink onto the front seat, I inhale a lungful of air before forcing it out again as Cole pulls away from the house that is no longer my home. A reluctant glance over my shoulder shows Dad on the front porch, his hands hanging limply at his sides as he watches us drive away. Once we round the corner, I swivel around before leaning back and closing my eyes.

That was so much worse than I could have imagined.

I'm so lost in the turmoil of my own thoughts that I jump at the sound of his soft voice.

"Are you okay?"

My eyelids snap open as I stare sightlessly out the front windshield. I can't bring myself to meet his gaze. Embarrassment bubbles up inside me like a geyser, until I want to sink through the leather seat.

"I'm fine."

But I'm not.

I'm so far from fine that it's not even funny. Now that I'm safely away from the situation, a fine tremble racks my body. Cole's fingers settle over my hand before clasping it. Only then do I force my gaze to meet his.

Questions, a million of them, swim around in his concerned depths.

He deserves the answers, but I can't bring myself to talk about it. I don't want his opinion of me to change. He knows, well...he's getting to know the girl I am now. I don't want him knowing anything about the girl I once was.

"That was certainly awkward," he says, pulling onto the highway and leaving behind the small city where I grew up in the rearview mirror.

A strangled laugh fizzes up inside me.

I have no idea why the comment strikes me as funny. It's either laugh or cry at this point, and I refuse to shed one more tear over last year.

"I'm really sorry about that."

When it becomes obvious that I won't be saying anything more, he clears his throat and glances at me. There's understanding within his gaze, but there's also a desire to figure out what I'm keeping from him.

"Are you going to tell me what that was all about?" His words are light, almost casually spoken, as if he knows how far he can push me.

There are a hundred different ways I could answer that question.

But...

"I'm sorry, I can't right now."

As I glance at our entwined fingers, Dr. Thompson's comments roll unwantedly through my head. Everything my father hurtled at me unwittingly echoes them.

Maybe they're right.

Maybe, in order to save myself, I need to pull back from Cole.

I need to show my family that I'm serious about getting my life back on track. And this year—this semester—is my chance to prove that what happened last year was a fluke. A series of poorly made decisions strung together into one giant clusterfuck.

As my gaze slides to Cole, my heart spasms, knowing it won't be the only thing I end up regretting.

15

CASSIDY

"What's up with your hockey hottie?"

Ever willing to force her nose where it doesn't belong, Brooklyn swipes some bright red lipstick on before shoving a finger into her mouth and dragging it out again.

My brows slide together as I watch her. "Maybe you'd like to be alone right now?"

She rolls her eyes before giving me a *you're so clueless* look. Since it's nothing out of the ordinary, I'm not offended by it.

"That's how you remove excess lipstick from the inside of your lips, so it doesn't end up on your teeth." She bares her sparkling white teeth in the mirror to make sure they pass inspection.

"Huh." Impressed with that beauty tip, I tilt my head. "Neat trick."

She winks before brushing out her thick blonde mane. Normally, Brooklyn leaves her hair loose so it can flow freely down her back because guys go crazy for her long glossy strands. They love it in a way that makes them want to wrap it around their fist and yank her head back (Brooklyn's words, not mine). Tonight, however, she twists it up into a topknot.

"Don't change the subject. What's up with you two? I want details. And lots of them."

My gaze skitters away as I shrug with a forced casualness.

I don't want to discuss Cole. Especially with Brooklyn. She and Austin are still going strong, which is a total shocker. After my last therapy session and the disastrous trip home, I've decided to take a step back from Cole. The thought of making another mistake is almost paralyzing.

"Nothing's up."

"Yeah, that's what I'm wondering about. You two were getting serious."

Even though it's not a question, it requires an explanation. And if I know Brooklyn, she won't let this go until she's been fully briefed.

With a sigh, I decide to go with something that loosely resembles the truth. "I need a little breathing room."

When her gaze settles on mine in the mirror, I get the feeling she's sifting through my eyes for the truth. "Is Cole aware of that?"

I break eye contact. "I don't know. We're not official or anything like that. We've been hanging out. We're just friends."

Lie.

Big lie.

Cole isn't interested in being *just friends*. Not that I've spoken to him about it. Instead, I've taken the coward's way out and have silently distanced myself from him.

Trust me, I'm aware of how shitty my behavior is.

As she whips around to face me, I'm startled by the irritation aimed in my direction. "You know that he really likes you, right?" There's a pause. "And you're just jerking him around." She purses her lips as if disappointed in my behavior.

I squeeze my eyes tight and shake my head.

It was never my intention to string Cole along. Even though I like him, I still can't bring myself to share the details of my past.

My own family loved me—supposedly unconditionally—and they turned their backs on me. It feels easier to push him away now rather than make another mistake or have him walk away from me.

He might not realize it, but it's better this way.

"That wasn't my intention."

Her lips flatten into a thin line. "You better think about what you're doing, because Cole is a really great guy and you're going to lose him if you keep this up."

Brooklyn isn't telling me anything I don't already know. Cole is one of the nicest guys I've ever met, let alone been with. Maybe that should be enough of a reason to take a leap of faith, but I'm too afraid to do it.

"Do you realize how many girls like him?" Anger ignites in her eyes. "Then throw in all the freaking hockey groupies." She scrunches her nose before spitting out the next words. "I swear, if I catch one more puck bunny hanging all over Austin, someone is getting bitch-slapped into next week." She gives me a hard-edged stare. "If you're smart, you'll get in there and stake your claim, because, trust me, someone else will be more than happy to do it."

A feeling of helplessness washes over me as I shake my head. I can't do that right now. Cole isn't mine to claim. I have no rights to him. In the end, I've decided it's best to let him go. He deserves a girl who has her shit together, and that's not me.

I get whiplash when she changes the subject. "Are you coming with us tonight?"

Already I know she'll be hanging out with Austin, which probably means Cole too. There's no way I can remain strong around him. He's become a pro at breaking down my defenses.

I tear my gaze away from hers before mumbling, "Sorry, can't. I've got homework to finish up."

Brooklyn stares at me for a long moment. "It's Friday night, and once again you're playing the lame card."

"Yup." I give her a thin smile, thankful she's accepted the excuse instead of arguing about it.

"Whatever. Don't bother waiting up for me. I'll probably crash at Austin's tonight."

"I figured."

A few minutes later, Brooklyn walks out the door, leaving behind a cloud of perfume in her wake. It's not like I was making up excuses to avoid running into Cole. I actually have a ton of reading to plow my way through, two homework assignments due on Monday, and an econ paper to outline. Can I start it all tomorrow and still have it done with enough time to spare?

Probably.

If I'm experiencing any remorse about pulling away from Cole, I try not to dwell on it. Instead, I bury myself in my work. Two hours later, I'm at the beginning stages of my outline for the econ paper when my phone chimes with an incoming text.

Ran into Brooklyn, she says you're staying in?

I freeze, unsure if I should answer the text. I don't want to get sucked into a conversation with him. I'm afraid of getting too wrapped up in him.

If I've learned anything, it's that being with Cole is easy.

Too easy.

It was the trip home that had me seriously reconsidering my decision to see Cole. Little did my father realize that he'd echoed the same concerns Dr. Thompson had broached during our session. I can't help but wonder if they're both right.

Maybe the best course of action is to focus on straightening out my life before getting involved with someone. At this point, I'm still finding my way. Even though everything seems to be going well, that doesn't mean it can't turn to shit at the drop of a hat.

Carefully, I set the phone on my desk before returning my attention to my econ outline. Ten minutes slide by and I can't seem to pick up the threads of my previous thoughts. Frustration roils through me because I know Cole is the reason for my inability to concentrate. I snap up the phone before reading over his text and tapping out a reply.

Lots of homework.

His response pops up almost immediately.

Can I come up?

My eyes widen.

Come up?

That would mean Cole is already here.

At the dorm.

I grip the thin device in my hand before squeezing my eyes tightly shut. I can't deny that part of me is leaping for joy, because I'm dying to see him. But I also realize that it's a slippery slope. The more time we spend together, the more difficult it is to keep my barriers firmly intact.

The phone chimes again, snapping me out of those thoughts.

Cassidy? Are you there?

Yes. Come up.

Ok. See you in a few.

I leap from the chair to pace, and worry my bottom lip with my teeth before straightening my hair.

Deep breath in. Slowly exhale out.

Deep breath in. Slowly exhale out.

Before I can do it a few more time, there's a knock on the door. Loud music pours in from the brightly lit hallway as I open it. People are laughing, yelling back and forth. Even though it's against the dorm rules, a few guys swig beer from cans as they toss a football from one end of the hall to the other.

"Hi."

When his gaze collides with mine, I'm once again struck by how good-looking he is. My fingers itch to plow their way through his dark shaggy strands. I have to shove my hands into the pockets of my jeans so I won't do exactly that. This already feels like a mistake.

Nerves flutter about in my belly. "Hey."

He glances around the room as if taking everything in before resettling on me again. His gaze is always so direct and forthright. Like he sees everything. Cole has already proven himself to be astute, always watching and anticipating my needs. He knows when to push and when to back off.

Two long-legged strides eat up the distance between us. He's so close that I have to crane my neck to hold his gaze. Again, the urge to touch him surges through me. All the memories of us snuggled up and kissing in his bed rush through my mind. It doesn't take long for desire to follow.

"I'm going to kiss you now, Cassidy."

Even as he murmurs the words, he's already on the verge of capturing my lips. My arms tangle around his neck before tugging him close, needing to feel more of him.

"I've missed you," he whispers before delving in for more.

I've missed him too.

Way too much.

"You've been MIA," he adds.

"I'm sorry, it's been really busy." It's more than that, and I wonder if he realizes it as well. My guess is that he does.

It's been almost a full week since we made that awkward drive back to the dorms. We haven't seen much of each other since that day. He's reached out, wanting to spend time together. I've kept him at a firm distance with excuses.

The truth is that I needed space.

Time and space to work through all the shit in my head.

I wasn't sure what he would do. Maybe get fed up or irritated? Instead, he backed off, giving me the time I needed. He didn't badger or hound me. If he had, it would have been much easier to get annoyed and cut things off.

When I'm wrapped up in his arms like this, all the protests grow silent. When I'm with him, a strange contentment washes over me.

"Do you have more work or are you finished for the night?"

My gaze darts away. I should keep working. I really should…

"No, I'm done."

Without warning, his lips lower to mine. When his tongue sweeps across the seam, I open and he delves inside. That's all it takes for me to melt against him. Unable to resist, I do what I've been dying to since I first opened the door. I tunnel my fingers through his hair.

A growl rumbles up from deep within his throat.

I don't want to stop touching him, and I certainly don't want him to backoff either. It's tempting to stake my claim just like Brooklyn suggested earlier.

He licks at my mouth, nipping at the corners until I'm the one whimpering, needing more. After a few breathless moments, he kisses his way down the column of my neck to the collar of my shirt.

"Cole…"

Barely can I force his name out.

What he's doing feels amazing.

"Hmmm?"

"I don't think we should take this any further." I pause, trying to catch my breath along with my scattered thoughts. "I'm sorry."

This is exactly what he does to me.

Instead of pushing for more, he nibbles his way back up to my mouth before pressing a lingering kiss against my lips.

"I know." He shrugs as if stopping isn't a big deal. One corner of his mouth hitches before he presses his forehead against mine. "I'm sorry. I don't want to force you into something you're not ready for."

I step away, searching his whiskey-colored eyes. Sometimes it feels as if I could stumble and fall right into them. I can't help but wonder what would happen if I did.

If I allowed myself to fall.

If I stopped retreating and took that leap of faith.

A thin shiver snakes its way down my spine as I continue to inch away.

16

COLE

"Hi sweetie," Mom calls out a greeting as I walk through the front door.

I pause, flooded with memories of what it felt like to walk into Cassidy's house. The tone and feel of our houses couldn't be more different. Even with no one there to greet us, the vibe had felt strangely tense.

"Hey, Mom."

Even though I'm nearly twenty, she wraps her arms around me and pulls me in for a hug. Other guys might fight the intimacy or grumble under their breaths, but I don't.

Honestly, I don't give a shit what anyone else thinks.

I know what it feels like to lose a parent.

So, if the woman wants to give me a hug every once in a while, I'm cool with it.

My mind tumbles back to Cassidy and her father. The stilted awkwardness of their interaction had felt like a suffocating blanket. Even though part of me hadn't wanted to leave her with him, it had been a relief to get the hell out of there.

His demeanor had been so cold and distant.

Angry.

I'm still trying to figure out what's going on, and Cassidy has remained tight-lipped about the situation.

That's an understatement. Cassidy is closemouthed about her past in general. Prying even the tiniest details from her is difficult. Other than she grew up playing hockey, I don't know much else about her.

She's a puzzle I want to solve.

All right, she's a puzzle I *need* to solve.

I'm not proud of myself, but I've done a little online snooping, hoping to gather a little more intel on this girl. The only thing I've been able to uncover is a few newspaper clippings and website pictures of her playing youth hockey.

Championship photos.

You could tell from the set of her jaw and glint in her eyes that she was one hell of a tough player. She wore her confidence as if she knew exactly where she belonged. Even in a group of rough and tumble boys, she'd known she was accepted.

What the hell had happened to change that?

Where had all that certainty disappeared to?

Why wasn't she still playing?

After being on the ice with her, I could tell she was good.

Talented.

I keep telling myself to be patient. That if I give her enough time, she'll open up. That hasn't happened. I'm beginning to wonder if it ever will. I'm not ready to give up on her yet, but the girl has to throw me a bone.

In every team picture I'd found online, her dad had been standing proudly behind her. He'd obviously been one of her coaches growing up. He'd looked different as well. Younger. Happier. Lighter.

It had taken a moment for recognition to dawn.

Whatever happened last year had affected both of them.

"That's a pensive look."

When my mom strokes a hand over my cheek, I snap out of my thoughts and force a smile. No matter how hard I try, I can't get that girl out of my mind.

"Everything okay?"

There's no way I'm discussing the Cassidy situation with my mother. There are just too many unknowns at this point. Half the time, I have no idea where I stand with her.

"It's nothing."

Plus, she'll want to talk it to death and I'm not in the mood for that.

She slips her arm through mine as we move into the kitchen.

"It smells good in here. What are you making this time?"

My mother loves to cook and is always trying out new recipes. Added bonus—she's really good at it.

"Braised beef roast, au gratin potatoes, glazed green beans with a freshly-baked rosemary infused bread." She flashes me a smile.

That's all it takes for my belly to grumble.

A full week of eating at school will make you appreciate a home-cooked meal.

"That sounds amazing. If there are any leftovers, can I take them back for the guys?"

Sadistic as it sounds, I enjoy watching them fight like jackals over the prepared dishes. It's the small things in life that you need to enjoy.

"You can invite them over any time. You know I don't mind."

I shrug.

She's right, I could have, but...

"I needed a break from the chaos."

Five guys sharing a house and playing hockey together is sometimes a little too much togetherness. Getting away for a few hours every Sunday is usually enough of a break before I head back to school for the week.

"That's understandable," she agrees.

I'm an only child. And while most moms feel a bit of relief when their children fly the coop, mine didn't. Hell, I'd still be living in my old room if she had her way. So, we compromised when I left for college. I stayed local, and live near campus instead of at home.

I swipe a chocolate chip cookie from a plate on the counter. "Where's Thomas?"

Mom waves a hand before glancing at the digital clock on the microwave. "He had an emergency at the hospital. Hopefully, he'll be back before we sit down to eat."

Thomas is an emergency department physician at the hospital in town. He's also my stepfather. Dad died in a car accident when I was ten years old. It was a drunk driver who took him out. A fucked-up college kid driving home from the bar at two in the morning. My father died on impact while that kid walked away without a scratch. He sat his ass in jail for a couple years, but so what?

It didn't bring dad back to us.

Mom married Thomas four years after that. He isn't my dad, and he doesn't try to be. What I will say is that he's a nice guy who treats my mother well, which is all that matters. If I need to talk or blow off steam, he's there.

It could be worse.

"That means I have you all to myself for a couple of hours," she says with a smile.

My father's death may have dampened her spirit, but over the years, it gradually returned and she persevered.

We both did.

"How's the team shaping up this season?"

I plow a hand through my hair as I turn the question over in my mind.

"I think we'll be solid. There are several strong players who've returned. Plus, we've got a tough defense and a fast offense. The freshmen and transfers we picked up seem to be talented, so that should help." I shrug. "So far, so good."

I open the fridge and grab a Gatorade before settling at the massive expanse of granite island as I twist off the cap. "You know, you don't have to buy these anymore."

That being said, I guzzle down half the bottle.

With a smile, she shakes her blonde head and continues to chop the green beans. "Of course, I'm going to buy the things you like. You're my son, I miss having you around. Seeing them in the fridge reminds me that you'll be popping home soon for a visit."

I raise a brow as an unmanly lump gets wedged in the middle of my throat.

Even so, I can't resist teasing. "Jeez, Mom. You're getting sappy in your old age."

A few seconds after the comment leaves my mouth, a dish towel hits me square in the face. No one can say that the woman doesn't have great aim. Although, I guess that's what happens when your dad dies, and your mother gets stuck pitching baseballs to you in the backyard.

"Have I taught you nothing?" Her voice turns sharp as her brows snap together. "Never call a woman old. *Especially* your mother."

My lips curve as a chuckle escapes. "Lesson learned."

Silence falls over us as she continues chopping and prepping the vegetables. My gaze gets drawn to the window that overlooks the yard. It doesn't take long for my thoughts to circle back to Cassidy. No matter how much I try to stop thinking about her, she's never far from my mind. It would be irritating, if I weren't so into her.

Even though we haven't been seeing each other long, I like her. She's a walking contradiction and I find that fascinating. At first, she struck me as a bit of a tough girl, but the more I get to know her, the more chinks I find in her armor. The vulnerability buried beneath that hard candy shell tears me up inside. It makes me want to do everything in my power to protect her.

"All right," Mom says, "who is she?"

My gaze snaps to hers. "What are you talking about?"

She gives me a patient smile as if I'm not fooling her for a moment. Already, I know she won't be letting this go until I tell her what's going on.

Whether I want to or not.

I clear my throat and glance away, attempting to downplay the situation. "It's just a girl I've been seeing."

One brow arches. "I didn't even know you were involved with someone."

I jerk my shoulders.

Aw, hell.

When I remain silent, she continues. "I take it there's a problem with this girl?"

I'm not even sure how to answer that question. For the life of me, I can't figure her out. All I know is that I want to crack the Cassidy code. It's just going to take some time to do it.

After mulling it over, I say, "She's a very private person."

"Umm hmm. Go on."

I almost groan.

Not the *go on*.

I seriously hate the *go on*.

It feels like I'm reliving my middle and high school years all over again with things like *open communication* and *dialogue*, and, god help me, *resolution*.

It's time to downplay the Cassidy situation before it spirals further out of control.

"It's just really new." I shrug, striving for nonchalant. "It might not even work out."

Sometimes I wonder if that's what Cassidy secretly wants. The girl has been dead set on pushing me away from day one. Five weeks later and she's still trying to do it. The problem is that I'm not going anywhere.

Sooner or later, she'll realize that.

"Nope, it might not." She gives me a small smile. "It's nice to see you back out there again after Jackie."

That name has my muscles tightening as I run a quick hand through my hair. My ex is the last person I want to discuss. Especially when my mind is so full of Cassidy.

"Let's not talk about Jackie," I say more gruffly than I mean to.

"It's important to talk about your feelings, Cole."

I roll my eyes.

What is it about being back in your childhood home that makes you feel and act like a sullen fourteen-year-old?

It's frustrating as hell, and one of the reasons I don't live here anymore.

"Trust me," I mutter, "I know that all too well. Besides, we've already hashed the whole Jackie thing to death. I'm over it."

Jackie is part of my past.

I'm hoping Cassidy will be my future.

Her gaze locks on mine, searches it carefully. "Are you?"

"Yup, I'm totally over it." I am totally over that lying, cheating—

"Hmmm."

It's a noncommittal sound that gets under my skin.

"Mom," I grit in warning, "I don't want to discuss Jackie." A topic change is exactly what's needed. "When's Thomas getting home again? Hopefully it'll be soon?"

She shoots me a frown. "Don't be a brat."

"I'm not, and you refrain from discussing our feelings when he's around." I'm starting to appreciate that more and more.

Another silence falls over us.

Just when I think she'll drop the topic of my ex, she says, "I ran into her at the grocery store last week."

I pause mid-sip of my Gatorade, waiting for her to continue. I'm almost afraid of what will come out of her mouth next.

"She said to tell you hello."

Mom watches me carefully from beneath a thick fringe of lashes.

I force out a snort. "Did you tell her to go take a flying fu—"

"Cole!" she snaps as her eyes widen. The knife she's holding clatters against the granite.

I hunch my shoulders. "I'm old enough to swear, Mom. I do it all the time." That's a lie but not one she needs to know about.

"When you're in my house, you'll refrain from doing so." She's remains silent as she transfers the potatoes into the oven. "She's living at home now."

That means she's right around the corner, only a block and a half up the street.

Jackie and I grew up together. We were best friends up until we began dating at the end of our sophomore year in high school. When Dad died, she was my rock. We'd hold hands and sit in the tree house. She'd try to distract me from the fact that he was no longer with us.

A bad feeling settles in the pit of my gut.

"I have no interest in seeing her if that's where all this is leading." I slam down the plastic bottle with more force than necessary. A few orange drops of liquid slosh from the top of the container onto the granite. "That's not where you're going with this, right?"

A long silence stretches between us.

"You need to stay out of this," I say with a grunt.

Jackie was like the daughter my mother never had. I can understand why she wants me to sweep everything under the rug and make nice, but that's not going to happen.

The sooner she accepts that, the better off we'll all be.

Now that the potatoes have been placed in the oven, she turns toward me before laying her palms flat on the counter so we end up at eye level.

"I think it would be good for both of you to sit down and talk. Closure can only help the situation. I hate what she did, but you were always such good friends." She watches me silently before adding softly, "She lost the baby."

Even though her words surprise me, I keep my face perfectly blank. I don't want any outward emotion to be misconstrued as me caring about the bomb she just dropped.

"I already told you that I'm over it."

"Obviously you aren't, or you wouldn't be reacting like this."

Instead of snapping the way I want to, I suck in a steady breath before exhaling it.

"I'm totally over Jackie and what she did. I wish her all the best, but I have zero interest in seeing her or being friends with her. What we had is over."

With a nod, she reaches out and squeezes my shoulder. "If that's the case, I'm happy for you." There's a pause as she switches the topic. "Tell me about this new girl. How long have you been seeing her?"

As much as I don't want to discuss Cassidy, it's better than continuing to rehash Jackie. In order to avoid one conversation, I'm opting to discuss the other. "A couple of weeks."

"And you like her?" she asks with genuine curiosity.

"I do."

"Am I detecting *a but* in your voice?"

I give her a pointed look. "Not *a but*."

I pause, carefully searching for the right word but it remains elusive. With a shake of my head, I give up. "Fine, a small *but*."

"And what is this small, practically nonexistent *but*?"

My eyes narrow at the humor in her tone. "You're making fun of me."

She straightens to her full height as a frown flashes across her face. "No, I'm not. I want to know what the issue is, because if there wasn't one, you would have said so by now." She raises her brows. "Am I right?"

"What you are, is annoying." I glance around the kitchen, wishing there was a way to escape from the conversation. "Seriously, where's Thomas when you need him?"

"Oh, just answer the question." She chuckles, clearly enjoying herself. The woman is totally in her element when she's attempting to drag information out of me.

"I don't know," I grumble. Before I can stop myself, everything that has been rolling around in the back of my brain is shooting out of my mouth. "She's a little closed off. I can't figure out what happened to her, and she refuses to tell me. It's like she doesn't trust me."

Mom is quiet for a long stretch of silent moments as she turns my words over in her head. That's the thing about her. She really does care and wants to help, which is exactly why she can't let the Jackie situation go.

She wants resolution.

Even if it's not her relationship.

Maybe it's my mom specifically, or it's females in general, who feel the need to smooth everything over in order to move on with their lives. Guys don't operate like that. If the relationship is over, it's done. No need to come to a good place.

A long time ago, we'd been friends. Now we're not.

End of story.

"Maybe she needs more time to feel comfortable with you in order to open up."

"Maybe. I'm just not sure it's ever going to happen."

Once I've released that into the atmosphere, I realize how true it is. No matter how much I like Cassidy, I can't force her into a relationship. "I'm not sure where this is headed." I drag a hand over my face. "Sometimes it feels unnecessarily complicated."

Her expression turns thoughtful. "You seem to really like this girl, but if it already feels difficult and you just started seeing each other, it's not going to magically get easier. Relationships don't work that way."

As much as I don't want her words to ring true, they do.

And that sucks.

I can't be the only one fighting for this.

17

CASSIY

*M*eet me downstairs ASAP with your hockey bag.

I stare at the phone in my hand before typing out a response.

Are you serious?

Just do it.

Bossy much?

The eye roll emoji pops up on the screen.

Fine. I'll be down in 5.

I grab my hockey bag from the closet and throw on a navy jacket before heading out the door. Once out on the sidewalk, I find Cole's Mustang idling at the curb in front of the dorm. When he sees me, he pops open the trunk before hopping out of the vehicle as I jog over.

He gives me a quick kiss on the lips. Before I can register the gesture, he pulls away, looking strangely hesitant.

"Ready to go?"

"Yeah. Why are we heading to the ice rink at nine in the morning?"

His expression becomes shuttered, as he holds open the door for me. "You'll see."

With our gazes locked, he hunkers down, grabbing the seatbelt before pulling it across my chest and clicking it into place.

My brows slide together as I study him. Even though he kissed me in greeting, he seems oddly distant.

It's a ten-minute drive to the arena and Cole is quiet the entire way.

My guess is that there's something on his mind, but, for whatever reason, he's keeping it to himself. One of the things I've grown to like about Cole is that he doesn't play games. Even though I've been less forthright with him, he's still straightforward with me. I always know where I stand and what to expect from him.

That, however, is not the case now.

It makes me feel strangely anxious.

When I can't stand another second of the silence that fills the cabin of the car, I force myself to ask, "Is something wrong?"

For some reason, that's how it feels.

If nothing were wrong, Cole would already have my hand firmly ensconced within his own. Instead, my fingers are twisting nervously in my lap.

And as much as I want to be the one to reach out first…

"Everything's fine." Even though he gives me a reassuring smile, he seems distracted.

Distant.

I can't get that word out of my head. I never realized how attentive Cole was until he wasn't.

"Are you sure?" I inhale a deep breath and try to find my nerve. It takes effort to reach out and lay my fingers over his larger hand. He glances at me, our gazes colliding, before shifting back to the ribbon of road in front of him.

"I'm sure." Even though he wraps his fingers around mine, giving them a brief squeeze, it still feels as if something sits uncomfortably between us.

It's a relief when we finally pull into the parking lot. Without a word spoken between us, we exit the vehicle. Cole pops open the trunk and grabs my bag, hoisting it over his shoulder.

Instead of focusing on the weird tension, I glance around the crowded lobby. "Are you going to tell me what we're doing here at nine o'clock on a Saturday morning?"

When we skate, it's usually five in the morning, before the arena is open to the public. I love when it's just the two of us on the ice.

"You'll see." He nods toward one of the rinks. "Come on."

Before I can ask any more questions, he strides toward rink number one. After a silent moment, I trail after him. As much as I don't like what's happening between us, I'm unsure how to smooth it over and make it better.

Cole holds open the door and I'm hit by a burst of frigid air.

He points to a door on the other side of the rink. "Use locker room number three and meet me back here."

I glance around and notice a team in the middle of a ninety-minute practice. There's still sixty minutes left running on the clock.

"Don't you think I'm a little old to play with these guys?" Actually, they're more like boys. Normally, on a Saturday morning, both sheets of ice are being used for hockey practice or games. I have no idea why he wants me to suit up.

The first full-fledged smile I've seen from him since he picked me up twenty minutes earlier curves his lips. My heart skips a painful beat in response.

"Just go change," he orders softly.

I give him one last searching look before reaching for my bag. Our fingers brush during the exchange and a sizzle of awareness shoots through me. My gaze rises to his only to find his attention already locked on me.

"I'll be right back," I whisper, feeling knocked off balance.

His expression turns serious. "I'll be waiting."

Unsure what else to say, I nod before scurrying to the locker room. Ten minutes later, I lace up my skates and am ready to go. It's a bittersweet feeling to be outfitted in my own hockey gear. It's been almost a year of not skating five to six days a week.

No drills.

No practices.

No dry-land work outs.

No games.

Nothing.

Before last year, my life had revolved around hockey to the exclusion of everything else.

And then it was gone.

I was left with vast stretches of time and nothing to fill it. No friends. I'd sacrificed all those to get to the next level of hockey. No boyfriend. There had never been time for that. No other hobbies, activities, or interests. There'd never been time to develop anything else. I may not have been an Olympian or professional athlete, but I trained like one.

I shake myself out of those thoughts and spot Cole standing where I'd left him. For just a moment, I allow my gaze to rove over him as he watches a team of twelve-and thirteen-year-olds skate up and down the ice while practicing a passing drill. The coach blows his whistle about every twenty seconds as a new set of kids take off down the sheet of ice.

A smile curves his lips as he watches them. With his attention focused elsewhere, I'm able to study him openly. From the navy beanie pulled low over his shaggy brown hair to his golden whiskey-colored eyes. There's a light stubble that covers both his chin and cheeks. His lips are full, and his face is handsomely chiseled. There isn't an ounce of boy there. Even though he's only a sophomore in college, he's all man. Something unexpected flutters in my belly as I silently acknowledge how gorgeous he is. His shoulders are impossibly broad. I love running my hands over them and down his muscular arms. They're all sinewy muscle.

And he's tall.

Solid.

My snap judgment about him when we'd met at that party couldn't have been more off base. Even though he's devastatingly handsome, he's the last guy I would call a D-bag. He's probably one of the nicest guys I've ever met.

And I'm ruining this. I can feel him pulling away.

The need to lighten the mood surges through me as I close the distance between us.

I point toward the ice. "Seems like a long time ago, doesn't it?"

He glances over at me, and one side of his mouth slides up. "Sometimes it feels like yesterday, and other days like a lifetime ago."

Understanding the sentiment, I nod in agreement. "Yeah, it does."

His gaze slides over me with more interest as he grins and shakes his head. "You look hot, Cassidy."

I roll my eyes as heat floods my cheeks. For one, I look massive with the shoulder pads and cushiony pants. Plus, my skates give me three inches of extra height. I probably look like a goon.

"Shut up."

He chuckles before reaching for my hand. "Come on."

I let him capture my fingers as we head toward the doors that lead to the lobby again.

"Where are we going now?" That's when I realize he hasn't changed out of his street clothes. "Wait a minute, you're not skating?"

When I slow my pace, he tugs my hand and pulls me through the double doors. "No more questions, you're late."

Instead of releasing my fingers, he tows me across the crowded lobby, weaving between parents with their morning cups of coffee. We continue walking to the second sheet of ice before pushing through another set of doors. I stop short as my gaze lands on players racing up and down the ice.

These players are older.

And they're girls.

Well, women.

Probably my age.

My wide gaze slices to his. "What is this?" Stupid question because it's obvious this is a girls' college-level hockey team. "Why did you bring me here?"

I don't know why I'm beginning to panic, but I am. My chest feels achy and my head light. The only thing that stops me from racing out of the rink is Cole, who still has my fingers tightly held in his grip.

His easy smile collapses as he searches my expression.

Before he's able to say anything, a girl flies across the ice and skids to a stop, spraying ice in a perfect arc. Her breathing is labored as she unlatches the door and steps outside.

With a quick tug of her gloves, she pulls them off before unbuckling the helmet and yanking it off her head. Her long blonde hair is secured at the back of her neck in a low ponytail. There's something familiar about her, but I'm not sure I actually know her.

With her gaze focused on me, she holds out her hand. "Hi, I'm Sammy. Cole's told me a lot about you."

The smile I give her is forced. "Hi," I say nervously, "Cassidy."

Even though it's tempting to tell her that Cole has told me nothing about her, I remain silent. I feel awkward and out of place as I gesture to the players skating through drills.

"What team is this?"

Her gaze flicks toward Cole before returning to mine. "He didn't tell you?"

I shake my head. "No."

Nope. Cole definitely didn't tell me anything.

I can't decide if I'm pissed off that he put me in such an uncomfortable position or not.

"This is Western's women's intramural hockey team." She shrugs. "Nothing fancy but it's a lot of fun. We've got a good bunch of girls, and practice three times a week. Cole thought you might want to check it out since you used to play."

I don't know what to say. My heart pounds painfully as I watch a couple of girls fly across the ice. It takes a moment to realize that Cole and Sammy are waiting for a response. I clear my throat, not wanting either to notice how affected I am by the offer.

"Um, yeah. I'd like that. Isn't the team set for the year?"

"Nah. Intramurals are pretty loose, and we can always use another body out on the ice."

She tilts her head, looking me up and down. "Forward or defense?"

"Forward, center," I reply with just a hint of pride in my voice.

"Excellent." She flashes me a grin before turning to Cole and kissing his cheek. "Thanks."

As he meets her gaze, a genuine smile lifts his lips. That's all it takes for a little pang of sadness to pierce my heart. I blink, surprised by their familiarity. And then Sammy is opening the heavy metal door and jumping back onto the ice before skating toward the team. All of the girls gather around her.

Cole's expression turns somber as he nods toward them. "You better get out there."

I glance at the ice. A few of the girls stare back with curiosity. "I haven't skated with a team in a long time." My voice dips as I reveal my worst fear. "What if I make a fool out of myself?"

His face softens. "We just skated last week, and you were great. Hardly rusty at all. Even with taking some time off, you're probably better than half the girls out there."

I nip my lower lip before glancing at the ice with a mixture of longing and fear. "I don't want to embarrass myself." The thought of these girls judging me—and ultimately finding me lacking—is almost debilitating.

Just like the Dartmouth team.

Once upon a time, hockey had been my passion. It was the one thing I'd excelled at. I don't know if that's the case any longer.

"Hey." His sharp voice pulls my attention back to him as he reaches out and takes a hold of my hand. "I promise, you'll be great. I wouldn't have asked Sammy to let you skate with them if I didn't think you were ready for this." He squeezes my fingers. "You know that, right?"

I force a smile. "Yeah."

He jerks his head toward the ice for a second time. "Then get out there."

Nerves prickle along my skin as I secure my helmet and shove my hands into my gloves before meeting his gaze. "Okay."

Even though it feels like I'm walking to my death, I inhale deeply before stepping onto the ice and skating toward the team.

Fifty minutes later, sweat is pouring down my face as I race with the black rubber puck toward the goal. Two defensive players are nipping at my heels. Their labored breaths fill my ears as one of them tries to backcheck me by knocking the puck from behind. Adrenaline pounds through my system. When I'm ten feet away from the net, I wind up before pulling my stick forward and hitting the puck toward the goal. The black disc lifts from the ice toward the five-hole between the goalie's legs. It flies past her as she dives for it.

I pump my fist into the air and circle the net. I can't believe how good this feels. Cole had been right. This wasn't the best group of girls I'd ever played with, but it was fun.

So much fun.

Sammy breathes hard as she stops next to me. "Damn, you're fast." She elbows me when I grin back in response.

She's not the only one breathing hard.

"You're going to play with us, right?"

"I'd love to," I say with a laugh, unable to believe how much I want that.

As I skate back to center ice, I realize that I haven't looked for Cole since I skated onto the ice almost an hour ago. Did he stick around and watch me practice with the team?

I'm not nearly as good as I once was, but I kind of want him to see me in action. My gaze coasts over the bleachers, only to realize that he isn't there. I shouldn't feel hurt that he didn't bother to stick around and share this moment with me.

But I do.

For some reason, it matters more than I want it to.

CASSIDY

I don't hear from Cole for the rest of the weekend. By Sunday night, I finally break down and shoot him a text. He answers it, but like the car ride to the rink, the distance is palpable. And because I'm unwilling to put myself out there, I don't bother to contact him again. It only confuses me more as to what we are to one another, if anything.

I thought for sure he'd be waiting outside the dorms early Monday morning for our usual run, but I failed to see the text he sent late Sunday night saying he wouldn't be able to make it. So, I ran by myself. Instead of being an easy and relaxing job, it just felt lonely.

He's pulling away.

I can feel it happening.

Even if I wanted to fix what's wrong, I wouldn't know how.

When he doesn't show for Psychology later that morning, I begin to wonder if something is really wrong with him. For ten solid minutes, I debate the merits of shooting him another text when someone in a back row barks out a laugh. As I swing around, my gaze slides over a familiar dark head.

My breath catches.

Cole is sitting at the back of the amphitheater-style lecture hall. I blink and realize that Sammy is parked next to him, and their heads are bent toward one another. Shock and hurt crash over me as I spin around, not wanting either of them to catch me staring.

After class is over, I purposely linger, slowly packing up my stuff before taking a deep breath and turning toward the exit.

It's a relief to find them both gone.

Tuesday night, I attend my first official practice for the women's intramural hockey team. Since Sammy owns a car, she offers to pick me up. Even though she's the last person I want to hitch a ride with, I don't have much of a choice in the matter. Not having my own transportation means I have to bum rides. And as much as I'd like to hate her, I can't blame her for wanting to be with him.

Cole is amazing.

Maybe I've only spent an hour or so with Sammy, but she's pretty and athletic. And she's nice. But not in a sweet, simpering, phony-baloney kind of way. It's more like a *I'll kick-your-ass-because-I-don't-take-any-shit-from-anyone* kind of way.

So, yeah. I bet Cole is totally into her.

Who wouldn't be?

They certainly looked all cozy sitting together in Psychology yesterday. It also explains why he hasn't bothered to call or text.

I can only gnash my teeth together. At this very moment, I'm being eaten alive by jealousy.

With a grumble under my breath, I toss my bag into the trunk of her rundown Honda Civic before slipping into the front seat beside her.

"Hey," she says with a grin before pulling away from the curb at breakneck speed.

My wide gaze flies to hers as a devilish smile curves her lips. All thoughts of Cole and her together disappear as I grab the oh-shit bar as she squeals around a corner.

"Holy crap, are you trying to kill us?" I gasp as she continues to pick up speed.

Oh my god, my life is literally flashing before my eyes as she takes another corner.

"I like to drive offensively," she says with a laugh. "And I like speed."

Her gaze locks on mine.

With my heart lodged in the middle of my throat, I point to the pavement that feels like it's hurtling toward us at warp speed. "Look at the road, look at the road!"

My gut roils. Any minute, I'm going to be sick.

"Jeez, Cassidy." She shakes her head. "Calm down. I'm actually a really good driver. I've never been the cause of a major accident."

The cause of...

A major accident?

Oh crap.

The arena is only five miles away, and we arrive in record time. Oblivious to the fact that I'm in the midst of a heart attack, Sammy chats about the girls on the team, practice schedule, and travel dates. Since this is an intramural team, the university doesn't provide transportation, and we need to arrange our own rides. Even though Sammy offers to drive me to all the games, I decide that I need to make friends fast with the other players.

I would die if I had to ride with her and Cole to a game.

No.

Way.

In.

Hell.

Just as we slam to a stop in the parking lot, she fires off questions, asking me about my hockey background. I can't help but freeze up, not wanting to give her too much information. As we walk into the arena and change into our hockey gear, I give her a Cliffs Notes version of my hockey career, making sure to gloss over my college experience, which means I don't tell her about it at all. By the end of my spiel, she seems satisfied, and we begin warmups by circling the ice.

The ninety-minute practice is over in the blink of an eye. Just like last time, it feels so good to lose myself in the drills and scrimmage. I pour all my heartache, uncertainty, and anger at myself onto the ice.

By the time it's over, I'm a sweaty, exhausted mess. I huff and puff my way off the ice, hoping I'll be tired enough to fall into bed and sleep without dreaming of Cole.

My stomach twists into knots as I walk toward Sammy's car before sliding onto the passenger seat. Before I can mentally prepare myself for the roller coaster that is Sammy's driving, we're hurtling toward campus. Maybe it's the exhaustion or the fact that I keep my eyes tightly closed, but her driving doesn't make me nearly as nauseous as the ride to the rink.

"Do you want me to drop you off at Cole's?"

My eyelids fly open as my head snaps around. "What?"

God no. I think about the text message I sent and his brief, impersonal response.

There is no way in hell I'm showing up on his doorstep like some kind of pathetic loser.

One side of her mouth hitches up as she refocuses her attention on the road. "You guys are seeing each other, aren't you?"

"Ummm."

How am I supposed to answer that question?

For starters…isn't *she* seeing Cole?

I saw them sitting together in class and it was pretty obvious from their interaction on Saturday morning that they're familiar with one another. I'd just assumed Cole had moved on…to her.

"I'm not really sure."

Sammy's dark gaze flicks to mine as her speed slows to ten miles above the legal limit. I no longer feel like I'm careening toward my death.

She smirks. "He likes you."

I don't want to ask.

I don't want to.

But I have to.

Could I be any more pathetic?

"So, how do you know Cole?" As soon as the question is out of my mouth, my teeth sink into my lower lip.

A few soft chuckles erupt from her. It makes me feel like an even bigger idiot. "He's my cousin."

For the second time in a matter of minutes, my head whips toward her as I repeat stupidly, "*Your cousin?*"

That's a plot twist I did not see coming.

Another burst of laughter follows. "Yeah, we're cousins. Our moms are sisters."

"Oh." There are so many thoughts crashing through my head.

"You thought we were something more, huh?"

The question is asked slyly, as if she didn't know exactly what I'd been thinking. The smile curving her lips, however, tells a different story.

"No, I didn't." Of course, I'd thought they were something more. They look ridiculously cute together.

She snorts before raising a brow. "Are you sure?" Her voice brims with undisguised humor. The girl is practically chortling.

It's not a good look.

"Okay," I finally reply through stiff lips, "maybe I thought you two had something going on."

"You could have just asked him." This time, when her gaze darts to mine, I don't think about the road in front of us. "Or me."

I shake my head and focus on the darkness flying past the car. "Maybe I should have."

Questioning Cole would have made me look jealous. Or like I actually cared about seeing him with other girls.

Crap. I really am in trouble.

"I'm making an executive decision and dropping you off at Cole's. It seems like you two have some serious shit to hash out."

What!

Eyes widening, I shake my head. "No, that's not a good idea." In fact, it's the worst idea I've ever heard. Even if they're not together, he's still distancing himself from me.

I'm struck with another thought that makes my chest spasm.

What if there's another girl at his place?

"Please," I plead, barely able to contain the anxiety roiling through me, "don't. Just take me back to the dorms."

"Well," she says, taking the corner onto his street so fast that I clutch at the handle, "I think it's a freaking fantastic idea."

My tongue darts out to lick at my lips as desperation claws at my insides. "I don't know if he wants to see me."

Already my chest is tightening up.

"He does."

At this point, I know there's no way to sway her and mentally scramble for a reasonable explanation as to why I'm showing up unannounced at nine o'clock at night. As his house comes into view, she shoots into the driveway before braking abruptly. Thankfully, I'm still strapped in, or my head would have crashed through the windshield.

Then again, maybe that would have been preferable to the humiliation she's forcing on me.

"You drive like shit," I whisper as my heartbeat hitches.

She throws the car into park before pulling out her phone and tapping the screen. A few seconds later, her phone dings in response and Cole jogs down the front steps toward the car.

I track his movements before whispering from the corner of my mouth to Sammy, "I don't know you very well, but I'm going to kick your ass for this."

Not taking the threat seriously, she bursts into laughter.

Her gaze slides to mine. "On the ice, I think you could probably do it. Right here and right now, not so much. I've got at least twenty pounds on you."

"But I have rage on my side," I mumble.

My cheeks heat as Cole's gaze settles on mine in the darkness.

I might have grown up playing hockey, and have even thrown a punch or two, but an all-out brawl—nope. I'm not a fighter. So, she's probably right about kicking my ass in a fight.

Sammy beams as Cole comes around the car before arriving at the passenger side.

As he pulls open the door, we stare at one another before he murmurs, "Hey."

"Hi," I say in return before shifting on the seat. Uncomfortable has nothing on this.

Maybe I can get him to drop me at the dorms as soon as Sammy takes off.

"Hi, Cole." Sammy waves from the seat next to me. "Just ignore me over here."

His gaze flicks from mine to hers before flashing a smile. "Hey, Sammy. Thanks for dropping her off."

She spears him with a knowing grin. "No problem. See you on Sunday for dinner."

"Yup."

Sammy pops open the trunk and Cole unloads my bag before slamming it shut again.

"You're welcome," she whispers as I sit frozen in place.

"I haven't thanked you for anything," I mutter.

"You will." With a wink, she unclasps my seatbelt. "Now get the hell out of here. I've got places to go and people to see."

I send one last glower in her direction before slipping from the car and watching in dread as she backs out, pulling away with a roar of her engine.

"Do you want to come inside for a bit?"

I paste a smile on my lips. "Sure."

Ten minutes tops and then I'm Ubering it home if I have to. Cole leaves my hockey bag on the porch before holding open the front door for me. We walk through the entryway and living room, arriving at the kitchen where he grabs two bottles of water before leading me up the staircase to his room.

Once there, Cole settles on the armchair in the corner as I sit at the edge of his bed. For a moment, we stare at one another before I break eye contact and glance away. This is so painfully awkward, it's almost unbearable. When I can't stand another moment, I shoot to my feet, anxious to leave.

"This was a bad idea. Would you mind driving me back to the

dorms?"

His brows furrow as he rises to his feet, eating up the distance separating us. "Is that what you really want, Cassidy?" There's a pause as his gaze searches mine. "Because I don't want you to leave."

My chest feels as if it's being squeezed in a vise.

I give my head a little shake. I'm so completely out of my element with him.

Being here feels wrong.

Or right.

I don't know anymore.

I don't know what I'm feeling. There are too many emotions churning within, making it impossible to separate them.

He draws me into his arms slowly as if giving me a chance to pull away. That's all it takes to break me down. Instead of fighting the closeness, I give in and allow my head to settle against the broad expanse of his chest. His heart thumps a steady rhythm beneath my ear as he presses a kiss to the crown of my head.

"I don't want you to go," he murmurs against my hair.

I squeeze my eyes shut and admit the truth. "I don't want to go."

His arms tighten around me. "I've missed you."

I blurt out the one question that has been eating me alive. "Have you been avoiding me?" Even though I know the answer, I want to hear it from him.

For a long moment, he remains quiet. "It seemed like you needed time to sort things out. I was trying to give you space."

The funny thing is, after the appointment with Dr. Thompson and the visit home, I'd needed time to straighten everything out in my head. Somehow, without me telling him, Cole had sensed it as well.

I'm knocked from those thoughts when he asks, "Do you need more time?" He drops another kiss on my head. "I promised that I wouldn't push you and I won't."

I think about how much I missed him this past week. It's more than I thought possible.

"No." I rise onto the tips of my toes until I can reach his mouth. "I don't need more time. I know what I want and that's you." Once the words are out of my mouth, I realize how true they are.

I want to be with Cole.

I've been miserable without him.

Lonely in a way I hadn't realized I was.

The corners of his lips tilt upward. "Good, because I want to be with you, too."

His mouth opens over mine, and before he's able to make the first move, I beat him to the punch. A surprised noise rumbles up from deep in his throat as his arms tighten around me again. My heartbeat speeds up as I caress him with my lips. We kiss for a few lazy moments before I pull back to lick and nip at him.

And he lets me do it.

He allows me to be the aggressor.

Which feels oddly empowering.

I'm the one in control.

I'm the one who decides how this will unfold.

Instead of making me feel scared or nervous, it feels good.

It feels right.

"Cassidy," he growls, "you have no idea how much I want you." The low scrape of his words arrow straight to my core before exploding on impact.

All of the sudden, I feel very powerful.

"Stay with me tonight."

Instead of answering, my lips steal over his as our tongues tangle. "Even if we don't do anything more than this, I just want to hold you in my arms."

His words have my heart thawing. Melting from the deep freeze that has encapsulated it for almost a year.

Cole isn't like anyone I've met before. He won't hurt me. Not deliberately. If anything, I'll end up hurting him. I'm the one who will try escaping from our intimacy when it becomes more than I can handle.

Maybe I don't deserve Cole Mathews, but I want him. I want to hold onto him for as long as I can. I want him to heal the broken pieces inside me.

With my lips pressed against his, I whisper, "I want to stay. I want..." my voice trails off. Even though I'm terrified, I force them out. "I want you."

He breaks our kiss before drawing away enough to search my eyes. "Are you sure? We don't have to have sex. I can wait. *We* can wait until you're ready." He brushes his lips across mine before adding, "You know this is more than just sex, right?"

Yeah, I do.

I think I've always known.

But hearing him say it out loud melts the last of the ice within me. His words sweep away all the doubts fluttering around the sharp edges of my mind.

"At some point, you'll have to tell me what happened."

My muscles tense as thin tendrils of anxiety thread their way through me, making my chest feel tight and achy.

"Not tonight," he says quickly as he searches my eyes, "but soon. You can't keep pushing me away when you get scared."

Can I do that?

Can I regurgitate everything that happened, and then wait for him to accept or reject me?

It's a frightening prospect.

But what other choice is there?

I want—no *need*—to give this a real chance.

I want Cole. And I want this to work between us. The only way that can happen is if I tell him the truth.

Full disclosure.

"Yes," I whisper thickly as my belly twists itself into a series of complicated knots.

Almost as soon as the answer escapes from me, he captures my lips before wrapping his arms around my body and carrying me to the bed where he lays me down. Once he settles on top of me, his lips feather over mine.

That's all he does.

Tastes my mouth a thousand different ways until I'm almost drunk with the sensation.

If this is going to happen, it needs to be on my terms. I push against the steely strength of his chest until he draws back and searches my gaze.

"Changed your mind?" Even though there's a raspy edge to his voice, I know he'll stop if I want him to.

"No."

Instead of explaining what I want, I push him back against the mattress until he's the one lying flat before I climb on top of him and straddle his hips. My heart gallops almost painfully as I stare down at him from this vantage point.

Have I mentioned just how much I love his chest?

It's so broad and muscular.

Firm and powerful.

Just like him.

I think that's what I like most about Cole. He's so big and strong, but there's a tenderness within him. An unexpected gentleness. A goodness you don't always find in people.

"You're so beautiful," he murmurs, gaze roving over my features.

Heat fills my cheeks as I lower my lashes. "I'm already in your bed, you don't need to tell me that."

His lips quirk as he shakes his head. "I saw you the first day in Psychology, sitting way up in front. I couldn't stop staring as you diligently took notes. You were listening so intently and seemed so serious. Almost like everything the professor said was important, and you didn't want to miss a word of it. I thought about talking to you but chickened out." His laugh is oddly self-deprecating. "And then I chickened out every day after that, until I saw you at that party. I watched you with Alex, and then suddenly you were pulling that girl over and the others joined you. It was the funny to watch. Instead of yelling at Alex, you stood there with a little smirk on your face. That was the moment I knew I had to meet you." The corners of his mouth lift as he chuckles. "And I'd already had a beer or two, so I was feeling confident."

It boggles my mind that Cole would be afraid to speak with me.

Me.

He has to know how girls look at him. The guy can't be that oblivious.

Unable to help myself, I bend down and take his mouth with my own before admitting, "I thought you were beautiful."

"Beautiful?" He gives me a mock frown. "Not ruggedly handsome?"

My lips tremble as I shake my head. "Nope, beautiful. Gorgeous, actually." Then I add so he doesn't get too swollen of a head, "I was pretty sure you'd be a douchebag."

Laughter bursts from him. "A D-bag, huh?" He scratches his chin and narrows his eyes. "I do remember you trying to blow me off. A few times, now that I think about it. Luckily for you, I'm persistent."

I press a kiss against his lips before straightening to meet his gaze. "You're the furthest thing from a D-bag." I suck in a steady breath before releasing it back into the atmosphere and admitting, "I like you, Cole. A lot."

His lips curve as his eyes soften. "I like you, too."

Still sitting astride him, I grab the hem of my long-sleeved shirt and yank it over my head. His gaze holds mine before dipping to my breasts. It occurs to me that I'm wearing a simple white bra and underwear. It's not even a matching set. It's functional, at best.

Heat leaps into Cole's eyes as he reaches up to cup my breasts through the thin white material. "You're absolutely beautiful, you know that? Just…beautiful."

His praise gives me the confidence to reach behind my back and unclasp the hooks. The straps fall down my arms as the cups fall away from my breasts. Even though the urge to cover myself pounds through me, I keep my arms at my sides and allow him to look his fill.

Slipping the bra free, I toss it on the floor as his hands rise to palm the soft flesh. His upper body rises from the mattress until he's able to capture one pebbled nipple between his lips and suck it into his mouth. Ribbons of arousal coil in the pit of my belly as a strangled noise escapes from me. His fingers stroke the other peaked tip. I gasp as heat explodes in my core, making me throb and ache with a restless need I've never experienced before.

Just when I don't think I can take another moment, he releases me with a soft pop. There is so much need crashing through my body, threatening to drag me to the bottom of the ocean. A fire burns its way through my system as I lean down and take his mouth with my own. It heats all the cold, dark places inside me that I didn't know existed.

I break free and sit up again before working his T-shirt up his torso and over his head until he's lying beneath me as bare-chested as I am. My gaze licks over all that chiseled strength.

And he thinks *I'm* the beautiful one?

I almost snort as my fingertips drift over his muscles. When I tweak one of his flat nipples, a deep growl rumbles up from him.

The throbbing between my legs grows.

Cole is probably the most beautiful guy I've ever seen. Inside and out.

My gaze trails after my fingers as I discover a large tattoo that wraps around his ribcage, and carefully trace the intricate patterns of ink.

"This is a surprise."

He shrugs as something darkens in his eyes.

Whatever the reason for this tattoo, it's important.

"I'd wanted one for a while, but my mom refused to let me get it until I turned eighteen. I think she was holding out hope I would change my mind. I got inked on my birthday. It was a present to myself."

I close the distance between us until I trace the tip of my tongue over the dark ink. Another groan falls from his lips.

"Very sexy," I whisper against his ribs.

"Then I'll get a couple more," he murmurs as my mouth slides over his flesh.

I shake my head. "What I like is that it's so unexpected." Just to prove my words, I lap at him. "A lovely little surprise."

He hisses out a sharp breath before shifting. That's when I become aware of the erection nestled between my legs. A whimper escapes from me as my fingers slide from the tattoo to the button of his jeans before flicking it open and lowering the zipper.

"We don't have to take this any further," he says in a voice that is whipcord tight. "We really don't. I want you to be sure about what we're doing."

When my fingers stroke over his hard length, he winces as if in pain.

"I am sure. I want this." My gaze locks on his. "I want you."

A muscle tics in his jaw as I tug at the denim before he takes over and slides the thick material down his legs, kicking his feet free. A moment later, he lies beneath me in nothing more than black boxer briefs that hug his muscular thighs. This is what years of skating will get you.

My breath catches as my gaze roams over him. With the guys I'd been with before, there'd never been an opportunity to sit and look my fill. This is an entirely new experience.

One I'm enjoying.

I can't believe how gorgeous Cole is. And so damn sexy. As cliché as it sounds, my breath actually catches at the back of my throat.

Thoughts I never expected tumble through my mind. I want to lick every inch, and feel him inside me.

Filling me up.

My belly hollows out at the thought of him buried deep inside my body.

His fingers slip to my jeans, popping the button free before peeling the zipper and sliding the material down my hips. I rise above him on my knees so he can pull the denim free, until only my panties remain. His attention dips to my plain pink underwear before he leans closer, pressing a delicate kiss against the vee between my legs.

"Are you sure?"

I nod.

His gaze holds mine as he pulls the thin fabric down my hips and legs until I'm totally bare.

I sink down until his thick length is nestled against me through his boxer briefs. A moan slips free as I stroke myself against him. His hands wrap around my hips, grasping them tightly as I move against him again. Sensation explodes in my core as my head lolls back. There is something so erotic about riding him like this. His hot gaze stays pinned to mine as his fingers bite into my hips.

"You have no fucking idea how much I want you right now," he growls.

Even though he's not inside me, already something is building deep within. Another guttural groan escapes from him as I roll my hips.

One hand drifts from my hip to the apex between my legs. I gasp as he grazes my sensitive flesh. It's not a conscious decision to widen my thighs so he can touch more of me. A whimper slips from my lips as he continues to stroke my pussy.

"Probably as much as I want you," I pant.

How is it possible that he's capable of giving me so much pleasure?

I'm so close to splintering apart. I can't imagine anything feeling better than this.

The need to lay my hands on him pounds through me as I lean forward and stroke my hands over the solid ridges of abdomen, moving upward to his chest and then down again. It doesn't surprise me that he has a six-pack.

Cole works out religiously.

When I reach the elastic band of his boxer briefs, I snap the stretchy material against his taut flesh. The entire time I've been learning his body, his fingers have kept up a steady rhythm, never dipping inside my heat.

"Take them off," I gasp.

Those three little words are all it takes for him to lift me from his body. A moment later he's sliding the underwear down his legs and tossing them to the floor. As soon as he relaxes onto the mattress, I climb on top of him so that his thick length is nestled against my slick core.

His gaze arrows to the place where our bodies are connected. He groans, a muscle in his jaw ticking as I roll my hips. Bright sparks of pleasure ricochet through every nerve ending of my body. The delicious friction sends a million tiny pulses of electricity skittering across my flesh before coiling tight in my center.

I've never wanted anyone the way I want Cole.

"Are you on anything?" he asks, voice strung tight.

I shake my head, thankful he's cognizant enough for the both of us to think about protection. Even though it shouldn't be, it's the last thing on my mind. It only proves how affected I am.

Pain flickers across his face as he grits, "I have a few condoms in the drawer next to the bed."

My lips lift as he slides against me. "Are we going to need more than one?"

"I really hope so." When my eyelids flutter closed, he grinds against me with a little more force. "Cassidy?"

My eyes open, locking on his. "I don't make a habit of sleeping around. That's not really my style. Maybe we should have talked about this already, but I wanted you to know that."

I force myself to give him the same honesty in return. "I haven't been with anyone in almost a year."

Unwilling to allow the past to intrude on the perfection of this moment, I close the distance between us until my lips can ghost over his. His mouth parts beneath the gentle pressure of my own. A couple of heartbeats later and I'm kissing a hot trail down his chest, over rock-hard abs, to the stiff length between his naked thighs. He groans as I lick him from root to tip and back down again.

"Cassidy..." he rumbles. "This won't last long if you spend any more time down there. Trust me, I'd like to last longer than a few desperate strokes. My self-esteem kind of depends on it."

I grin, continuing to lick his cock. There's something powerful about hearing a guy growl, his voice scraped raw with need, when you have the most precious part of him in your hands and mouth.

He groans when I slip his blunt head between my lips. Once, twice, three times I slide over him before he snarls, grabbing me beneath my arms and hauling me up his body until I'm draped across him, hard shaft nestled between my thighs. Before I can say anything, he flips me onto my back. A gasp slips free as my heart races with anticipation.

"Do you really think you're the only one who can play games?" he rasps, crawling down my body, sucking each hard nipple into his mouth.

My eyelids close as I arch into him, wanting more. He nips and licks at my flesh until I'm squirming with the pulsing need that has gathered in my core. His lips create a fiery trail across my ribs and belly before sinking lower, until his hot breath feathers across my core.

He presses a small kiss at the juncture of my thighs before muttering, "You're so fucking gorgeous." His mouth sinks lower with each swipe of his tongue. "I want to spread you open and take my time with you."

A shiver dances down my spine as his deep voice crashes over me. The slick heat between my legs grows as my pussy throbs with need.

My gaze fastens on him as he slips between my spread thighs. The image he makes with his dark, mussed hair against the juncture of my legs is the most erotic thing I've seen. A few strokes of his tongue and my legs are falling impossibly wide.

He groans, kissing my wet flesh as his heated gaze captures mine. There is such a strange seriousness held within their gorgeous tawny depths. I'm powerless to look away from the picture he makes as he presses his lips against me.

The fine tremble that racks my body has nothing to do with his touch. It's about the way his penetrating gaze pierces mine, never once releasing me as he continues to stroke my pussy. I shift beneath him as his tongue dips inside me, lapping at me until I'm teetering on the brink of falling apart.

These sensations are almost too much to feel within the confines of my own flesh. It's as if something inside me is attempting to claw its way out. And still, he holds my gaze the entire time, watching as I'm forced closer to the precipice. Watching every moment of pleasure as it roars through me.

His hands settle on my thighs, pinning me to the bed as he gently sucks my throbbing clit into his mouth. My fingers twist into the covers, fisting the thick material as my back arches.

A whimper escapes from my lips as he continues to torment me. The need to pull back from the thick waves of pleasure that pummel my senses pounds through me until I'm squeezing my eyes tightly shut, attempting to escape within myself to regain control. This feeling of coming unhinged is so strange and new. No one has ever played my body as if it were a fine instrument.

It's almost too much to bear.

His tongue swipes over me once more before disappearing. When the heat of his mouth doesn't return, I moan as the agony of his withdrawal leaves me feeling bereft. I arch my hips, wanting to feel the delicious pressure of his lips. I've never felt like a slave to the needs of my own body.

"I want your eyes on me," he growls.

When I don't immediately comply, his heated breath drifts against my wet flesh. I groan in frustration. It's as if I'm perched precariously on the brink of something new and amazing.

"Open them, Cassidy. I want you to see exactly what I'm doing to you."

With a whimper, I force my gaze to his. A knowing glint fills his eyes. Before I can rasp out one incoherent word, his lips return, driving me relentlessly toward the precipice.

When I finally explode, I nearly scream with the force of it. My fingers bite into the comforter as my body arches, shuddering and spasming under the firm pressure of his mouth. He doesn't stop until every last shockwave has subsided and I lay spent, staring at the dark ceiling, questioning every sexual experience that now feels sadly lacking.

I'm barely cognizant of Cole rising from the bed and moving to the nightstand where he rips open a small package before quickly sheathing himself in latex. Before I'm fully able to miss him, he returns, heavy weight pinning me to the mattress. His thick length pushes against my entrance.

Need sparks in my core as his lips settle over mine. The taste of my arousal should be repulsive.

It's not.

I deepen the kiss, remembering what it felt like to have the velvety softness of his tongue stealing over me, his gentle yet punishing lips stroking my inner thighs, spreading me open and sucking my clit.

"I can't wait any longer," he rasps, cock poised at the edge of my swollen lips.

With a moan, I squirm beneath him, desperate to feel every thick inch buried deep inside my body. "You don't have to."

Not a heartbeat later, he drives inside me. Once buried to the hilt, he stills, allowing my inner muscles to adjust to his size.

"You're so damn tight." He kisses me before lifting his hips and moving inside my body. "It feels like you're strangling my cock," he growls as his body rocks against mine.

Everything about this moment feels so right.

He joked earlier that it would only take three desperate strokes and he'd be coming. It takes nine. Nine smooth strokes before he comes inside me. Every single groan that falls from is lips is for me. For the pleasure he feels at being buried deep inside my body.

With my gaze pinned to him, I watch as pleasure unfolds across his features.

I squeeze my inner muscles around his cock, reluctant for the moment to end. I want to savor it for a few more blissful seconds. I want to feel him inside me, filling me up, showing me exactly what sex can feel like between people who care about each other.

And that orgasm…

Holy crap.

I've secretly never understood all the fuss about sex. All my experiences were mediocre at best. That being said, I understand the appeal of it now. When it's right, there's nothing quite like it.

Cole rolls onto his side and collapses on his back before pulling me along with him until my exhausted body is draped across his. As I lay on top of him, my ear pressed against his chest, I can't help but think about what just happened, and marvel at the unexpectedness of it all.

His harsh breathing fills my ears as he drops a kiss against my forehead before trailing his fingers through my hair. "I'm sorry, I'd wanted it to last longer. I hope it was still good."

A lazy smile curves my lips as I tiredly pick up my head to stare at him. I can't resist teasing him just a bit. "Fishing for compliments, are you?"

He chuckles and his chest rumbles. "Just tell me it was good."

I snuggle against him before allowing my fingertips to drift across the light sprinkle of hair covering his chest. "I've had better."

Lie.

I've never experienced anything like it before in my life.

I yelp when he flips me over, gaze searing into mine. "You've," he echoes in disbelief, "had *better?*"

"It was good. Really. A solid performance. A definite seven or seven point five."

His eyes widen as his mouth falls open.

"Look," I continue, "you're young. I wouldn't worry about it. With enough practice, you'll improve."

"Well, fuck…" A determined expression settles over his face as he reaches over and opens the drawer of his nightstand.

I grumble, not appreciating the way he's jostling me. "What are you doing?"

"Clearly, I need to redeem myself. I knew it'd been a while, but honestly, I thought…" his voice trails off in embarrassment.

Laughter bursts from my lips. "You know I was joking, right? It was spectacular."

He swings around and cages my upper body before staring down at me. "You were seriously messing with me?"

I nod as a slow smile curves my face.

The lure of his bulging biceps is too much to resist, and I find myself running my fingers over them. I want nothing more than to reach up and nip at the firm flesh with my teeth before laving at them with my lips and tongue. That thought is enough to make me groan.

"Yup."

Before I realize it, his fingers are drifting over my ribs and under my arms. As they attack, I squeal and try to catch my breath. "I'm sorry, okay? Please stop," I breathe, still laughing, "please!"

After he ceases the torment, his hands glide over my pliant body as he shifts to his side, pulling me against him. "It was good?"

A chuckle slips free as I roll my eyes. "Cole, it was amazing." I press a kiss against his throat. "I've never had an orgasm before."

His brows shoot up. "Never?"

Why this should make him happy is ridiculous, but apparently it does.

"Nope." I've never come close to feeling like I was going to explode.

"Not even by yourself?"

"No." Under normal circumstances, talking about something so private would embarrass me. With him, it doesn't. I pull away enough to meet his inquisitive gaze.

He smirks with obvious pride. "I'm glad I was able to give you your first big O." He closes the distance that separates us before capturing my mouth in a scalding kiss that nearly burns me alive. "The first of many," he whispers.

"Yes," I agree, wanting that just as much as he does.

A comfortable silence falls over us as we lay entwined in each other's arms, and my mind begins to wander. Wrapped up in him, I feel more safe and secure than ever before.

He drops a tender kiss against the top of my head. "You're mine now. There's no more running away."

My eyelids flutter open as I stare into the swirling darkness. Instead of responding, I keep my breathing deep and even, pretending to be asleep. When he doesn't say anything more, I close my eyes again before drifting off.

As much as I want to give him that assurance, I can't. What I do know is that

I want Cole for as long as I can hold onto him.

19

CASSIDY

"Hey, look who decided to pop over for a visit. It's my phantom roommate." Even though these words are muttered, they're still loud enough for me to hear.

I hesitate over the threshold before closing the door behind me. My gaze settles on Brooklyn as she sits in the middle of her bed and paints her toenails. Unsure what the issue is, I hover near the exit and wonder if it's too late to retreat.

The corners of her lips sink into a frown as she continues to ignore me.

With a sigh, I set my leather bag on the floor beside my desk before settling on my twin bed. She doesn't spare me a glance, which only reinforces my suspicions that she's pissed at me.

As I comb through my thoughts, I realize I haven't seen or spoken to Brooklyn in a couple of days. I've spent the past few nights with Cole, and have been on the go with class, practice, and tutoring.

The last time we spoke, everything was fine. By the look on her face, that's no longer the case.

As Brooklyn applies a second coat of eye-popping blue polish to her nails, she blinks a few times as if focusing her attention on the task. A frown creases my brow. It almost looks like she's about to burst into tears.

But how can that be?

Brooklyn never cries. She's usually over-the-top-happy.

Unless she's hung over.

Then, not so much.

I rise to my feet before gingerly settling next to her on the bed and laying a hand on her shoulder. "What's wrong, Brook. You look upset."

When she finishes up, she tightens the cap on her polish before setting the bottle on the table and swinging toward me. As her gaze catches mine, I see an ocean of sadness swimming around within their depths.

"When you called to tell me that you were leaving Dartmouth and applying at Western, I knew something must have happened. I mean, come on, who leaves Dartmouth midway through the year?" She allows that question to hang in the air for a long moment.

Something painful coils in the pit of my gut. Unable to hold her gaze, I drop mine to my fingers that are twisting the hem of my sweater. When I remain silent, she continues. "At the same time, I was excited you were going to be here, and we could get to know each other all over again. You know, be friends the way we used to be before hockey took over your life."

I shake my head, offering up a weak protest. "I never pushed our friendship to the side for hockey." At least, it had never been a conscious decision on my part. Unfortunately, the older I got, the more time-consuming hockey and training became.

She levels me with a hard stare. "But that's the way it felt. You were always busy with your teams. And then there was school and your family. Over the years, we drifted apart. I don't blame you." Her gaze slides to the large picture window of our dorm room. "It's just some-thing that happened."

"No matter what, I always considered you my closest friend." Anxiety swirls through me as my fingers tangle together, fidgeting with the soft fabric.

Disregarding the comment, she says, "When you decided to

transfer here, I thought we'd finally get a chance to mend our friend-ship, but that hasn't worked out. If you're not with Cole, you're playing hockey or tutoring. There's never time for us to just hang out."

I suck in a deep breath and consider what she's just unloaded on me. As difficult as it is to admit, she's right. I allowed our friendship to fall by the side of the road when we were younger, and now, I'm making the same mistake. I've become too wrapped up in Cole, hockey, classes, and tutoring. I'm trying to juggle everything, but obviously, I haven't been making enough time for Brooklyn.

"I'm sorry, Brook. I didn't realize you felt this way and just assumed you were spending all your free time with Austin."

Her shoulders collapse as she breaks eye contact and stares down at her freshly polished nails. "I was." She shrugs. It's just a little jerk of her shoulders, but I feel the words coming before she gives voice to them. "We broke up two days ago."

It's official. I'm definitely a shitty friend. I've been so wrapped up in my own life that I haven't been paying attention to what's been happening with Brooklyn.

"I'm so sorry." Hesitantly, I ask, "Do you want to talk about it?"

Tears pool in her green eyes before she swipes the moisture away. "I caught him kissing someone else."

"You did?" My mouth falls open. There's no way that can be true. Austin is crazy about Brooklyn, and everyone knows it. I can't imagine him cheating on her.

Misery swamps her features as I wrap my arms around her.

"I'm so sorry. He seemed so into you." I give her a little squeeze before silently vowing to be a better friend.

Brooklyn sniffs before giving a watery laugh that's just a shade above bitter. "Yeah, well, I guess he wasn't into me enough. It's those freaking hockey whores, always hanging around the house. There's five or six of them that get passed around between the guys. Don't they have a single shred of self-respect or dignity?" Crystal-looking tears shimmer on her long lashes.

A lot of the men's teams on campus have die-hard groupies who want nothing more than the notoriety of saying they'd slept their way through the roster.

"So, that's it? You guys are over?"

"Cass, I can't be with a guy who cheats." She sucks in a big breath before slowly blowing it out again. "I just can't."

"Does he want to work it out?" Austin is so crazy about her. I can't imagine him walking away without a fight.

She scrunches her face before picking up her phone and scrolling through a few things before handing it over. My eyes widen before darting back to hers.

"Forty-two missed calls?" That's, umm, excessive.

"And fifty-five unanswered text messages," she adds before huffing out a breath.

"Wow." It takes a moment to gather my scattered thoughts. "I don't know if that's romantic or cause for a restraining order," I say with a bit of humor, but I'm not entirely joking.

She glares out the window. "I've told him there wasn't anything more for us to talk about, but he won't leave me alone." She shakes her head in exasperation. "He keeps showing up at my classes and the cafeteria…" She pauses. "It's just getting embarrassing."

I can't believe all this was going on and I didn't have a clue.

"What are you going to do?" I point to the cell. "Did you give him a chance to explain his side of the story?"

Just as I ask the questions, her phone chirps with an incoming call.

One glance at the screen has her rolling her eyes. "Guess who."

Even though I don't want to get involved in this mess, I'd do it for Brooklyn, because that's what friends do. They help each other out. And I haven't been a very good friend to her.

"Do you want me to answer it? Maybe if I talk to him, tell him that you need some space, he'll get the message and leave you alone."

She hits the decline button before tossing the phone on her bed. "No." Her brows pinch together as she scoffs, "His side of the story? Give me a break! What could he possibly say? That he was so shit-faced, he thought Mandi Richards was me? Ha! That he accidently slipped and fell onto her face?" Jaw tightening, she shakes her head. "I don't think so."

"But you can't keep living like this with all the calls and texts, and him following you around campus." I don't even know what to tell her. This is completely out of my depth. "Maybe he just needs to hear you tell him it's over. That there's no coming back from this."

"I can't talk to him right now. I'm still too angry." Sadness and hurt lurk in her eyes. She may be furious with him, but she still cares.

Unsure what the answer is, I pull her in for an embrace. "How about we plan a girls' weekend? We can stay at the dorm and binge-watch reality TV or check out a party." I quickly tack on, "But definitely not any hockey parties."

Her lips flatten. "I think I'm done with hockey players...for now." After a moment, her lips curve into a smile. "Thanks."

"I'm really sorry about being such a crappy friend."

Even though I'm nearly twenty, sometimes it still feels like I'm navigating through the pitfalls of how to be a good friend. This is the stuff people learn in grade school. Not college.

"It's all good. We'll have fun this weekend, just the two of us."

"Definitely."

20

CASSIDY

e stay in Friday night and stuff our faces with pepperoni pizza while marathoning reality TV shows. Saturday afternoon is more of the same. I fill Cole in on the situation with Brooklyn and Austin, and he says he'll speak with his friend. Hopefully, get him to back off for a while.

Even though I love spending time with Cole, it's nice that we can do our own thing and still be good. After this weekend, I need to carve out more time for Brooklyn.

By eight o'clock on Saturday night, my roommate is climbing the walls with the need to escape our dorm and hit one of the fraternity parties that seem to be a constant around here. Since Cole and Austin are throwing a bash of their own, she won't have to worry about running into her ex, which is a relief.

Looking to draw as much male attention as possible, Brooklyn chooses a short, black skirt and a low-cut, red shirt that clings to her curves and does amazing things for her boobs. They almost defy gravity with their perkiness.

Not wanting to encourage any male attention, I throw on a pair of skinny jeans and a pretty pink cashmere sweater that is soft and well-loved. But not exactly sexy. I leave that to Brooklyn, who has decided to pull out all the stops tonight. Since this is clearly a hunting expedition, Brooklyn leaves her long blonde hair free to float around her shoulders in big soft curls. It's her secret weapon. Not that she needs one. She's gorgeous and never lacks for male attention no matter what she's wearing. How she manages to look like sex on a stick, all the while appearing angelic, is beyond me.

I leave my hair down because the weather has turned cold, and I want my neck and ears to be warm. You never know if a party will be inside or outdoors.

She sprays us both with perfume and pronounces us ready to go.

We meet up with a bunch of girls from our floor before walking to fraternity row. I've seen most of them around but don't know any the way Brooklyn seems to. It only slams home the fact that I've been spending a lot of time with Cole and not enough with Brooklyn or trying to make new friends.

By the time we reach the party, the house is already bursting at the seams with people. I scan the street and notice quite a few parties happening up and down the block.

Brooklyn scopes out the talent—her words not mine—as we make our way through the first floor to the backyard where the beer is flowing freely. The guy in charge of the keg takes one look at Brooklyn before giving her a Solo cup on the house. With a flirty smile tipping the corners of her lips, she tells him that mine should be free as well. He agrees, and we both walk away with full cups of beer.

I stare down at the frothy bubbles dancing along the rim of my red plastic cup and silently debate whether to drink it. It's obvious that Brooklyn is pulling out all the stops tonight, and I'm not exactly a big drinker. I haven't been trashed since last year. That experience left a bitter taste lingering in my mouth, and I've steered clear of alcohol ever since. Getting kicked out of another school isn't high on my priority list.

Brooklyn holds up her cup before tapping the rim against mine as her gaze scans the thick crowd. "Drink up, Cassidy. One beer won't kill you."

"I know." But still…

It feels like a slippery slope.

Her fingers wrap around my arm before she gives me a pleading look. "We hardly go out anymore. Just this one night, let's have fun together, okay?"

One of my brows jerks up. "Are you seriously trying to peer pressure me into drinking?"

"Ha! That's not peer pressure, *this* is peer pressure." She closes the distance between us before getting in my face. "I won't be your friend unless you toss back a couple of cold ones with me. Don't you want to be cool like the rest of us? Don't be a loser, Cassidy. Come on, drink up."

We both burst out laughing as she retreats a few steps, her eyes sparkling with humor. It's nice to see her smile and forget about all the Austin drama for even a few minutes.

Deep down, I know she's right.

One beer won't kill me.

My mind tumbles back over the previous few weeks and I run through a quick self-check. I haven't felt any real anxiousness or nervousness. Everything has been going well. Would it really hurt to have a beer or two?

I blow out a steady breath and decide to go for it before taking a small sip and allowing the yeasty flavor to trickle down the back of my throat.

You know what it tastes like?

Failure.

I almost snort.

"See?" Brooklyn snaps her fingers. "Works like a charm every time." She drains her beer in one thirsty gulp. "Guess I better get a refill."

Dangling the cup in her fingers, she swings toward the silver barrel. I bring the beer to my lips for another drink and watch as the guy manning the keg waves Brooklyn to the front of the line. Much to the grumbling protests of the people she just cut in front of, he refills her cup. With a bright smile, she gives him a peck on the cheek before whispering something in his ear that leaves him smiling.

With a shake of my head, I narrow my eyes as Brooklyn makes her way back to me. "I hope you're not promising sexual favors in return for quick service at the keg."

It's a joke.

Kind of.

That angelic expression is back in place. "I promised no such thing." She loops her arm through mine before towing me through the thick, jostling crowd. "Let's go find some hot guys to flirt with."

"I don't need a hot guy." I refrain from mentioning that I already have one.

A chuckle falls from her lips as she tugs me along. "I meant for me, silly."

Thirty minutes later, we're dancing, laughing, and singing along obnoxiously to the loud music. Brooklyn isn't drunk, but she certainly isn't feeling any pain. I'm sure tomorrow morning will be a different story. I've had two drinks, and although I'm nowhere near drunk, I'm pleasantly buzzed. It's just enough to make me feel loose and happy.

Brooklyn is grinding up against a cute fraternity guy and I'm dancing with another. He seems harmless so I'm not overly concerned. I haven't let him put his hands on me, so I don't feel like I'm giving him any mixed signals. It's all just lighthearted fun.

After a couple of songs, the guy I'm dancing with leans closer so he can be heard over the pounding beat. Even though he's tall, muscular, and good-looking with short blond hair.

"Do you want another drink?"

I shake my head. One of us needs to be sober enough to get us home tonight, and it isn't going to be Brooklyn. "No, I've had enough, but thanks."

With a smile, he inches closer until there's only a handful of inches that separate us. His eyes fill with questions as he studies me as if trying to guess where he knows me from. I have to admit, there's something strangely familiar about him as well. Even though Western is a big school, you tend to run into the same people on campus or at parties.

Unease blooms inside me as he continues his intense perusal.

"You're really pretty," he says.

With a nervous smile, I take a hasty step in retreat, wanting to create more distance between us. "Thanks."

"You said that your name is Cassidy, right?" A thoughtful expression flickers across his face.

I nod, unable to remember his name. Or if he even told it to me.

"Can I get your number? Maybe we could hang out some time?"

The last thing I want to do is lead him on. "Sorry, I have a boyfriend."

Honestly, I'm not sorry at all. Even the thought of Cole is enough to have me fighting back a smile. As happy as I am to be here with Brooklyn, it's Cole I'd rather be dancing with.

He glances around before raising a brow. "If you were my girlfriend, I wouldn't let you go to a fraternity party all by yourself."

Irritation sparks to life inside me. "He trusts me." Then I add so we're perfectly clear, "And I like him. I wouldn't do anything to mess that up."

He jerks his head into a nod as if accepting that I'm not interested. "He's a lucky guy."

Relief rushes through me as my muscles loosen. "Thanks."

He stares at me for a long moment before giving his head a little shake. "Give me your phone."

"Why?"

Instead of answering, his fingers curl into a *give it to me* gesture. "Just hand it over."

Uncertain what to do, I slide my phone from the back pocket of my jeans before holding it out to him. He plucks the slim device from my fingers. My teeth sink into my lower lip as I watch him scroll through my contacts list before tapping in his information. A second later, his phone buzzes with an incoming message.

"When you break up with that guy, give me a call and we'll go out."

Just as my fingers wrap around the cell, he brushes his lips across my cheek before disappearing into the crowd. Almost absently, my fingers drift over the spot. I can't believe he did that. As I slip the phone back into my pocket, I glance around for Brooklyn. I catch sight of a few girls from our floor but not her.

For the next ten minutes, I scour the backyard before moving inside the house. I'm busy scanning the crowded kitchen when I smack into a hard body. An apology sits on the tip of my tongue as I glance up and lock gazes with the last person I expected to see.

"Austin, what are you doing here?"

Instead of responding, he pulls out his phone and taps the screen a couple of times before turning it toward me. My eyes widen as I stare at a picture of Brooklyn and the guy she'd been dancing with. In the photo, his arms are wrapped tightly around her. One hand is curved around her backside as she laughs.

My gaze flicks back to his. "You two aren't together. Brooklyn can do whatever she wants." I'm not trying to twist the knife in any deeper, but he needs to realize that he made this mess. And stalking her around campus won't change anything. It'll only make matters worse. "You cheated on her."

"For fuck's sake, I didn't cheat on her!" He plows one hand through his dark hair in frustration.

"Cassidy."

My attention locks on Cole who I didn't realize was standing behind Austin. "You guys showed up here because someone texted a picture of Brooklyn?"

"It wasn't just of Brooklyn," he says.

Austin scrolls to the next picture. It's one of me and the guy I'd been dancing with. My profile is clear in the shot, but his isn't. It's a little shocking to realize that someone snapped a picture of us and sent it to Austin. A pit grows at the bottom of my belly as I glance from Austin's phone to Cole. He doesn't look upset, but he doesn't look happy either.

"We were just dancing." Cole and I are in such a good place. I don't want to do anything to ruin that.

He searches my gaze for a silent moment before his expression lightens. "Okay."

Air rushes from my lungs in relief that he's dropped the subject so easily.

"Where's Brooklyn?" The question is clipped out as Austin scans the sea of revelers.

I nibble at my lower lip. My fear is that she's still with that guy. Austin is already tap dancing on edge. I don't want anything to push him over the precipice.

"I'm not sure," I hedge. "I was looking for her."

His expression darkens. "Call her. See if she answers her phone, because I've been trying to reach her all night and she won't pick up."

Well, duh. You cheated on her.

I wisely keep that comment to myself.

I nod before pulling out my phone. Hopefully, I can warn her that Austin is here. After four rings, it goes to voicemail. I don't have any other choice but to leave a message.

Once I shove the phone back into my pocket, I clear my throat. "I've already searched the backyard and she's not there."

He swears under his breath, continuing to crane his neck and look around.

Cole slips his arm around my shoulders before tugging me close as we push our way through the mob of people. "Why is Austin here? They aren't together anymore."

He nods toward his friend, who is clearing a path for us. The way his warm breath feathers across my ear sends a little shiver of awareness dancing down my spine.

"Austin swears he didn't cheat on her. He just wants a chance to explain that to Brooklyn, but she won't listen to him."

My eyes narrow as I give him a skeptical look.

Cole returns the expression before raising a brow. "That photo of you didn't exactly look innocent."

My eyes widen. "We were dancing. Absolutely nothing else happened."

Cole releases a steady breath. "I don't want to talk about this right now. Let's find Brooklyn and get out of here, because I can already tell Austin won't be leaving without her."

That's exactly what I was afraid of.

Just as we round the corner into the living room, Austin grounds to a halt before bellowing Brooklyn's name and charging toward the couch. As the crowd separates, I catch sight of Brooklyn sitting on a guy's lap. It's the same cute frat boy she'd been dancing with earlier. One of his hands is stroking her thigh beneath the short black skirt she's wearing. Laughter falls from her lips as he whispers in her ear.

Before Brooklyn realizes what's happening, Austin is yanking her up until she tumbles unsteadily into his arms. The guy she's with jerks to his feet. When they'd been dancing earlier, I hadn't realized how big he was.

He's huge.

Then again, so is Austin. They square off, getting in each other's faces. Brooklyn looks shellshocked before quickly snapping out of it.

"What the hell are you doing?" she yells. "You have no right to come here and pull me away! I can be with whoever I want. We're not together anymore!"

Ignoring the angry frat guy, Austin attempts to cajole her with a soft voice and puppy dog eyes. "Babe, you're just angry. You don't really want to be with this douche. Please come home so we can work this out."

The frat guy takes offense to being called a douche and knocks Austin in the chest, pushing him back a step. "Dude, she doesn't want you. You and your friend need to get the hell out of here before this gets ugly."

By the look on his face, he wouldn't mind if things get ugly.

My gaze slides to the other guys in the room who have taken an interest in the confrontation. My guess is that his friends wouldn't mind it getting ugly either.

We're drawing all sorts of unwanted attention. People are craning their necks, trying to see what's going on.

When my fingers settle on Cole's forearm, his gaze flickers to mine. He doesn't strike me as a brawler, but I know he'll back Austin up if it becomes necessary.

Only wanting to deescalate the situation, I step forward and slide my arm around Brooklyn. "We should probably head home, it's late."

If we don't get Austin out of here, a fight will erupt. And he's not going anywhere unless Brooklyn leaves with us.

Her eyes flash as she snaps, "I don't want to go anywhere with him."

"That's fine, but it's still time to go." I drop my voice. "You don't know anything about that guy."

She levels a hard look at Austin. "Maybe not, but I bet he doesn't screw around with hockey whores."

"I didn't cheat on you," Austin explodes. "You won't even give me a chance to explain what happened. You just assumed I cheated and cut me off."

Brooklyn's eyes narrow to slits. "I saw enough to know what was going down. If I'd stumbled across you five minutes later, it would have been that hockey whore!"

Even though he's simmering with anger, Austin takes a moment to get control of himself before stepping closer to her. "Baby, please, I wouldn't cheat on you. You have to know that. Give me a chance to explain my side of the story and if you don't want to see me after that, I'll leave you alone. Don't go home with this tool just because you're pissed off at me."

Brooklyn still looks like a firework ready to go off, but she doesn't seem quite so angry. With a sigh of relief, I loop my arm through hers. "Let's go, Brook."

She continues to scowl at him. "Fine."

Austin takes his own life in his hands when he reaches out and strokes his fingers down her arm. "Come home with me and we can talk. If you want me to drive you home after that, I will. Promise."

"No." A look of resolve settles across her face as she shakes her head. "We can meet for coffee in the morning. There's no way I'm going home with you." There's a pause before she mutters, "I want to be clear-headed when we discuss this, otherwise, you'll just talk me into bed."

One corner of Austin's mouth hitches. "Would that really be so bad?"

"Yes," she snarls. "I'd hate myself in the morning." She levels him with a hard glare. "And you."

With a shrug, he holds up his hands. "Then we'll discuss it in the morning over breakfast. I'll pick you up at nine."

She purses her lips before stomping away.

"Brooklyn," the frat guy she'd been dancing with calls after her. "You know where to find me when you're done with his cheating ass." He gives her a wink with a smug smile.

Austin growls, his hands tightening, before stalking after Brooklyn as Cole wraps his arm around me. We walk half a block to Cole's car. The short drive to the dorms is an uncomfortable one as Brooklyn stares out the window while Austin tries to coax her into a more receptive mood. Just as Cole parks in front of the dorms, Brooklyn shoots out of the Mustang with her ex hot on her heels.

I glance at Cole and find his attention already locked on mine. His fingers rise to trace the fullness of my lower lip. "Stay with me tonight."

As much as I want to...

"I can't. Brooklyn needs me."

Instead of trying to talk me out of my decision, he reaches over and drags my hand onto his lap. "Are we okay?"

My heart stutters before pounding into overdrive. "I'd thought so."

He nods before glancing at our entwined fingers. "I'm not some crazy jealous guy, and I don't want you to think that I don't trust you. It's just..." his voice trails off as his gaze settles on mine. "I've been burned before, and I'm not interested in going through that again. Does that make sense?"

"Of course, it does."

His expression becomes more closed off. "You have your issues and I have mine."

For some reason, it never occurred to me that Cole might have been hurt before or have triggers of his own.

The thought of another girl causing him pain makes me want to be even more careful with him and what's unfolding between us. Cole has always been so cautious with me and my feeling. I want to be just as careful with his.

My hand rises to drift across his cheek. "I'm sorry. I didn't realize."

"There's still a lot we don't know about each other."

I suck in a deep breath, knowing that he's referring to my past.

An idea takes shape in my brain. Before I can overthink it, I force out the words. "Why don't we go out to dinner on Wednesday. We can sit down and talk everything out."

A smile tugs at the corners of his lips. It's the first time tonight I've seen him look genuinely happy. "Yeah, that sounds good. How about I pick you up at seven after practice?"

I nod.

The need to be close to him thrums through me, and I close the distance between us until my lips can settle on his. With a groan, he hauls me closer until I can straddle his lap in the driver's seat. His hands slip under my sweater as he nips at my mouth. A whimper escapes as his thick cock presses against my core. Thoughts of what it felt like to have him buried deep inside me roll through my head as I flex my hips.

"Come home with me, Cassidy," he begs between deep kisses that leave me breathless and achy.

I moan as he grinds his erection against me. My eyes are on the verge of crossing. It's so tempting to go back to his place. But how can I leave Brooklyn?

The answer is that I can't. Especially when I was already MIA during the actual breakup.

Just as I open my mouth, the passenger door is wrenched open, and Austin stares down at us with a raised brow and a smirk.

"Sorry, dude. If I'm not getting any tonight, neither are you." He jerks his thumb at me. "Out of the car, Cassidy."

He doesn't seem all that sorry to have disturbed us. It's probably for the best. Ten more minutes and we might have taken this further.

I make a noise that is a cross between a groan and a chuckle as Cole kisses me one last time.

"For fuck's sake, let's go," Austin snaps. "I'd tell you to get a room, but I think you'd actually do it."

"Give us a minute," Cole grumbles before his lips stroke over mine and heat me up all over again.

His kisses are seriously dangerous. And I love it. Love that they now belong to me.

Austin pounds on the top of the car with his hand as he waits for me to climb out. As I do, I straighten my clothing. I should probably be embarrassed to be caught straddling Cole, but I'm not.

Instead of smiling at the realization, my expression turns stern as I hold Austin's gaze. "I really hope, for your sake, that you didn't cheat on her. She'll never forgive you."

The smirk falls away as a solemn expression replaces it. "I swear that I didn't cheat on her, Cassidy."

With nothing left to say, I nod before turning toward the dorms.

Even though Brooklyn is angry, I think she really cares about him. I've never seen her upset over a guy. She usually flits from one boy to the next without so much as a backward glance.

That doesn't seem to be the case this time.

21

CASSIDY

"It's been two weeks since I last saw you, tell me how everything is going." Dr. Thompson skims over her notes before her gaze settles on mine.

I draw in a steady breath and silently marvel at my answer. "It's been good." My mind tumbles over the past couple of weeks before reiterating, "It's actually been really good."

When was the last time I could say that?

It feels like forever.

Six months ago, I'd been teetering on the brink of depression and feeling anxious most of the time.

Her lips lift into a smile. "And school? That's going well?"

"I've still got straight A's. I'm going to talk to a couple of my professors about changing my courses for next semester. I need something more challenging. What I'm enjoying most is my Psych class. The subject matter is so interesting." I pause before admitting the path I've been considering. "I'm thinking about changing my major to Psychology, and maybe going into counseling."

A thoughtful expression crosses her face as she nods. "That's a wonderful idea, Cassidy. I know the university has excellent internship opportunities available to their students. What about tutoring? Are you still able to make that mesh with your schedule?"

"I'm working about ten hours a week at the tutoring center, and I still enjoy it." A smile hovers at the corners of my lips as I shrug. "There are so many people who hate math, but I love it. I like being able to help other students grasp the concepts."

"You're right, not many people feel that way about mathematics. You might want to consider going into a teaching program. I think you'd be an excellent teacher. It's just another option to consider."

For the first time in more than a year, I feel like the possibilities for my future are limitless. I can achieve whatever I set my mind to, as long as I commit myself and work hard.

"After failing out last year, I wasn't sure if I'd have the grades to get into a teaching program." What happened last year still embarrasses me, but with time and distance, it's fading.

"I can understand your concern. Acceptance into the School of Education is competitive. If it's something you're interested in, we'll find a way. Think it over. You have time before you need to make any big decisions. I would also suggest that you set up an appointment at the career counseling center. They could help you research both professions."

Optimism fills me. "Okay, I'll do that."

"How's hockey going? Still enjoying it as much as you were before?"

When a wide grin spreads across my face, she says with a chuckle, "I can see that you are."

"I love it. There's no longer any pressure for me to perform, and it feels fun again. Just like it used to before my dad started planning my entire future around it." My mind drifts back to the past. "Where I'd go to college. The camps and clinics I needed to attend. All the extra practices and workouts." Somewhere along the way, hockey stopped being enjoyable and became more of a job. One I had to be perfect at. "After getting kicked off the team last year, I never expected to play again, but it feels great to be out there."

"Isn't that nice? To play for yourself and have fun. It seems like somewhere along the way, that piece got lost. I'm glad you were able to rediscover that. When was the last time you actually enjoyed playing hockey?"

I scour my brain before shaking my head. "I don't remember. Probably elementary school, before I started playing on a travel team." Even though I enjoyed being part of a girls' team, that was when the pressure to stand out intensified. Every game had to be my best.

Her eyes sharpen as they hold mine. "Now it's about the joy you feel on the ice."

"Yes, it is. I don't have to worry about impressing coaches or scouts," there's a pause before I add in a softer voice, "or my dad." As soon as the words leave my lips, my heart constricts.

She nods as if understanding how painful the admission was. "I'm glad you realize that. In a way, flunking out released you from the constant pressure you'd been operating under for years."

Taken aback, I whisper, "Are you saying I sabotaged myself on purpose?"

A heavy silence falls over us before she says, "I don't have that answer."

I drop my gaze, staring down at my fingers as they twist in my lap. I've spent a lot of time thinking about how I self-destructed last year.

It's only in hindsight that I realize I've been a ticking time bomb. And when I'd detonated, not only had I destroyed myself, but my relationship with my family. All these thoughts circle through my head before I force myself to meet her gaze.

"I think the pressure of playing at such a high level, attending such a rigorous school, needing to be perfect…it all just got to me until I couldn't deal with it anymore."

"But that's not the case here?"

"No. Everything feels different. It's like night and day."

I'm not worried about self-destructing. I'm more in control than I was before. I have a better understanding of myself and what I can handle." I gulp in a breath before forcing it out again. "And my father is no longer controlling everything. I think that had a lot to do with it. Up until I'd left for college, he'd regimented my entire life. I followed the schedule and didn't ask questions. Without him there, I'd fallen apart."

Giving voice to the words makes me feel pathetic. I'd been eighteen years old. I should have been able to handle everything on my own.

"Have you learned anything from that experience? Is there anything good you can take away from it?"

Anything good?

As soon as the snort escape, my eyes widen. Dr. Thompson's lips tremble in response.

"I don't know," I finally say when it becomes apparent she's waiting for a response. "Failing out, losing everything the way I did, was the worst experience of my life. But it did make me realize that, ultimately, I'm the one in control. It also taught me that I'm stronger than I thought. I can get through anything if I take it one step at a time and stay focused on what's important." I pause for a moment, processing what I've just verbalized. "I've learned that ignoring an issue won't make it go away. It's better to tackle problems head-on instead of trying to sweep them under the rug. Realizing you need help and seeking out assistance doesn't make you weak. Maybe if I'd talked with my coach or adviser, everything wouldn't have spiraled so far out of control."

Dr. Thompson nods, agreeing with everything I've voiced. "It certainly sounds like you've learned a lot about yourself and what you're capable of doing when life doesn't go your way. You need to give yourself a little credit. It took a lot of courage for you to return to school this fall after failing. Not to mention, you've picked up a hockey stick and are playing again."

A lump settles in the middle of my throat.

She leans forward. "You should be proud of yourself. Everything you've achieved this semester has been hard-fought, and you shouldn't discount that because you perceive your freshman year to be a failure. From where I'm sitting, you've grown quite a bit as a person, and you've learned a lot of important life lessons that will stick with you for the rest of your life."

I wish my parents could see everything through her lens.

She straightens on her seat before changing the subject. "How is everything going with the boy you've been seeing?"

I'm about to say his name before she stops me. "Just use a first initial. I see a lot of students on campus, and I want to keep things as private and separate as I can, okay?"

"Yeah." Knowing that she's safeguarding my personal information as well, makes me feel more at ease. I decide to use the initial of his last name. "Umm, M."

"Are you and M still seeing each other?"

Sometimes it's difficult to believe how much Cole has come to mean to me in such a short period of time. "Yes, we're still going out."

"Tell me how the relationship is progressing."

She jots down a few notes as I talk. "It's really good." I laugh just a little bit before shaking my head. "I know I keep saying that everything is good, but it really is. I like him a lot. He's so different from any other guy I've been with."

She studies me before asking, "Are you being careful?"

It takes a moment for her meaning to sink in. When it finally does, I shift uncomfortably in my seat. "We're using condoms and I've made an appointment at the student clinic on campus for birth control." Heat floods my cheeks as I force myself to hold her gaze.

"Have you opened up about last year?"

My mouth turns cottony. "We're going out to dinner tonight, and I'm going to tell him everything."

"How does that make you feel?"

"Nervous."

"Being vulnerable with another person can be difficult. But it's the only way to have an honest relationship." She pauses before searching my eyes. "Do you feel panicky? I know discussing this subject with M probably feels scary."

I close my eyes to better assess the way my body feels. My heart is pounding a little harder than normal and my chest is a bit tight, but it's not terrible. It certainly isn't debilitating. I can breathe through it using the techniques I've learned.

"I'm all right, but I know I'll be nervous when it comes time to tell him."

"Maybe you should consider having this conversation when you're alone and not in the middle of a crowded restaurant being interrupted by the waitstaff. What do you think about that?"

I turn her words over in my head. "Yeah, that might work better. Maybe we can stop somewhere on the way home or go back to his place and talk."

"That sounds like a good plan." She searches my gaze. "If this boy is the person you think he is, then he'll understand that everyone makes mistakes. No one is perfect." There's a pause before she adds, "At some point, *you* need to forgive yourself for what happened."

I nod, praying she's right and Cole will understand that I'm not the same girl I was last year.

As far as forgiving myself…

Well, I'm nowhere ready to do that. Sometimes I wonder if I'll ever be able to forgive myself for throwing everything away.

22

CASSIDY

"I've never been here before." My fingers fidget with my skirt before smoothing the fabric out. The only thing I can focus on is that by the end of the evening, Cole will know all of my secrets.

As the hostess seats us in the dining room, her gaze continuously strays to Cole. It's almost comical how oblivious he is to her lingering looks. A grin springs to my lips as she returns to the front of the restaurant.

"What?" A smile curves his lips upward as his golden-hued eyes lock on mine. Cole has such a direct, unflinching stare. Sometimes I wonder if he can see straight down to my soul.

"Nothing." Glancing away from him, I look around the cute Italian restaurant Cole chose for us. "This place is really nice."

There are crisp white cloths covering each table and the lighting is dim. Even though the atmosphere is intimate, I notice other students dining here as well. It seems like a strangely popular place for being so far from campus. My guess is that the aroma permeating from the kitchen is the reason for that. Although, it's doubtful I'll be able to force much down.

Cole takes in the interior as if seeing it through my eyes. I'm surprised by the hint of sadness that lurks in his eyes. "My parents used to take me here when I was a kid. It was my dad's favorite restaurant."

Not understanding the pensive look or somber tone, I ask, "Do you still come here with your family?"

His gaze falls to the menu on the table. Silence falls over us as he sucks in a breath before releasing it. Only then does he glance up again. There's a heaviness to the atmosphere that wasn't there before.

"My dad died when I was ten."

Stunned by the admission, I reach across the table and cover his hand with my own. "I'm so sorry," I whisper, "I didn't know."

How is it that I didn't know something so important?

The loss of a parent…that devastating.

He gives me a forced smile, one that's meant to be reassuring. "It happened a long time ago."

I shake my head unable to fathom what it would be like to lose my mom or dad. "That must have been really difficult." I gulp as hot waves of emotion flood my chest. Difficult doesn't begin to describe that kind of loss.

Devastating.

"He was hit by a drunk driver and died at the scene. There wasn't anything that could have been done for him. The kid who caused the accident walked away without a scratch."

My heart twists as I squeeze his hand. "That's terrible. I'm so sorry."

The sentiment feels flimsy. There's nothing I can say that will dull the pain of his loss. Losing a parent so abruptly…

I can't imagine it.

My parents and I are going through a rough patch, but they're still there if I need them. Hopefully, with enough time, we'll be able to mend what's broken between us.

Cole doesn't have that luxury.

"For a long time, life really sucked." His gaze drops to the table. "I guess that's why I have a hard time understanding how people can just cut each other off. No one would do that if they understood what it felt like to have someone ripped from their lives. There are no second chances to repair relationships. You have to make peace with their death the best you can and move on."

A wet lump of sawdust settles in the middle of my throat, making it impossible to breathe as his words churn through my head.

What can I say to that?

Cole doesn't have a father, and would probably give anything to have him back in his life, while my family is barely on speaking terms.

It all feels so pointless.

A heavy silence falls over us as we sit quietly, each lost in our own private thoughts.

When he clears his throat, I glance up. "The tattoo on my side is for my dad. It's the Mathews family coat of arms. I wanted something permanent that would be with me forever since he couldn't be. Every time I look at it, I'm reminded of how much he meant to me and how much I loved him."

His thickly spoken words have unspent emotion pricking the backs of my eyes. My heart twists for the little boy Cole had once been.

The one who'd lost his father.

The one who still misses him.

"I'm sorry. I wanted this to be a nice dinner. I didn't mean for our conversation to get so heavy." He reaches for my hand before bringing my fingers to his lips and pressing a soft kiss against my knuckles.

"So...any idea what you want to order?"

I blink, trying to shake off the oppressiveness of the moment.

Pasta is out of the question. There's no way I can stomach something so heavy. "I think I'll just get a salad."

His brows pinch together. "The spaghetti and meatballs are amazing. Sure you don't want to try it?"

I shake my head before giving him a slight smile. Attempting to steer our conversation toward lighter terrain feels impossible after what Cole shared. Part of me wants to come clean and blurt out everything just to get it out in the open.

Our server stops by to take our order, and within fifteen minutes, our plates are bought out. I'm even less hungry than I was before. I don't know how much longer I can sit here and nervously pick at my salad.

Cole notices my lack of appetite. "Are you okay?"

"Yeah, I'm fine." This dinner hasn't gone as expected.

He reaches across the table and nabs my fingers with his own. "I'm sorry, I wanted tonight to be nice. We've never really gone out before, and I wanted it to be special. That's why I brought you here." A hint of a smile curves his lips upward. "Note to self—don't talk about dead father on first real date. Total buzzkill."

I shake my head, unwilling to make light of such tragedy. My heart aches for Cole and all the things he missed out on with his father. It makes my own situation seem foolish because it's self-inflicted.

"No, I'm glad you told me." It doesn't escape me that I want to know everything about him, even though I'd rather keep certain pieces of my past buried where no one can find them.

He squeezes my hand. "Are you ready to get out of here?"

I hate to admit it, but I'm relieved that dinner is over. At this point, I want to find a quiet place where we can talk.

"I need to use the bathroom and then we can leave."

He nods as I slide from the booth and find the ladies' room at the back of the restaurant. As I stand in front of the mirror, I give myself a silent pep talk.

I can do this.

I'll tell him and everything will be just fine.

He'll understand.

I straighten my shoulders before heading back to the table. My pace slows when I notice someone sitting across from Cole. A prickle of unease snakes down my spine as I realize it's the guy I was dancing with at the party.

What's he doing here, and why is he sitting with Cole?

My gaze flits to Cole just in time to see him shake his head as confusion settles across his features.

My feet feel frozen in place. I'm almost afraid to join them. It's no more than a heartbeat later when Cole glances away from the guy and our gazes collide. I don't have a clue what's going on between them, but I can tell that something isn't right.

"Cassidy."

When he holds out his hand, I have no choice but to cross the space. As I reach the table, Cole grabs my fingers and pulls me down beside him in the booth.

Anxiety bubbles up inside me until it feels like I'll choke on it.

Cole gestures toward the guy sitting across from him. "Cassidy, this is Luke Wellington. He plays hockey with me."

I glance at Luke before my gaze snaps back to Cole. I have to remind myself that I didn't do anything wrong when I danced with him a few nights ago. Other than that one interaction, what else could this be about?

"Luke thinks you two know each other."

My heart pounds painfully against my ribcage as I admit, "He's the one I danced with at the party Saturday night."

Strangely enough, that explanation has Cole's muscles relaxing. "I'm sure that's it." His gaze flickers to Luke before sliding to mine. "He thinks you two went to the same school last year. Luke is a junior and just transferred from out-of-state. I keep telling him that you're a freshman and it's your first year at Western."

And just like that, the bottom falls out of my world and I'm in freefall. The acidic taste of bile rises up in my throat as my wide gaze settles on Luke again and I search his face with more care. It's only then that something clicks in the far recesses of my brain. If he hadn't pushed the issue, it's doubtful I would have recognized him. It makes me wonder if a small part inside me had tried to mentally block it out.

But I see it now.

Luke played on the men's hockey team at Dartmouth last year. Maybe second or third string. He hadn't been clean shaven like he is now. As recognition sets in, my stomach sinks to the bottom of my toes as it all falls jarringly into place. My breath hitches painfully. In that moment, I want to bolt from the restaurant.

"You look just like someone I went to school with. The resemblance is kind of freaky." He continues to scrutinize every inch of my face, just like when we'd danced together. "Do you have a sister or cousin who plays women's hockey at Dartmouth?"

A fine sweat breaks out across my palms as I shake my head. "Nope, no sisters or cousins at Dartmouth."

Even though he shrugs, the look in his eyes says he doesn't believe me. The silence at the table turns stifling.

"I guess you've got a doppelgänger out there, Cassidy," he says nonchalantly.

It takes effort to pull my stiff lips into a thin smile. "Yeah, maybe."

Bile churns at the bottom of my belly like a washing machine on spin cycle.

Gaze holding mine captive, he leans toward me, pressing against the table that separates us. "The similarities are almost uncanny."

I need to get out of here right now.

He remembers that horrible night.

Even thinking about it makes me cringe as panic spreads through me like poison.

Breathe in through your nose and out through your mouth.

Breathe in through your nose and out through your mouth.

The last thing I want is for Cole to hear the entire sordid story from Luke.

As if in slow-motion, I turn to Cole. "I'm ready to go, if you are."

Relief washes over his expression as he nods. As we come to our feet, I scoot away from the table. Nerves prickle along my skin.

Luke rises to his feet and nods to a table full of guys across the restaurant.

Cole gives them a chin lift in greeting before clapping Luke on the shoulder. "All right, I'll see you at practice tomorrow."

"Yup. Catch you later, man." His gaze locks on me. "It was nice seeing you again, Cassidy." His words are light, but there's an undercurrent woven throughout them.

"You, too." I force a slight smile before hightailing it from the dining area and shoving through the glass doors. As soon as I'm outside, I inhale gulps of chilly air, needing to calm my racing heart.

How can I turn around and tell Cole the truth when I just lied? And Luke didn't look convinced either. He remembers the night I've tried so hard to forget.

It's one thing for me to rehash last year without anyone else knowing the details, but now Luke is at Western. He saw me at my absolute worst and probably knows things I can't remember.

Even if I could have gone back to Dartmouth, I wouldn't have. Western was supposed to be a fresh start. No rumors or whispers. No ghosts from the past to haunt me.

The little bit of salad I'd forced myself to choke down roils in my belly, and for one awful moment, I wonder if I'll be sick in the middle of the parking lot.

"Cassidy?" I jump as Cole lays a hand on my shoulder. "Are you okay? You don't look so good." He searches my eyes in the darkness under the bright parking lot lights.

I glance away, not wanting him to see too much. I can't tell him the truth.

Not now.

My plan had been to get it all out in the open so there wouldn't be any more secrets between us, but the words are sticking in my throat like a lump of wet sawdust.

With fingers that tremble, I stroke my temple. "I had a bit of a headache before you picked me up and it's gotten worse. Would you mind if we cut this short and you drop me at the dorms? I'll feel better if I lie down for a while." It's not a total lie. A massive headache is brewing.

He wraps his arm around my shoulders before pressing a kiss against the top of my head. "Of course. I'm sorry about tonight." A weak chuckle escapes from him. "It didn't exactly go the way I planned."

It's a relief to know that in less than fifteen minutes I'll be at the dorms. And then I can sort through this whole mess and figure out what I'm going to do.

As we drive back to campus, I stare out the passenger side window. Just like Cole, I'd imagined tonight going differently. Instead, all I've managed to do is heap more lies onto the ones that need to be untangled.

23

CASSIDY

"Cass, tell me what's wrong."

Brooklyn strokes my back as I lie curled up in the middle of my bed. Once I returned to my room, the tears started flowing and refused to stop.

"I can't help you if you won't talk to me," she says.

Luke Wellington is here at Western.

That thought plays on a constant loop inside my head.

He should be at Dartmouth. What happened should be a distant memory. But that's clearly not the case, because he's here. If the look in his eyes is any indication, he remembers everything.

"Did you and Cole have a fight?" Her voice dips, becoming low. "Did you break up?"

I shake my head, unable to get the words out.

I had come to Western to forget about the mistakes I've made. I didn't want to be *that girl*. And now there was someone here who could breathe life into the rumors all over again.

"Just tell me what's wrong and we'll work it out, I promise." She squeezes one shoulder. "You know that I'm here for you and I'll help any way I can."

With a swipe at my eyes, I haul myself up into a sitting position before searching Brooklyn's concerned face. Since rooming together this semester, Brooklyn and I have become closer friends than we were in high school. She'd been right when she'd said that I allowed our friendship to fall by the wayside.

It hadn't been intentional, but it had happened, nevertheless. If there weren't hockey practice or games to attend, there'd been a strict gym schedule to adhere to and schoolwork to plow my way through. There'd never been time for anything or anyone else.

Including Brooklyn.

As I search her earnest gaze, I realize exactly what I'd forfeited. Where had my hard work and sacrifice gotten me? What did I have to show for myself?

No hockey scholarship.

No prestigious college.

No friends.

No family to stand behind me.

Maybe I owed it to Brooklyn to tell her the truth. Even though I hadn't been a good friend, she's still here, standing by my side. Ready to offer her support.

Once I start talking, it's impossible to stop.

If the wide-eyed expression is any indication, then I've completely shocked her. Throughout the entire story she remains silent. No comments, no questions, no judgment. She sits beside me and listens to every word as it pours out of my mouth. When I'm finished, I collapse onto the stack of pillows behind me.

"Jeez, Cass, I had no idea. I'm sorry you went through all that by yourself. I wish you would have called me."

I sniffle, relieved the tears have long since dried.

Even though I'm emotionally exhausted, opening up and getting it all out has made me feel lighter. Unfortunately, I'm still unsure what to do about Cole. Or Luke, for that matter. Now that I've shared everything with Brooklyn, I no longer feel so alone. It helps to know that my friend's opinion of me hasn't changed.

"You're right, I should have." I glance away. "Any idea how I should handle this with Cole?"

She presses her lips together before saying, "I think you need to tell him everything before Luke beats you to the punch, because he obviously remembers you."

Deep down, I knew that would be her answer. In hindsight, I realize Luke hadn't just stopped by our table to say hello to his teammate. My brows draw together, because he could have forced the issue and outed me if he'd wanted to.

So...why hadn't he?

Nausea hits me like a punch to the gut. Even before Brooklyn gave me her opinion, I realized that telling Cole the truth was the only option available to me.

She adds, "The only other thing would be to stop seeing him altogether and distance yourself from the team. If you're not around, then maybe Luke will forget about you."

Even though I don't want to lose Cole, I turn the idea over in my head.

"He could still tell people what he knows." My heart twists at the thought of all this resurfacing again when I'd hoped it was behind me. "I can't stay at Western if he starts spreading rumors."

Her face falls. "I don't want you to leave."

The idea of starting over again at a different college is daunting. Brooklyn is the only one I can count on right now. "I don't want to leave, either. I like it here."

Western now feels like home. I'm enjoying my classes and rooming with Brooklyn. We're closer than ever. I love tutoring, and the women's hockey team. After last year, I never thought I'd play again and it's turning out to be so much fun.

And then there's Cole. I think I fell for him that first night, and I'm still falling.

It would be difficult to leave all this behind.

"Maybe you should talk to him."

A wave of exhaustion crashes over me. "Who, Cole?"

"No." There's a pause as she shakes her head. "Luke."

My eyes widen as my heartbeat thunders under my breast.

No way. I don't even want to see the guy again. I want to pretend he doesn't exist.

"I can't talk to him. I can't relive that again. Even though we're strangers, he was there. He saw…" I shake my head, willing away the images. "I can't do it."

As painful as it is, I know what needs to be done.

"If Cole and I are going to be together, then I need to tell him the truth so he can decide if I'm still the girl he thinks I am."

"It won't change anything." Her fingers wrap around mine before squeezing them. "He likes you, Cass. What happened last year doesn't change who you are." Brooklyn seems so sure of the outcome. I wish I felt half as confident.

"He likes who he *thinks* I am," I whisper. "He doesn't know the real me." I've kept those pieces of myself buried deep down where he couldn't see.

"Yes, he does, and so do I. What you told me hasn't changed my opinion." After a beat of silence, she adds, "Everyone makes mistakes." Her green eyes flash with fire. "If he can't see how wonderful you are, then screw him. You're better off without the guy."

Tears well in my eyes. Her words are exactly what I needed to hear. "Thank you. That means a lot to me."

Brooklyn's lips lift into a slight smile. "It's the truth." There's a pause before she takes us right back to where we started. "So…what are you going to do now?"

24

CASSIDY

*N*erves prickle at the bottom of my belly as I stand on the front porch and knock on the door. A few seconds tick by before it swings open and Alex stares down at me.

"Hi." It takes effort to force out the question. "Is Cole here?"

"Hey." lex jerks his head toward the second floor. "He's up in his room. Go on up."

With that, he swings around and leaves me standing on the porch before walking into the living room where a bunch of guys from the hockey team are sitting around playing video games.

Avoiding eye contact, I slip past them before racing up the stairs and taking them two at a time. I need to get this over with before I chicken out.

Or Luke suddenly decides to tell him first.

I suck in a breath, trying to settle everything inside me before wrapping my knuckles against the thick wood. When his muffled voice greets me from the other side, I push it open and find Cole at his desk, bent over a textbook. He does a double take before rising to his feet and closing the distance that separates us.

His brows draw together as his gaze searches my face. "Are you feeling better?"

I almost wince. It's just another lie for me to untangle. My shoulders collapse at the thought.

Avoiding the question, I say instead, "Do you have a few minutes to talk?" Another round of nerves detonates in my belly as I gesture to the books on his desk. "It won't take long."

"I'm never too busy for you." Expression softening, he reaches out and grabs my hand before towing me to him. Once his arms wrap around me, I squeeze my eyes shut and pray this won't be the last time we're together like this. "I'm glad you stopped by."

I hope he feels that way after I've gotten everything out.

Untangling himself from me, Cole walks us to the bed so we can sit down. My hands are still clasped within his. The physical connection is all that's keeping me going. Unable to hold his searching gaze, mine skitters away as I try to remember what I want to say and how I want to say it.

A long silence stretches between us.

"Cassidy?" He reaches out, touching the side of my face with gentle fingers. "Tell me what's going on. I can tell that you're being eaten up with something."

Now that I'm here, I have no idea how to begin. It feels as if everything in my life led up to that one turning point. One bad mistake spiraling into another and then another until I was all but drowning in them.

"Baby?"

The soft way he says the endearment tears me up inside. I shake my head and stare at my knotted fingers until they blur before my eyes.

"You wanted to know what happened to me..." my voice trails off as I peek at him.

He strokes the side of my face as concern floods his eyes. "I want to know because I want to understand you better."

My insides feel just as tangled as my fingers.

When I remain silent, he presses his lips to mine.

I shudder, needing to feel his warmth flooding through my veins, filling all the cold dark places inside me. I'd thought it would be a quick kiss, a bit of reassurance to give me the strength I needed to continue. As it unfolds, he deepens the caress. Or maybe I do.

What I know is that I need to feel the intimate connection between us.

I whimper when his tongue slips inside my mouth. Sparks of desire shoot through my body. His hands slide from my face to my shirt before he quickly tugs it over my head. Needing to feel his bare skin, I do the same, yanking his shirt up as he unhooks my bra, until we're both naked from the waist up.

"God, baby, I want you so badly."

Before I can say anything, his mouth claims mine as he palms my breasts, stroking the pebbled nipples before leaning down to suck one stiff bud between his lips. With a groan, my fingers tunnel through his messy strands. He releases the tightened peak before kissing his way down to the waistband of my skirt.

A few heartbeats later, I find myself flat on my back with my skirt being pulled down my hips and thighs. My panties quickly follow suit until I'm completely bared to him.

"I need to be inside you."

Intensity brims in his whiskey-colored eyes as they linger over every inch of me before locking on mine. "You're so fucking beautiful, Cassidy."

The thickness of his murmured words does strange things to my insides.

One hand settles between my legs before he parts them. His attention drops to my wet heat. Air gets clogged in my throat as he presses a kiss against my core, dragging the velvety softness of his tongue across me. He widens my thighs before circling my clit and sucking it into his mouth. My body tightens, arching off the mattress, as every nerve ending throbs and sizzles at the intensity that crashes over me, threatening to suck me under.

"So fucking beautiful," he whispers against my heated flesh before adding, "and mine."

I squeeze my eyes shut, wanting that sentiment to be true. I've never wanted anything more in my life. In a short amount of time, Cole has come to mean everything to me.

He plunges his tongue deep inside my body as he rubs the pad of his thumb against my clit in tiny circles that make me feel as if I'll burst out of my skin. A moan escapes as I come undone and splinter apart. Even after my body settles, he continues to stroke my oversensitive flesh with both his fingers and mouth until I can't bear another moment of it.

"I need you inside me." I want him to fill me up until he's all I can think about. All I can remember.

With one last kiss pressed against my pussy, he rolls away, grabs a condom from the nightstand, and crawls up my body. Once his cock nudges my entrance, he sinks inside me one inch at a time until he's buried deep, filling me to the brim. Our gazes stay fastened as he begins to move.

"I think I'm falling for you, Cassidy," he whispers before taking my lips with his own. The way his body rocks against mine makes me feel like we are connected in the most intimate way possible.

When he finally comes, I follow him over the edge. Even though my body is exhausted by our lovemaking, my mind is restless with what still needs to be said.

After returning from the bathroom, I strip off the oversized T-shirt he'd given me and crawl naked into bed with him. He gathers me up in his arms and presses me against his chest, where my head settles. The steady beating of his heart fills my ears. It takes everything I have inside me to gather my courage. As much as I don't want to ruin this perfect interlude, I can't allow everything to linger between us any longer.

"Cole?" I whisper into the darkness.

I still, straining to hear any sound.

"Cole? Are you awake?"

The question is met with silence. Not a moment later, his deep, even breathing fills the void and I realize with a sinking heart that he's already fallen asleep. For a long time, I stare at the ceiling before finally drifting into a restless slumber.

When I wake the next morning, the sheets beside me are empty and Cole is gone. There's a piece of paper propped up on his nightstand that lets me know he's at an early morning practice.

I rub the sleep from my eyes and stare at the note before flopping back onto the pillow. My intention had been to get everything out into the open so I could finally breathe again. Instead, we'd tumbled into bed, and I'd allowed myself to get wrapped up in his body and the way he makes me feel. A shiver dances down my spine even remembering the delicious way he had played with my body.

Irritated with myself for prolonging the inevitable, I throw an arm over my eyes and wonder if I'll ever find the courage to tell him. The longer I allow my past to linger between us, the more difficult it becomes to force out the truth.

CASSIDY

"Hey, Cassidy, wait up."

Not recognizing the voice, I turn at the sound of my name. My muscles freeze as I catch sight of Luke trotting toward me. Unable to move, I hitch the brown leather bag higher onto my shoulder as if clutching it for dear life.

When he reaches my side, he flashes a bright smile as if we're life-long friends.

"Hey." Even though it's difficult, I force my stiff lips into something that hopefully resembles a smile as my heart jackhammers a painful staccato beneath my breast.

"I've been looking all over for you."

Why?

My mouth turns cottony, making it impossible to swallow. What could we possibly have to say to one another?

Nothing good. Certainly nothing I want to discuss. Especially with him.

"Are you headed this way." He nods in the direction I've been walking.

It's tempting to shake my head and take off down another path. I don't want to spend another moment in his company. Already my chest is tightening.

I open my mouth to lie and hear myself blurt instead, "Yeah."

He gives me another smile as if totally oblivious to the tension that permeates the atmosphere. "I have Poli-sci in ten minutes."

"Econ," I respond grudgingly as my mind races, trying to figure a way out of this mess.

When my brain remains frustratingly blank, I hasten my steps, hoping that if I walk fast enough, there won't be enough time for us to talk.

"How long have you been seeing Cole?"

The unexpected question makes me stumble. He reaches out, his fingers wrapping around my elbow to steady me. A shiver of awareness slides through me at the unexpected contact.

"I'm all right," I mumble, feeling like an idiot.

It takes a few moments for his hand to fall away. I give him a bit of side-eye as I quicken my pace. At this point, I'm practically jogging across campus. It won't be long before I break into a run.

I'm reluctant to give him any information about myself. "For about a month or so." Even though the weather is chilly, sweat pops out across my brow.

A thoughtful expression crosses his face as he nods. His gaze returns to mine and like before, I feel it sharpen as if he's searching for something. Air gets lodged in my throat as I wait for an indication as to which direction this conversation will veer.

But he remains silent.

Tension continues to ratchet up inside me as we walk side by side. A scream builds within. Any moment it's going to burst free. Just when I'm about to lose it, Luke reaches out and grabs my hand, pulling me off the concrete pathway onto the grassy stretch of lawn so we're no longer caught up in the swiftly moving foot traffic.

My wide gaze lands on his as everything inside me freezes.

"My class is in Danners," he says in explanation before nodding to the left. "I need to head this way."

Instead of releasing me, his grip tightens. My skin prickles with unease at the intent way he continues to stare.

"All right," I say lightly, carefully trying to tug my hand free. He closes the distance between us until there's no more than a few inches that separate us. My breath hitches at his proximity as I lift my chin to hold his gaze. The way he invades my personal space sets my nerves even more on edge.

With his attention locked on me, he cocks his head. "I realize you're seeing Cole, but can we grab coffee later?"

I blink before slowly shaking my head.

No.

Absolutely not.

I can't imagine sitting down with him. What the hell would we talk about?

That thought has my belly hollowing out because I know *exactly* what he wants to discuss.

"No, I don't think that's a good idea."

"Just as friends," he adds as if that will change my mind.

Again, I shake my head. The urge to flee pounds through me.

As I hold his gaze, memories from last year flood back to me. I remember seeing him around campus before that night. He was on the men's hockey team and had caught my attention. With his short blond hair and blue-gray hazel eyes, there'd been plenty of girls vying for his attention.

Knowing that we both attended Dartmouth last year, and that he had a front row seat to what happened makes me sick to my stomach. Instead of feeling attracted to him, I'm repelled. I want to get away from him as quickly as possible.

"Just think about it, okay?" His voice dips. "I'd like to get together so we can talk."

He leans over and brushes a soft kiss across my cheek. Even when his lips leave my skin, he doesn't retreat. His muscular body invades my space as his gaze searches mine for a long, breathless moment.

Just when I'm afraid he'll push the issue, he squeezes my fingers before saying goodbye, disappearing through the crowd. I'm left standing on the grass next to the walkway as people rush past. It takes a couple of heartbeats before I'm able to gather my scattered thoughts and hurry to class.

The rest of the day passes by in a blur. Later that afternoon, I meet up with Brooklyn for dinner at the Union.

We both order taco salads before sliding into an empty booth buried deep in a corner. I haven't seen her since last night, and I'm sure she'll be brimming with questions.

I'm not wrong.

"How did it go? You told him, right?"

Indie rock plays in the background as other students grab something to eat.

I shake my head before shoving a forkful of lettuce and taco seasoned ground turkey into my mouth. Just like last night at the restaurant, my appetite pulls another vanishing act, leaving only queasiness in its place. At the rate I'm going, I'll lose all the weight I've gained from not working out.

I wince when Brooklyn purses her lips. I know what's going to fly out of her mouth before the words leave her lips.

"Cassidy, you have to tell him before Luke does!"

"I know." With an unhappy huff of breath, I stare at my bowl of leafy greens.

I can't help but wonder how Cole and I veered so offtrack last night. All right, I know exactly what happened.

And you know what?

I can't bring myself to regret it. I never dreamed I could feel so close to another human being.

No longer interested in eating the salad, I drag my fork through it. "I'll talk to him tonight. I promise."

Brooklyn levels me with a hard stare. "I know it's hard, but you have to do it. It'll be so much better coming from you. If Luke says something first, it'll seem like you were keeping the relationship from him." She pauses, brows pinching together as her voice drops. "It might even look like you and Luke had something going on."

My eyes bulge as my mouth tumbles open. "Why would you say that?"

She jerks her shoulders. "I don't know. You both attended the same college last year. He was there the night everything went down. And you were dancing together at that party when someone snapped a picture. At the restaurant, he tried to get you to admit that you knew him." A thoughtful expression flickers across her face. "It's almost like he wants Cole to find out you two know each other."

Everything she just said circles through my head as a fresh wave of nerves ripple across my flesh.

Is Brooklyn right?

Will it now seem like I'm trying to hide our nonexistent relationship from Cole?

My teeth sink into my lower lip as I lean closer to the table. "Want to hear something weird?"

One of her perfectly manicured brows slinks upward. "If it has anything to do with Luke, I don't think so. The situation is already bad enough." When I remain silent, she gestures with her hand to continue. "All right, lay it on me."

"Luke caught up with me when I was walking to Econ earlier this afternoon." I'm still unsure what to think about the encounter. It had been so uncomfortable and stilted.

Her brows nearly hit the ceiling as she shoves a forkful of salad into her mouth. Her expression turns contemplative. "You want my honest opinion?" Before I can say anything, she blurts, "I think he has a thing for you."

Not that I want to feed into her speculations, but I need to tell her everything. "He asked me to grab coffee with him so we could talk."

She holds her fork midair as a knowing glint fills her eyes. "I knew it. He's definitely got a thing for you. My guess is that he's trying to cause trouble between you and Cole."

I shake my head, hoping she's wrong. "I don't think that's the case."

"All right, let's say you're right and I'm totally off base. The only way you'll get it figured out is if you sit down and talk to him."

The look Brooklyn spears me with says that she doesn't think she's wrong.

What I hate most is that she could be right.

"I'm not interested in anything he has to say. I came to Western for a fresh start, and now it feels like everything from last year will be dredged up again." The thought of that happening makes me want to cry. It must show on my face because Brooklyn reaches across the table and lays her hand over mine before giving it a squeeze.

"I know. I swear we'll get through this together." There's a pause before she adds, "You have to tell Cole what happened. Once you do that, it'll make dealing with Luke easier."

She's right.

"Thanks, Brook. It helps talking with you about this." I give her a half-hearted smile as everything swims around in my head. Not wanting to dwell on the situation any longer, I ask, "Anything new on the Austin front?"

"He," she sets her fork down before making exaggerated air quotes with her fingers "claims that Mandi was hanging all over him and wanted to whisper something in his ear, but kissed him instead." Her lips flatten before she tacks, "Which is when I oh-so-conveniently walked in."

"Do you believe him?"

"I don't know. He keeps swearing that he's not interested in Mandi and had no intention of kissing her." She huffs out a breath. "The last thing I want is to spend time worrying that he's screwing around behind my back."

I can understand where she's coming from. No one wants to feel like a paranoid, jealous bitch. Nothing ruins a relationship faster than distrust.

"I still have a hard time believing he would throw your relationship away by messing around with another girl. Especially out in the open, where it could easily get back to you."

Her expression turns thoughtful. "I guess that's true."

"Are you thinking about giving him another chance?"

I like Austin, and them together.

"I haven't made any decisions." She shrugs. "I told him that I needed time to think about it."

"You should take as much time as you need to sort out your feelings."

A smile trembles around her lips. "I'm just not sure how much longer I can hold out. Sex with Austin is seriously hot." Her eyes take on a mischievous glint as she warms to the subject. "Have I mentioned the amazing things he can do with his tongue?"

I lift a hand to stop her. "Unfortunately, you have. And I don't need to hear about it again, thank you very much. Once was more than enough."

A chuckle escapes from her. "Oh, come on, Cass. You can give me all the sexy details on Cole, and I'll dish about Austin. We can compare notes." She waggles her brows. "Maybe exchange some ideas."

Eyes widening, I sputter, "No way!" Then I add, "Absolutely not!"

When she dissolves into a fit of giggles, I consider the possibility that she's messing with me. Although, knowing Brooklyn...probably not. She's already given me the lowdown on several guys she's been with this semester. I have to avert my gaze every time I run into one of them around campus.

Just as my shoulders shake with laughter, a muscular body slides onto the bench next to me. Surprised, I find myself staring into Cole's golden-hued eyes. Not a heartbeat later, he leans over and smacks a kiss against my lips. Even though it's nothing more than a peck, it's enough to get my blood pumping.

"Hey." He pulls away enough to flash a smile at me.

"You'd disappeared before I got back this morning," he murmurs.

The heated look filling his eyes tells me exactly what would have happened had I stuck around.

"Yeah, I had to take off and study for a test."

He reaches out and grabs my bottle of water before taking a long drink. My gaze drops to the column of his throat, watching as the muscles constrict with every swallow.

How can that be so sexy?

"How'd that go?"

My attention snaps back to his face.

His lips lift into another smile as his fingers gravitate to mine, tracing delicate patterns across my skin. A thin shiver works its way through me as he continues to play with my hand.

I clear my throat and focus on the question. "Good." His nearness has my nervousness draining away. It's just so easy to be with him. "It went really well."

He closes the distance between us before kissing me again and whispering against my lips, "Are you going to stay over tonight?"

Desire flashes in his eyes as an answering heat flares to life in my core. For someone who wanted nothing to do with sex a few short months ago, he's flicked a switch inside me. I want him all the time and I love that he's so openly affectionate. I never thought I'd be someone who enjoyed PDA.

Turns out that I do.

My gaze flicks to Brooklyn as Austin slides in next to her. Even though his lips curve into a hopeful smile, her scowl is enough to knock the expression off his face.

I have to nip my lower lip with my teeth to keep from laughing. I get the feeling this is her way of torturing him.

"Um, I'm not sure," I murmur in return.

Not caring about the audience we have, Cole presses his lips against mine. "Last night wasn't enough to persuade you to sleep in my bed from now on?"

It was more than enough to convince me that I never want to sleep anywhere else.

Ever.

When I remain silent, he says, "Cassidy?"

"Yes."

When I finally rip my gaze from his, I find Brooklyn using her fork to shred the last of her salad, and Austin is staring at her with a pensive expression.

"How about I pick you up after practice?" His fingers continue to toy with mine.

I nod, knowing that I can't allow him to distract me as easily as he did last night. No matter what, I have to get everything out in the open so we can move forward.

"All right, I'll see you then." He glances at his teammate before giving me a wink. "You ready to go?"

Austin gives Brooklyn puppy dog eyes as if that will thaw her iciness toward him.

It doesn't.

"Yeah." He sighs in frustration. "Let's get out of here."

CASSIDY

It feels amazing to fly down the ice with the puck before snapping it into the net with a flick of my wrist. When I'm out here, I can shut off everything in my head, and lose myself in the physical exertion.

"You suck, Cassidy!"

Our goalie shakes her head, irritated that I was able to slip another puck past her. I grin around my neon-pink mouth guard before skating to center ice. Sammy glides over before slapping me on the shoulder. I wince from the impact of it. The girl doesn't know her own strength.

"Nice goal. The team really seems to be shaping up. I think we're going to have an awesome season this year. I'm glad you decided to join us."

That makes two of us. Playing with this group of girls has quickly become everything to me. I never thought I'd enjoy hockey again. I wasn't even sure if I'd skate. And I owe it to Cole. He figured it out and found a way to give it to me.

I huff out a tired breath as both of us glide to center ice for another face-off. We scrimmage for another forty minutes. Halfway through the practice, I glance at the bleachers and almost stumble as my gaze zeros in on a lone figure sitting in the stands.

Squinting, I try to get a better look. It can't be who I think it is.

It just can't be.

A thin shiver of unease slithers down my spine. It feels as if Luke's gaze is focused on me. I spin away, thankful there's a number plastered across the back of my practice jersey and not my name.

Why is he here?

Is he actually watching me?

Brooklyn's words from earlier echo throughout my head. The last thing I want is for him to cause problems with Cole.

Seeing him here at practice and running into him on campus earlier…it can't be a coincidence. Gulping down my fear, I try to force him from my mind, but that turns out to be impossible. For the remainder of practice, I can't stop wondering about what he wants from me. The question circles through my head, shooting my focus to hell. It causes me to miss shots I could easily make in my sleep, or misjudge the edge of my skate, which sends me crashing onto the ice.

Every few minutes, I find myself glancing over my shoulder, checking to see if he's still there.

Each time I do, my gaze catches his.

As soon as the buzzer sounds, I jump off the ice and race to the locker room where I quickly shower and change. I'm almost afraid to return to the rink. I'm terrified he'll be waiting for me.

How did he know I was playing hockey again?

Is he following me?

Nausea blooms to life at the bottom of my belly.

Sammy is yanking up her skinny jeans when I ask, "Did you notice the guy in the stands?" Even though I strive for nonchalant, a slight tremble threads its way through my voice.

Not picking up on my anxiety, she shrugs. "Sometimes people like to watch practice. It's not a big deal." Her gaze settles on me with more interest. "Do you know who it was?"

I glance away as my teeth sink into my lower lip. I'm not sure if I should tell her. It's always possible I'm overreacting, right?

"I think it was one of the guys from the men's hockey team." I clear my throat and force out the rest. "Luke something or other."

With a nod, she finishes tying her shoes. "I know who he is. He just transferred in. I think he went to a big school out East. From what I heard, he wasn't getting enough playing time, so he left." She flashes me a sly smile. "I got the lowdown from Cole cause that boy is smoking hot with a capital H."

"Does he have a girlfriend?" For all I know, he was here watching someone else. Maybe he's here watching someone else and I'm just a paranoid freak.

"Not that I know of." Her smile fades as her eyes narrow. "Why? Are you interested?"

I shake my head. As much as I like Sammy, I'm not about to bring up my past with her. "No, not at all."

After shoving gear into her locker, she slams the door shut with a resounding thud. "Good, because my cousin really likes you and," she pauses to flex her pipes, "I'd have to kick your ass if you hurt him. Cole is like a brother to me."

There's no doubt in my mind that Sammy could wipe the floor with me. Even though she's a total hard ass, she's a likable one.

As long as you stay on her good side, that is.

"I won't hurt him." Even as the words spill from my lips, I pray they're true.

"Good, because that guy has been through enough." She gives me a bit of side-eye before packing up her bag. "Has he told you anything about Jackie?"

Jackie?

I would have remembered if Cole brought up another girl.

"No, he hasn't mentioned her."

My mind tumbles over our previous conversations and I wonder if she's the one he'd alluded to after the party when we'd been sitting in his car outside the dorm. I'd gotten the feeling he'd been cheated on.

Sammy nods as if she's not surprised. "He doesn't like to talk about her."

It feels wrong to pump Sammy for information about her cousin when I haven't been forthcoming with my own background. I resist for a handful of seconds before the question shoots out of my mouth.

"Were they together long?"

Sammy remains quiet for a long stretch of moment. Just when I think she'll ignore me, she says, "Yeah. They were friends for most of their lives before dating in high school. They ended up splitting last year. It got pretty ugly."

I sink onto the wooden bench in surprise. "Oh."

I have no idea what I'd been expecting, but that hadn't been it. I'm almost sorry I asked.

They'd been friends their entire lives and dated in high school?

That sounds serious.

Really serious.

"What happened?"

"Never mind. I shouldn't have mentioned anything." She pulls her long blonde hair up into a high ponytail. "If you have questions, you should talk to Cole. I just wanted you to know that he hasn't dated anyone seriously since Jackie, and he really seems into you. After that bitch put him through the wringer last year, he deserves a nice girl." Her lips quirk at the corners as if to soften the heaviness that permeates the air. "And I think that girl is you."

My insides twist painfully as I nod.

She hauls her bag onto her shoulder before asking, "Are you ready to head out? Do you need a ride home?"

The thought of getting into the deathtrap that Sammy calls a car is enough to unsettle my stomach even more than it already is. "No, Cole is picking me up."

I can't stop thinking about what she just revealed.

I guess we both have our secrets.

Oblivious to my inner turmoil, a smile spreads across her face. "Come on, let's get the hell out of here."

As we push out of the locker room door and into the ice arena, my gaze goes to the bleachers. Air gets trapped in my lungs as I scan them. Another team is warming up and skating through drills. A few people dot the stands, but there's no sign of Luke.

Once we push through another set of doors into the lobby, tension leaks from my muscles. When there's still no sign of Luke, I begin to wonder if it was just a figment of my imagination. Instead of dwelling on my paranoia, I shake it off and head to the parking lot with Sammy where we find Cole's Mustang idling at the curb.

He pops open the trunk so I can throw my bag inside before closing it. I give Sammy a wave and slide onto the front seat. As soon as my ass hits the leather, Cole pulls me to him before greeting me with a kiss.

After a heated moment, he whispers, "I missed you."

Not giving me a chance to respond, his mouth crashes onto mine again. As much as I want to lose myself in him, I can't. It feels like my past and future are on a collision course. I need to get everything out before this goes any further.

My palms settle on his chest as I push against him. It takes a moment for Cole to pull back and meet my gaze.

"We need to talk," I say.

"All right, what do you want to talk about?" His attention falls to my mouth as his tongue darts out to lick at his bottom lip.

I glance around the semi-crowded parking lot. "Is there somewhere more private we can go?"

His gaze snaps to mine before he searches my eyes with more care as if only now realizing that what I need to tell him is important.

"Sure." He reaches over and slides the seatbelt across my chest. "This sounds kind of serious."

I draw a deep breath as the familiar feelings of anxiety prickle along my skin, and a thick ball of tension settles in my belly. "I promised to tell you what happened last year and that's what I'm going to do."

The heat filling his eyes moments ago dissipates as he pulls my hand onto his lap and holds it there. A heavy silence falls over us as we drive. By the time he pulls into a gravel parking lot that faces a small lake, I'm so tightly strung with nerves that my stomach is queasy. He cuts the engine before releasing his seatbelt and then doing the same to mine. Silvery moonlight filters in through the windshield, illuminating his eyes as they settle on mine.

My heart riots painfully as if it'll beat right out of my chest.

I need to get this over with.

Cole tightens his grip on my fingers like he will never let me go, as the other hand slides across my cheek until he can cradle it in his palm. Not wanting to see the questions that flood his eyes, I squeeze mine shut.

"Cassidy."

It's only when I open them to meet his steady gaze that he says, "Whatever you have to tell me doesn't matter. All right?" There's a pause. "It doesn't matter at all."

"It does." He needs to understand how the past has shaped me into the person I am today.

"I've already told you that I'm falling for you. Whatever you have to tell me won't change that. I promise."

"Just let me get this out, okay? I want you to understand what happened last year and then you can decide if it matters."

In answer, he leans over and takes my lips with his own. His tongue slips inside my mouth to mingle and dance with my own. A whimper escapes from me as he attempts to suck me under until I can't think straight. I lose track of how much time passes as his lips coast over mine and he licks at the inside of my mouth.

"Please," I gasp, breaking away from him, "let me get this out. It's eating me up inside."

Instead of backing away, his gaze holds mine as one hand settles on my shoulder and the other continues to stroke my cheek. The intensity of his stare makes me feel like a ball of tightly wound nerves. When a tremor slides through me, Cole's grip tightens as if trying to anchor me to him.

"I'm not a freshman like you think I am. Well, credit-wise I am,but age-wise, I'm almost twenty…like you."

"Okay," he says slowly.

I gulp in another breath before forcing it out. "I graduated from high school the same year as you, and then I started at Dartmouth in the fall."

"Dartmouth?" He repeats the word as if it's foreign. I can almost see his mind tumble back to the restaurant and Luke asking if I'd attended that school. And me lying about it.

"You and Luke were at the same school last year?"

Heat fills my cheeks. "Just for the first semester."

Confusion floods his voice and fills his eyes. "I don't understand why you'd lie about it."

Of course, he doesn't.

"That's what I need to explain." My heart pounds into overdrive until it becomes painful. I remind myself to take slow, even breaths. If I don't calm myself from the inside out, there's no way I'll get through this. When I start, it's from the beginning. I don't know any other way to make him understand.

"Ever since I was a little girl, my dad talked about me playing college hockey out East. Once I became older, that school became Dartmouth. It was the goal I spent my teenage years working toward. You probably understand what that's like," my gaze sifts through his in the darkness, searching for some measure of understanding, "to commit yourself so completely to a sport."

When he nods, I continue. "I ate, slept, practiced, and went to school. That was the extent of my existence. There was always so much pressure to succeed, excel, push through to the next level."

Cole dips his chin but otherwise remains silent.

"When I committed to Dartmouth in the fall of my senior year, I'd assumed some of the pressure would be off and I could ease up. Maybe even relax and have some fun. Instead, everything become more intense. I needed to keep my grades high, and my dad had me working out every day, in addition to team practices. He said playing at the next level would be tough, the competition more challenging, and I needed to train harder in order to be physically and mentally prepared." I shrug as my mind tumbles back to all the work and sacrifices that have been required of me.

Sacrifices I'd ended up pissing away.

"I spent the summer working out with trainers and skating with private coaches. I swam and ran for extra conditioning. When I finally left for college in August, I was exhausted and burned out." I'd been in the best physical shape of my life, but mentally, I was a miserable, stressed-out mess. "And my dad had been right. Playing at the next level was more challenging. I was skating with and against girls who'd been playing for two or three years in college. Instead of being at the top of my game and one of the best players out on the ice, I was barely holding my own. No matter how hard I worked, it was never enough. It didn't take long before I was drowning in my classes."

I shake my head, remembering how rigorous the workload had been. "In hindsight, if I hadn't been playing hockey, I would have been able to focus more on school. My grades wouldn't have been perfect but at least they would have been..." my voice trails off as I get tangled up in the memories.

For a moment, I sit in silence before mentally shaking myself out of the past as it slyly wraps around me. "Not only was I failing academically, but I was also failing at something I'd always excelled at. The one thing I was talented at and took pride in. Hockey."

Regret and shame sink their sharp teeth into me. It's Cole's soft voice that breaks through the chaotic whirl of my thoughts.

"I can understand all of that, Cassidy. I've felt the same kind of pressure to succeed. What I don't understand is why you'd lie to me about it."

"There's more."

"Okay. Tell me the worst of it so I can understand what changed you so much."

I inhale a breath, prepared to purge the rest from my body. "About a month into the semester, I was already failing a couple of my classes. Even though I studied, it didn't seem to matter. I was always behind and trying to play catch up. No matter how hard I worked in practice, it wasn't enough. The coach barely noticed me, and the other girls didn't respect me. I'd never..."

It was so hard to wrap my lips around the words.

Even now, almost a year later.

"I'd never failed at anything. And now, I was failing across the board. I didn't know how to handle it. I couldn't tell my dad what was going on because he was so proud of me. Of what I'd accomplished. The coaches didn't care, and I didn't have any friends. I was far away from home, and felt," I shake my head, remembering how alone and lonely I'd felt, "isolated."

"That's nothing to be ashamed of," Cole cuts in quietly. "I understand how that could happen. Going away, all the pressure to succeed. I just wish you hadn't felt like you needed to hide all this from me."

Pulling me to him, he presses his lips against my forehead.

As much as I appreciate the gesture, I untangle myself so I can continue. "Even though I'd requested a room with another hockey player, that didn't happen. My roommate's name was Amy. She was really nice, but we didn't have a lot in common. She liked to party, and I'd always considered myself a serious athlete. I didn't drink or do drugs. I worked out all the time and was focused on my sport. In the beginning, she'd ask if I wanted to go out, but I always declined the offers. The weekends were for getting caught up on homework. After a while, she stopped asking. When everything started to fall apart, she noticed how stressed out I was and asked if I wanted to go out. Normally, I'd say no, but it felt like my life was imploding. And I needed a break from reality."

My gaze flicks to the windshield before settling on his again. "I got so wasted. I couldn't get out of bed until two o'clock the next afternoon." I shake my head, remembering how hung over I'd been. I'd never had a drop of alcohol, so it hadn't taken much. "That night was the first time in forever I remember having fun. I wasn't obsessing about my classes, playing hockey, or my father. Instead of feeling alone, I felt good. So good, that when next Thursday evening rolled around, I went out with Amy and her friends again. And I continued doing that. A few weeks later, I met Nate. He was in a fraternity, and I'd seen him around campus. Up until Nate, I'd never been with anyone." Heat fills my cheeks. "I'd barely kissed a guy."

Even though Cole remains silent, tension fills his muscles.

"Nate was my first." Unable to hold his stare, I drop my gaze to my hands. "Honestly, I don't remember much about the experience except that it was fast." I grimace at how awkward and painful it'd felt. "Big surprise, I never heard from him again. There were a few other guys after that. Just random hookups. None of them meant anything, but they dulled the pain and took my mind off everything else that was going on." Embarrassment heats my cheeks as I stare out the windshield. "I'd get so trashed that I usually couldn't remember what happened the next morning."

His shuttered expression scares me more than anything, because I have absolutely no idea what he's thinking. Cole has such an expressive face and he's always so open with his feelings. That's no longer the case.

Even though my throat feels as if it is closing up, I continue, needing to get it over with. "I was still going to classes because I thought by some miracle, I'd be able to pull off passing grades." I shake my head before forcing out a mirthless laugh. What an idiot I'd been.

"I must have been in denial. Hockey, though, was different. Instead of showing up for practice every day, I started blowing it off. My teammates wouldn't talk to me, but they sure enjoyed talking about me. By that time, rumors were already flying around campus. All the girls on the team knew what was going on, and I'm sure they talked to the coaches about it, but no one bothered to reach out or try to help. I just kept sinking further and further. Toward the end of the semester, I'd missed so many practices that the coach kicked me off the team. I had no idea how to tell my father. I knew he'd be furious."

Even though Cole's hands are still on me, I no longer feel connected to him. In the moonlight that filters in through the windows, his expression remains unreadable.

"A few weeks before winter break, my dad called me." A thin shiver works its way down my spine as I recall that horrible phone call. "My coach had spoken to my parents and filled them in on everything. *Everything.* That I'd been kicked off the team, was failing my classes, along with all the rumors surrounding the partying. She put it all out there without ever saying a word to me." A bitter laugh escapes from me as I recall the conversation. He's screamed for fifteen minutes as I silently sobbed on the phone.

"My dad told me that they were picking me up the following weekend since there wasn't any point to finishing out the semester. In a way, it was a relief that everything was finally out in the open. I didn't have to pretend anymore. Mentally and emotionally, I shut down. I stopped going to classes altogether and partied instead. It was so much easier to numb the pain. I stayed with a few friends who lived off campus. Just some random guys I'd met through Amy. On the night before my parents picked me up, they threw a huge party. I was drunk out of my mind and went upstairs with some guy. We were fooling around," unable to hold his gaze, I glance away before forcing out the rest, "and the next thing I remember is that my clothes were off."

I shake my head as images from that night flash through my head like a slow-motion picture show. "He was stretched out on top of me when the bedroom door opened, and two guys walked in." I blink as the memories crash over me. "I think they were all friends, but I don't know. I remember them staring down at me with smiles on their faces." I suck in a shuddering breath, wishing I could skip the rest. "I didn't mind screwing around with the guy I was with, but I couldn't understand what the other two were doing there."

It's the feel of Cole's fingers biting into my shoulder that has me snapping out of the daze. "At that point, I just wanted to get dressed and go. The way they were watching us was weird. I remember telling them to leave, but they wouldn't. And the guy on top of me didn't seem to care. I tried to push him off me so I could get out of there, but he wouldn't budge. And then the other two guys grabbed my arms to hold me down. I remember yelling, trying to break loose, but I wasn't strong enough. One of them covered my mouth with his hand. I bit him and kept screaming for help, but I knew no one would hear me. The party was so loud. Music was blasting, people were laughing and dancing downstairs."

I'd give anything to wipe that night from my memory.

"I knew they were going to rape me, and that there wasn't a damn thing I could do about it," I whisper.

It took over three months of therapy to stop waking in the middle of the night drenched in a cold sweat, and more than half a year for me to stop flinching when someone laid a hand on me. One touch was all it took for me to be transported back to that bedroom.

My belly roils as I tell him the rest of the story. "The door must have been left open and someone saw what was going on inside. He came in and…" I shake my head because what happened after that is still fuzzy around the edges. "I remember him punching the two guys who were holding me down, and then the guy on top of me was ripped away. Before I could understand what was happening, I was being bundled up in a shirt and carried down the steps. He got me out of the house and took me back to the dorms." It takes effort to summon the courage to meet his gaze. "The guy who rescued me was Luke."

Cole's eyes widen as he releases an unsteady breath.

"He stayed with me until I fell asleep. When I woke up the next morning, he was gone. Thankfully, my parents picked me up a couple hours later. I don't think I could have stayed on campus for another day. Not with what happened. My dad was so angry, he refused to speak with me." I hunch my shoulders as memories of the uncomfortable drive home flood through me. "I'd never been close with my mom, but I thought, maybe, if I told her what had happened, she'd understand all the pressure I'd been under and could help mend everything with my father. The first thing she did was take me to the doctor so I could get tested for pregnancy and STD's." My face heats as another wave of mortification crashes over me.

When I continue, my voice is smaller, thinner, and I just want it over with. I can't talk about this anymore. "All the tests turned out to be negative. Honestly, I don't have much to be thankful for, but I am about that. After the dust settled, my parents shipped me off to my grandparents' house. They were worried about what kind of influence I'd be on my younger sisters." It's a bitter memory that still has the power to inflict damage.

When Cole drags another breath into his lungs, something inside me grows colder. His gaze searches mine for a long moment before he pulls me to him and wraps his arms around me. He presses me so close that I have to fight for breath. That's all it takes for me to burst into tears.

"Don't cry, baby." His voice is nothing more than a rough scrape of emotion before he presses a kiss against my hair. "Please don't cry."

I'm too far gone to rein it back in. All the anxiety and sadness pours out of me in noisy sobs.

His fingers settle under my chin before lifting it until our gazes lock. "I told you that whatever you had to say wouldn't make a damn bit of difference, and it doesn't. I don't care about the mistakes you made last year. They don't define you." He presses a kiss against my lips. "I'm just sorry you felt so alone and had no one to turn to." Concern flashes in his eyes. "I hate that you were placed in such a dangerous situation." He tugs me back into the warm circle of his arms. "Thank God Luke found you when he did."

"I know." My lips tug down at the corners as I stare beyond the window and into the darkness that surrounds us. Instead of mentioning that Luke showed up at practice tonight or tracked me down on the way to class this afternoon and brushed his lips across my cheek, I remain silent.

Am I being paranoid where Luke is concerned?

I'm not sure.

At some point, I'll have to sit down with Luke. Even though he swooped in and saved me, the night that binds us together is difficult to rehash. His presence is a constant reminder of what happened.

Of what *almost* happened.

I can't imagine what Luke sees when he looks at me. All I know is that every time I catch sight of him, hot waves of humiliation crash over me, threatening to drag me under. He's tied to the worst night of my life. And seeing him, being around him, reminds me of it.

27

CASSIDY

Cole drops a kiss against the crown of my head. "You're going to be great out there."

His arms band around me as people walk past on the way to the stands. Excitement charges the frigid air around us.

"I'll be in the bleachers the entire time," he murmurs when I remain silent.

He's doing everything he can to help settle my nerves. I haven't played in a real game since high school. Last year, I rode the bench during the season. Even though this is just an intramural game, I'm choking on my nerves. Cole will be watching, and I don't want to embarrass myself or disappoint him. More than anything, I want to make him proud.

He presses another kiss against the top of my head before whispering, "Just have fun out there. That's what it's all about. That's what it's always been about."

I know he's giving me solid advice, but the nerves won't stop churning in my belly. They probably won't stop until I get out on the ice for warm-ups.

No pep talk is going to change that.

With a smile that makes his dimples pop, he slaps my ass. "Now get in the locker room and I'll see you after the game."

I reach up onto my tiptoes before stroking my lips across his in a way that drives him crazy.

A low growl rumbles up from deep within his chest. "You better get going before I scoop you up and carry your ass out of here."

I grab my hockey bag and head to the locker room. Just as I'm about ten strides away, he calls my name.

"Cassidy."

Swinging around, my brows lift in silent question.

A smile curves his lips as his gaze locks on mine. "I love you."

Unable to hold back the flood of emotion, my bag gets dropped to the floor as I fly into his arms. He wraps me up tight before picking me up and spinning me around in a circle.

"I love you too," I whisper.

"But I loved you first."

"I'm good with that." I laugh before his lips collide with mine.

When he nibbles at my neck, I squeal. As excited as I was for this game, I wish we could head home and get lost in each other for the rest of the night.

"Oh, for fuck's sake," Sammy rolls her eyes as she walks past, "get a room." Then she adds, "After the game. Get a room *after* the game."

After she disappears, I say, "I'd better go." With a grin, I back away, "I got me a game to win tonight."

Gaze pinned to mine, the smile fades from his face as heat flashes in his gorgeous, whiskey-colored eyes. "And I'll be here, waiting to get that room afterward."

A grin overtakes my features. "I certainly hope so."

For a second time, I pick up my bag before blowing him a kiss and pushing my way into the locker room. Rock music blasts from a speaker as the girls talk and laugh, trying to get pumped up. My feet grind to a halt as I take in the moment.

The comradery of a team.

The sisterhood of hockey players.

Girls who have your back.

The Dartmouth team hadn't been like that, or maybe I wasn't there long enough to experience it. But I have it now with this group of girls, and it makes me feel blessed. It doesn't matter that I'm not playing for a top college program. These girls, these *women*, are who I belong with.

I'm struck all over again that none of this would be possible without Cole setting it in motion. I'm lucky he understood what I needed before I was able to realize it for myself. Honestly, I feel so damn lucky to have him in my life. He's quickly becoming my everything. Sometimes, that's a scary prospect. But it's way scarier to imagine my life without him in it.

Sammy knocks me from my thoughts when she jostles me with her elbow. I grunt before rubbing my side.

"You two are seriously barfy."

Her disgusted words are enough to bring a smile to my face. Life seems really good right now. I'm not used to this kind of happiness.

"It's nice to see, Cass. Now get your head out of your ass and into the game where it belongs." She leaps onto one of the benches before surveying the crowd of girls and shouting over the music, "Let's show them whose house they're in by kicking a little ass out there tonight!"

A loud cheer goes up as I grin, stripping down and suiting up.

Two hours later, we're in the final minutes of the third period. The team we're versing is better than any of us anticipated. But that's all right, because we're pretty damn good, too.

With three minutes left on the clock, we're tied.

Again.

There's never been a moment when we weren't separated by more than a goal. The crowd is on their feet, going nuts, because this game has turned out to be a real nail-biter.

All I know is that I want to end this perfect night with a win. As the clock runs down, I line up at center ice and wait for the ref to drop the puck. As soon as it does, I scramble and win the face-off before sliding it to my right winger. With the puck on her stick, she surges forward, her skates digging into the ice. My gaze flickers to the clock as I skate with her, careful not to cross the blue line before she clears it.

As soon as she does, I fly toward the net. She glances up, meeting my gaze before faking a pass to the left wing. Instead, she shoots it to me. Two defensive players swarm, trying to block a clear shot to the net. I do the only thing I can and pass it back to her. Another glance at the clock tells me that time is quickly running out. We're down to thirty seconds. Thirty seconds until the game is over, and I don't want it to end like this.

We're so close to winning.

We need to work together and make it happen.

Nicole watches Lucy, the left wing, and me for an opportunity to pass. She fakes another pass to Lucy before slamming it to me again. I'm about eight feet from the net. As soon as the puck touches my stick, I lift it toward the top right corner and send it flying with as much power as I can muster.

Everything happens in slow-motion. My breath catches at the back of my throat as I watch the puck sail through the air. The goalie reaches out to block the shot, but she misses, and it hits the back of the net.

The buzzer goes off a second later.

Both wingers surround me, slapping me on the back. The crowd roars their approval, until the noise that fills the arena is deafening. The bench clears, as our teammates crowd around us on the ice.

It's the best feeling in the world.

I scan the packed stands, wanting to share this moment with Cole. When I find him, I smile and raise my stick in the air. He grins in response, clapping and whistling. Just as I'm about to glance away, my gaze settles on the person next to him.

My eyes widen as my mouth tumbles open. I blink and continue to stare.

It doesn't seem possible that my father is parked next to Cole.

When he notices that I'm staring at him, he gives me a thumbs-up sign, which was always his way of letting me know I played a solid game.

Tears prick the backs of my eyes.

I can't believe he's here.

It's only when Sammy wraps her arm around my neck that I blink back to the present. "Come on, Jameson. We've got some major celebrating to do tonight!"

I smile as my gaze strays to my dad. He and Cole are talking as they leave their seats. I can't get over the fact that he's actually here.

With Cole.

Twenty minutes later, my new team walks out of the locker room to the sound of clapping and cheering. I search the crowd until my gaze lands on Cole and my father. They look deep in conversation.

Cole's face breaks into a smile when he spots me. Awkwardness descends as I join them. Memories of our last interaction flood through me.

Dad is the first one to break the uncomfortable silence. "That was a good game, Cassidy. You played well."

My eyes widen at the unexpected praise. "Thanks, Dad." There's a pause before I blurt, "What are you doing here?"

His smile falters, and I squeeze my eyes shut before sucking in a breath. "What I meant to ask is how did you know I was playing tonight?"

It means a lot that he carved out time to see my first game with my new team. After all the heartache we've been through, it feels like we have a real shot at fixing our fractured relationship.

Dad claps Cole on the shoulder as if they're longtime friends. "Cole called last week, and we had a good talk." His gaze shifts to Cole before resettling on mine. "He mentioned you'd joined the intramural team, and that your first scrimmage was coming up."

There's a pause. It's almost as if he's gathering himself. My dad has never been overly demonstrative, but there's something about his expression that has a thick lump settling in the middle of my throat, making it impossible to breathe.

"I'm glad he did." His blue eyes flicker away before locking on mine. "I was hoping we could get together sometime next week. Maybe go out for dinner and talk."

Emotion swells inside me. "I'd like that."

I want more than anything to heal the wounds between us. This year has been rough for a lot of reasons. Not having the support of my parents is definitely one of them. Even though nothing has been resolved, it feels like a step in the right direction.

His lips lift into more of a smile. "Good. I'll call you this weekend and we can set something up."

"That sounds good."

My gaze slides to Cole's in a mixture of amazement and disbelief. He gives me a wink in return.

Dad pulls the brim of an old travel team cap low over his eyes before clearing his throat. "I'm going to head back home. Seems like your team has a victory to celebrate." Our gazes stay locked for a long moment. "It was a really good game, Cassidy. Hard-fought. You should be proud of yourself."

"Thanks, Dad."

His praise has always meant so much to me. I worked my entire life for it. After last year, I never expected to hear it again.

I'm surprised when he closes the distance between us and pulls me into his arms. Tears gather in my eyes as I hold on tight. After he sets me free, Dad shakes Cole's hand and thanks him again before disappearing through the crowd. I can only stare at his retreating back before my gaze slides to Cole.

"I can't believe you did that," I whisper, barely able to force out the words.

In this moment, everything feels damn near perfect. I played a good hockey game, spoke with my dad, and Cole told me that he loved me—for the first time. I can't imagine life getting any better than this.

Last year, my life imploded. A year later, I'm still struggling to put the shattered fragments back together again, and make an even better one for myself.

Concern flares in his eyes. "Are you mad that I reached out to him?"

A gurgle of laughter escapes from me as I shake my head. "Of course not. It was just weird to see him in the stands watching me. And then when he gave me a thumbs up after the game…" my voice trails off as emotion rises within me and tears trek down my cheeks.

I can't believe how full my heart feels.

Almost like it might explode.

"Aw, babe. Please don't cry. It was a great night." He gathers me into his arms before pressing a kiss against the top of my head. "I wasn't sure how you'd feel about me calling your dad. And I didn't want to get your hopes up if he was a no-show. So, I didn't mention anything. But he really wanted to be here to support you, Cassidy."

I don't understand how I got so lucky.

How did I find one of the best guys in the entire world?

It doesn't make any sense.

Last year had been a dismal failure. I wasn't sure if I'd ever pull my shit together and now…here I am…all because of Cole. I'm happier than I've ever been in my life.

"Thank you." I stretch onto my tiptoes before stroking my lips across his. "If I didn't already love you, what you did tonight would have clenched it for me."

The way his dimples flash sends an arrow of heat straight down to the pit of my belly. All right, so maybe it ignites a little lower.

"I was hedging my bets just in case you weren't impressed by my declaration of love earlier this evening."

"Well, it worked," I say with a chuckle.

"Good." His mouth drifts over mine. "Let's get out of here and cele-brate, because then I'm taking your ass home and having my wicked way with you."

I can't help but marvel at how damn perfect life feels.

And that has everything to do with Cole.

The man I love.

Who loves me in return.

Faults and all.

The End...For Now.

Read the second part of Cassidy & Cole's story in Don't Leave.
You can buy it here -) https://books2read.com/Dontleave

DON'T LEAVE

CASSIDY

"Wake up, babe." Cole kisses his way across my naked shoulder. "We've got class in an hour."

Still sleepy, I stretch against the firm length of his body. "Not yet," I mumble, "we don't have to get up just yet."

Twenty-five minutes. That's all we need to roll out of bed and still have roughly thirty seconds to slide into our seats for Psych 201. Unable to pry my eyelids open, I turn in his arms as my palms find the solid planes of his chest before stroking over them. It isn't long before my wandering fingers trail down his body.

Have I mentioned just how amazingly hard and cut he is?

Hours spent on the ice playing hockey and lifting in the gym have made him into the chiseled god that he is. A few heartbeats later and my hand is delving into his boxer briefs before gliding over the rigid length of his morning wood.

Well, hello there.

"Looks like we won't be making it out of bed on time after all," he growls, warm breath feathering across the outer shell of my ear as he rolls me onto my back. Before I can offer up a response, his lips crash onto mine as my fingers caress his thick erection before sliding further down to play with the only soft part of him.

Squeezing, petting, and teasing.

God, I love the feel of him.

I love the barely harnessed power that hums beneath the surface of flesh, bone, and muscle. It's something that used to make me nervous. But I know Cole would never use that well-honed strength against me. After what happened last year, being touched or manhandled can send me spiraling into a panic.

I hate when the icy tendrils of anxiety flood through every cell of my being before wrapping around me and squeezing tight. My heart jackhammers a painful tattoo against my chest. Nerves careen and skitter across my flesh. Nausea churns in the pit of my gut...

Until I can't breathe.

I.

Can't.

Breathe.

I've been working on that with my therapist and it's getting better.

I'm getting better.

The attacks don't happen with nearly as much frequency as they used to. I'm controlling it instead of being controlled *by* it.

Cole is always so careful and patient with me. Right from the start, he was gentle and kind. It's probably the reason I fell so easily for him.

Well, maybe not *easily* because in the beginning, I fought against the attraction. Fought against getting to know him. I tried to shut him down at every turn. But the guy is seriously persistent.

After my life imploded last year, it was important that I get my life back on track. And a boyfriend or even a hookup situation wasn't part of the plan.

No distractions.

That was my mantra.

What I've found is that the best laid plans never quite turn out the way you expect them to. If you'd asked me a year and a half ago, I would have told you that I'd be dominating on the ice at Dartmouth. Succeeding academically because that's what I'd always done. I had worked hard my entire life to get to a Division I college. I'd sacrificed friendships and a social life to make that dream come true.

Instead of taking Dartmouth by storm, I'd crashed and burned spectacularly.

Too much pressure and stress.

I'd ended up losing everything.

Including my family.

It's the way Cole's tongue tangles with my own that pulls me from those dark thoughts. Instead of allowing me to get stuck inside my head, he forces me to be present by hovering over my body and caging me in beneath him. I love the way it feels to be surrounded by his body. We've spent hours in bed, exploring one another. Learning what the other likes and doesn't like.

I curl my fingers around him, stroking his hard length in a way that drives him to distraction. I might be new at this, but I've caught on quickly. With a groan, he slips his fingers into my dampened panties.

"You're so damn wet." He sucks my lower lip into his mouth before nipping at it. "So fucking hot," he groans.

A whimper escapes from me when his fingers drift over my core before sinking inside me. His tongue and fingers move in tandem, driving me higher. And then higher still.

My hand tightens around him, pumping harder.

Faster.

Cole tugs my tank top over my head before tossing it to the floor. His heated gaze holds mine for a heartbeat before kissing his way down my body until he can suck my nipple into his mouth. He continues the onslaught until I'm shifting beneath him, needy for more. With a soft pop, he gives the same ardent attention to the other side.

I love the feel of his hot mouth as it roves over my naked body and the way he makes me feel when we're wrapped up in each other. It's as if the world around us shrinks down until everything else ceases to exist.

Releasing the other stiffened bud, he sinks lower until he's nipping at my navel. His lips ghost over my belly before reaching my hip bones and peppering me with kisses. Anticipation spirals through me as he reached the elastic band of my panties. Instead of stripping off the cotton material, he presses his lips against my throbbing center.

I shift restlessly beneath him, desperate for the thin barrier to be ripped away. All I want is to feel his mouth as he brands me. It drives me crazy when he teases me like this, and he knows it.

But that's just part of the fun.

When he presses another kiss against my damp panties, I groan and arch toward him. I'm precariously close to begging for it.

The chuckle that escapes from him is deep and low as if he knows exactly what he's doing to me right before his finger slips beneath the lacy edge to brush over my slick heat. He yanks the panties aside until the material stretches across my exposed flesh. A moment later, his mouth descends, warm breath feathering against me until I'm aching with need.

It's always like this between us.

Hot and explosive.

There are times when it's slow and gentle, and others when it's fast and hard. With anyone else, that would scare me.

But not with Cole.

Never with Cole.

He's like a drug careening through my system and I crave only what he can give me. Every thought swirling through my head disappears as he laps at my pussy until my entire body trembles with the need he's ignited to life.

A month ago, this kind of intimacy would have freaked me out. It would have unleashed the anxiety I keep tightly under wraps. That's no longer the case. I love surrendering to him. I love the way he makes my body throb and pulse.

Most of all, I love that Cole Mathews is mine.

And I'm his.

"You like that, baby?"

"You know I do," I whisper as he strokes his tongue over me, playing my body like a fine instrument. I bow my back, wanting to feel him buried deep inside my body, filling me to the brim. The ache within is growing. Pulsing and throbbing until it feels like it could consume me.

I've never felt anything like this before.

"Cole, please.." Desperation bleeds from me.

"Please, what?"

His voice is raw, scraped low with just as much pent-up desire as mine. His tongue steals over me before plunging deep inside and making me moan. As his talented tongue dances over me, my body tightens. He swirls around my clit, scraping it lightly with his teeth before sucking it gently into his mouth.

That's all it takes for me to teeter at the edge. My hips move restlessly against him as need floods through every cell of my body. I'm panting and pleading for him to push me over the precipice and into oblivion.

I'm.

So.

Close.

So close to shattering into a million little jagged pieces.

With an orgasm poised to crash over my body, his mouth disappears. I gasp, my eyelids flying open, as his warm breath ghosts over my pulsing flesh.

"Cole," I ground out. "I'm so close." Desperation threads its way through my voice. My neediness should embarrass me, but I don't give a damn. I want to scream in frustration.

I can't help but arch toward him, trying to close the distance. Even though he's intent on teasing me, I know how affected he is by my body. He tells me all the time how much he loves being buried deep inside me.

And I love his hard length filling me up and how perfectly we fit together.

None of my drunken hookups ever came close to feeling like this. What we have is rare.

A hungry look fills his eyes as he stares down at me. "One more taste."

He thrusts his tongue deep inside me. As a whimper falls from my lips, he pulls away for a second time.

"Stop teasing!" I growl.

With a soft chuckle, he crawls up my body before pressing a kiss against my mouth. "Delicious." There is so much intensity filling his eyes. "And I love teasing you. It's my new favorite pastime."

As soon as those husky words escape from him, he flips me over onto my belly before dragging my body to the edge of the mattress. With his hands sinking into my hips, he pulls my naked backside into the air. I groan as his fingers glide over me, swirling around my entrance before sinking deep inside. He slides his fingers in and out until I'm pushing against him. Whimpers falls from my lips as he pushes me closer to the edge.

Just as a wave of pleasure crests inside me, his touch vanishes.

"Cole," I groan as tears of frustration prick my eyes. "Please, I need you!"

The sound that escapes from him is strained around the edges as he moves behind me. The blunt head of his cock teases my slick heat, stroking against my lips, caressing them gently. I can just imagine what he looks like, holding his thick erection in his hand as it glides across my flesh. That picture will forever be branded into my brain.

When he finally sinks inside me, my eyelids feather closed as I strain against him.

He's buried so deep.

And it feels so damn good.

But then again, it always does.

Hovering over me, he wraps his hard body around mine. His hands drift across my ribcage until he's able to palm my breasts. He toys with my nipples all the while thrusting inside me. After a few moments, one hand trails down my body until he's able to play with my clit. I whimper as an orgasm builds with each flick of his fingers and stroke of his cock.

We stand at the precipice before careening over the edge. I have to bite down on my lower lip to keep the screams locked deep inside as pleasure streaks through my body. It's so tempting to let go and release the intensity, but I refuse to endure the shit eating grins, sly looks, and obnoxious comments from a houseful of his hockey team-mates over a bowl of cereal at the kitchen table.

Been there, done that.

As the last aftershocks reverberate through me, exhaustion takes hold and I hang my head between my shoulder blades as my panting breaths even out. Cole relaxes against me, his body curving around mine.

"I love you, Cassidy," he whispers before pressing a kiss against my neck.

"I love you, too."

Want to read more of Cassidy & Cole's story?
You can buy it here -)
https://books2read.com/Dontleave

JUST FRIENDS

REED

With a sigh, I collapse onto the couch in the living room of the house I share with a couple of guys from the hockey team and pop open a can of cold beer, guzzling down half of it in one thirsty swig.

Goddamn, but that hits the spot.

Know what else would hit the spot?

Yeah, you do.

It's the second week of September, and Coach Richards has us skating two-a-days, lifting weights, and running five miles for extra cardio.

As if we need it.

Oh…and he added yoga to this year's regimen.

Fucking yoga.

Can you believe that shit?

Let me be perfectly clear—I'm not into contorting my body into a pretzel and breathing deeply from my diaphragm. Sure, I get it. He wants us to work on our flexibility. And I'll do it, but that doesn't mean I have to like it.

Coach R is a total masochist.

Or is it sadist?

I can never keep those two straight.

No matter. Whatever kind of *ist* he is, the man thoroughly enjoys working our asses over. The only amusement I get is from listening to all the incoming freshmen piss and moan about what a tough schedule we have.

Welcome to Division I hockey, boys. Buckle up, it's going to be a bumpy ride.

Pile on fifteen credit hours and I don't have time for much else.

"Reed, baby, I've been waiting all night for you to return."

A curvy female drops onto my lap like an angel falling from heaven before she twines her slender arms around my neck and pulls me close.

I stand corrected. There's always time for *that*.

Hell, half the time, *that's* what gets me through the grind. Sex is an amazing stress reliever, and don't let anyone tell you differently. I'm way more chill after I've blown my load. And if I'm fortunate enough to do it twice in one night, then it's like I've slipped into a damn coma.

Pure bliss, baby.

Luckily for us, the Red Devils hockey team has its fair share of puck bunnies on campus who are always willing to provide some much-needed stress relief on a regular basis. God bless every last one of those ladies. They have no idea how much their *team spirit* is appreciated.

That being said, there are always exceptions to the rule.

And the girl currently cozied up on my lap is exactly that.

Megan thrusts out her lower lip in a sexy pout. "How is it possible that we've never hooked up before?"

The answer is simple. I go to great lengths to avoid her like a particularly nasty case of crabs.

She flutters her mascara-laden lashes and tilts her head. Her voice becomes lispy and toddler-like as she twirls a dark curl around her finger. "Don't you think I'm pretty?"

Pretty?

No, Megan is flat-out gorgeous.

Her long, black hair is as shiny as a crow's wing as it floats around her shoulders in soft waves. She has dark eyes that are tipped at the corners, giving her an exotic look. And her skin is sun-kissed all year round. And if that weren't enough to have any guy giving her a full-on salute, she's also got gravity-defying tits and a nice round ass.

Have I imagined fucking her from behind and smacking that bubble butt a few times before blowing my wad?

You bet Megan's perfectly round ass I have. The girl is a walking wet dream.

And from what the guys on the team tell me (because they're a bunch of loudmouth assholes who like to brag), she can suck a dick like nobody's business. That being said, I won't be finding that out firsthand anytime soon.

I've made it a point to steer clear of Megan because every time I look at her, I see Emerson.

And imagining that I'm nailing my best friend is a definite no-no.

When I don't immediately respond, Megan grinds her bubble butt against my junk—which is something I really don't need, because just the thought of Emerson alone is enough to have me popping wood.

It's a messed-up situation.

One that Em is blissfully unaware of. Which is exactly the way it needs to stay. She can't find out that I've got the hots for her. Emerson Shaw is one of the first friends I made when Mom and I moved to Lakefield the summer before freshman year of high school. And we've been tight ever since.

While I enjoy having a casual, friends-with-benefits relationship with a number of girls on campus, I've never considered sleeping with Em.

Okay, maybe I've *considered* having sex with her. It would be hard not to imagine stripping her naked and getting jiggy with a girl who looks like that, but I've never done anything about it.

I've screwed too many women not to know that getting naked changes a relationship. And I like Em way too much to risk sleeping with her. She's the one person who has always had my back. And let's face it, I can be a hell of a lot more honest with her than my teammates.

Can you imagine me baring my soul to those assholes?

Exactly. I'd never hear the end of it.

My friendship with Emerson also gives me all this insight into the female psyche that I wouldn't otherwise be privy to. It's like taking a peek behind the magic curtain. I'm not willing to throw that away when there are plenty of random chicks I can get my rocks off with.

Moral of the story? Friends are a lot harder to come by than hookups.

"Reed?" Megan nips my lower lip between her sharp teeth before giving it a gentle tug and releasing it.

I blink back to the girl wriggling around on my lap. "Yeah?"

Her hands flutter to my shoulders before settling on them. "You're so tense."

Damn right I am. All I can think about is Emerson, and that's all kinds of wrong.

"Let's go upstairs." Her tongue darts out to moisten her lips as she whispers, "I know *exactly* what will fix that."

If any other girl were making the offer, I'd already be dragging her up the staircase to my bedroom. But that's not going to happen with Megan.

I just can't do it. Maybe I'm not *technically* doing anything wrong, but it still feels like I'm breaking some kind of friendship rule. Emerson may not realize I'm thinking about her like that, but I do.

And that's all that matters.

Guess I'll have to find a different girl to get busy with. Preferably a flat-chested blonde with big blue eyes who doesn't resemble Em. Or maybe a redhead, just to mix things up a bit.

Megan's eyes light up when I set my beer down and wrap my hands around her waist, until I carefully remove her from my lap. "Sorry, sweetheart. I've got homework to finish up for tomorrow." I tack on the lie to soften the blow. "Maybe another time?"

Her face falls. "Sure, no problem."

Before she can pin me down on a time and place, I beat a hasty retreat from the living room and head upstairs. Once I've taken refuge in my room, I fire off a text to one of my go-to girls.

Fifteen minutes later, my booty-call for the evening strolls through the door.

Know what I like most about Candace?

The girl gets right down to business. There's no need for small talk, and that I can appreciate. I'm in the mood to fuck, not debate world politics or climate change.

The door hasn't even closed and Candace is already shedding her clothes. Since she hasn't bothered with a bra, her titties bounce free as soon as her shirt is discarded. Her nips stiffen right up when the cool air hits them.

It's a beautiful sight to behold.

Except…

Nothing stirs south of the border. Not like it did when I was thinking about a certain someone downstairs who shall remain nameless. But I'm not concerned. I just need to harness my mental capabilities and focus on the task at hand. Which is getting my dick to work properly.

I yank off my T-shirt and toss it to the floor as Candace flicks open the button of her teeny-tiny shorts before unzipping them. With her gaze locked on mine, she shimmies out of them.

And wouldn't you know it…

No panties in sight.

Just a gloriously bare pussy.

Works for me.

Well, that's what *normally* works for me.

At the moment, limp dick-itis has set in.

Once Candace has stripped down to her birthday suit, she struts her sexy stuff toward the bed where I've made myself comfortable. Her eyelids lower as a knowing smirk curves her red-slicked lips. I rake my gaze over her toned body.

The girl is absolutely perfect.

"I've missed you." She crawls across the mattress until her hands are resting against my bare chest. "I'm glad you texted."

She says that now, but it probably won't be the case when she gets her hands on my junk.

What the hell is wrong with me?

I thought this kind of thing only happened to older dudes. I'm way too young for Viagra. I've seen first-hand how that shit can mess you up.

As a joke last year, one of the jackasses on my team got his hands on a couple of those little blue pills and slipped them to one of the freshman players. The poor guy was sporting wood for days. Unfortunately, a trip to the emergency room became necessary. When Coach R was apprised of the situation, he reamed our asses good and threatened to bench the entire team for the season. We skated suicides until our legs practically fell off.

No, thank you.

Candy trails her purple-tipped fingernails down my chest before pushing me against the mattress and straddling my torso. Then she leans over and licks a wet trail down my body until reaching the waistband of my athletic shorts. This encounter is going to nosedive real quick if I can't get it up in record speed. Not knowing what else to do, I squeeze my eyes tight as an unwanted image of Emerson pops into my head.

Dark hair, lush curves, bright smile.

Candace chuckles as she pulls my hard length from my boxer briefs like it's a much-anticipated Christmas gift. "There's my big boy!"

I groan.

I am *so* screwed.

Want to reed more of Reed and Emerson's story? You can buy it here -
) https://books2read.com/u/me7oeE

ABOUT THE AUTHOR

Jennifer Sucevic is a USA Today bestselling author who has published twenty New Adult novels. Her work has been translated into German, Dutch, and Italian. Jen has a bachelor's degree in History and a master's degree in Educational Psychology. Both are from the University of Wisconsin-Milwaukee. She started out her career as a high school counselor, which she loved. She lives in the Midwest with her husband, four kids, and a menagerie of animals. If you would like to receive regular updates regarding new releases, please subscribe to her newsletter here-

Jennifer Sucevic Newsletter (subscribepage.com)

Or contact Jen through email, at her website, or on Facebook.

sucevicjennifer@gmail.com

Want to join her reader group? Do it here -)

J Sucevic's Book Boyfriends | Facebook

Social media links-

https://www.tiktok.com/@jennifersucevicauthor

www.jennifersucevic.com

https://www.instagram.com/jennifersucevicauthor

https://www.facebook.com/jennifer.sucevic

Amazon.com: Jennifer Sucevic: Books, Biography, Blog, Audiobooks, Kindle

Jennifer Sucevic Books - BookBub